THE LIES SHE TOLD

TOLD

PAULA JOHNSTON

Louisa Johnston x

Praise for Paula Johnston

'Twisty, clever, pacy and fun!' - Best-Selling Author of Little White Lies, Philippa East

'An emotional thriller, full of suspense. It leaves you on the edge of your seat wanting more!'

'Just when you think you have a handle on where this book is going, it takes you in the complete opposite direction!'

'I was hooked from the beginning and could not put it down. Gripping, full of twists, and just brilliantly written. An outstanding debut novel.'

'A book you simply can't put down. Smart, gripping, and full of characters you don't know whether to love or hate.'

'Brings the reality of modern-day relationships to life. A psychological thriller that's every girl's worst nightmare.'

'Twists and turns like you'd never believe!'

Dedication
To my Grandparents, for always pushing me to follow my dream.

PROLOGUE

*W*e connect with people because they understand something about us; something that we possess that's enjoyable.

Even the most toxic relationships begin with a foundation of untainted trust and pleasantries. These relationships can flourish gracefully, allowing new levels to be built, but sometimes these foundations eventually show signs of wear and tear and inevitably start to crumble.

I like to think that I'm a good judge of character, but sometimes people don't take me just quite as seriously as they should. I give myself to people wholeheartedly with no inhibitions and to my own fault; I expect the same to be reciprocated.

When I found out, I wasn't mad at you. I wasn't even sad; there were no tears shed, my eyes were bone dry. You shouldn't have treated me this way. You made a big mistake, one I privately promised you would ultimately pay for.

As the wind blows sharply across my face today and I look down at you, I'm still not mad, I'm still not sad. I'm something else, something between satisfied and amused. I know that I'm a good

1

person. This – all of this – has no reflection on me as a person because you did this, not me.

This was all your fault.

PART ONE

CHAPTER ONE

KARLY

The sun pierces brightly through a small gap in the curtains, sending a sharp ray of light across the length of my bedroom. I always sleep with the window open with the curtains closed, but it's perfectly normal for a gust of wind to have blown them open slightly during the night.

It doesn't matter if it's not the height of summer, it could be a menacing autumn or a freezing cold winter. I never falter from routine. There's no spectacularly interesting reason behind it. I simply enjoy listening to all the different sounds of the outside world as I fall asleep at night: the buzzing of cars that have ventured out on a late-night journey, the click of shoes on the pavement as they pass by, the whistling of the wind through the trees. I find all of it comforting; the way each little insignificant noise disrupts the blanketed silence that attempts to capture and envelop me each night. These noises are a precious gift of illusion that I'm not entirely on my own.

Today is the seventeenth of July, my birthday, and I've just turned twenty-nine years old. My birthday however makes no difference to me, everything remains the same. There are no frills, no surprises, no fuss, and so it's easy for me to carry on as normal.

There is an empty space beside me in my king-size bed – a choice that was entirely my own. I could have extended an invitation to any one of my puppy dog eyed admirers to spend the night with me, just so I had someone to wake up to this morning, but I didn't, I don't need them.

Of course, I know that any one of them would have fallen over themselves to accept if I'd asked. I suppose I should be flattered by their attempts to woo me with lavish tricks and expensive gifts, all in a desperate bid to claim me as their own, but I'm not. I'm not interested in a serious relationship with any of them. That's not what I keep them around for. They have no sentimental value to me, merely playthings to accommodate my free time because everyone gets a little lonely from time to time. I'm only human after all, and admittedly, as much as I enjoy and am used to my own company, I'm not ashamed to have dabbled in more than a few meaningless flings over the years to fill some gaps. Most of them have been aesthetically pleasing, but dead between the eyes. The pretty ones you could stare at forever, but God forbid you ever try to engage in some intellectual conversation with. They don't have that brain capacity, which makes them meaningless, and so meaningless flings are exactly all they're good for.

Occasionally a rarity crosses my path and successfully piques my interest. They stand out from the crowd because they have something more to them than just their handsome smiles and chiselled jaw lines. They have that wit, that Jack the lad charm I find oh so endearing – but only because it reminds me so much of *him*. Despite my best efforts to mould something special between us, even just a sliver of resemblance to what we have, my time with them is always short lived with the outcome always the same, because deep down I know my efforts are futile. There is no one like him.

The annoying, repetitive buzz of my phone on the bedside table closest to me interrupts my train of thought. I wonder who could be texting me so early. I foolishly allow myself a moment of excitement and I'm not sure why because it's out of character for me, but the optimistic feeling evaporates just as quickly as it surfaced. Reality is always there to starkly remind me that it's not likely to be anyone important sending me birthday wishes. There isn't anyone important, not really.

I don't have any living parents to celebrate the day of my birth with. No one to tell me sweet little anecdotes about how I took forever to arrive or how much I weighed. I don't even have any brothers or sisters to take me out for a special meal or surprise me with sentimental gifts because I was an only child, and my dear old granny – for all she was worth – passed away just a couple of months after I turned twenty, which left me a sort of orphan, I suppose.

I don't remember all my birthdays that I was lucky enough to spend with my mum and dad as I was much too young; only the last one before their accident. The two of them burst into my pastel pink bedroom early in the morning with a gigantic, delicious looking chocolate cake in the shape of a caterpillar with a pink smiley face. It had five little purple and white striped candles poking out from its body; one for each year Mum had said.

I giggled excitedly and clapped my hands as they sang happy birthday to me in those funny voices that they knew I loved, and then I sprang from my bed to blow out the flames and make a special wish. Mum asked me what I'd wished for, but I told her not to be silly, that I couldn't tell her that or it wouldn't come true. She smiled down at me warmly and ruffled my then sandy blonde hair that has now darkened substantially over the years.

'Well, we wouldn't want that would we? Time to get up now, Keeks, you can have some of your cake for your breakfast. But just for today.'

I followed her and Dad out of the room and into the kitchen where she cut me a large slice of the caterpillar's body and put it on a paper plate that had lots of colourful balloons on it. I was so happy sitting at our kitchen table with the wonky wooden leg, eating my chocolate cake with my fingers as Mum and Dad pottered around getting themselves ready for work. My birthday was special then, and I felt special as I licked the gooey chocolate off my fingers.

Unfortunately, it turned out that my mum was right after all, having cake for breakfast that morning was just for that day. If I'd known that, I would have made a different wish.

It was in October that same year, only three measly months after my birthday that both my parents were taken from me. They weren't famous by any means, but the events which led to their deaths were so

7

horrific that it ended up on the television and splashed all over the front pages of the local papers. A tragic five car pileup on the motorway where three people lost their lives, and the surviving drivers and passengers were left critically injured. I wasn't told too much about it all at the time, just that there had been an accident and that I wouldn't see my mummy and daddy any more. Granny used to always change the channel when she caught me watching the news and I remember being annoyed that she was hiding things from me, but the curiosity never left me and so I looked it up on the Internet when I was a bit older and able to use a computer. Sometimes I wish I hadn't.

'*The car was crushed like a tin of beans*', one article reported. I hated the journalist who wrote those horrible words, they made it sound almost comical when it was anything but, and for so many years after I experienced the most horrific nightmares of my parents being trapped inside a compact metal tin; their twisted, lifeless bodies helpless with their beautiful limbs bent and broken, their blood spattering the interior.

It was simply a tragic freak accident, but one that might never have happened if things had worked out differently. My parents always took the train to work, less hassle with traffic they always said, but on this particular day, heavy construction works were taking place on the railway line and so they decided to car share into the city to avoid any delays. They should have left the car behind. Instead, they left me.

I don't know if they would have woken me up every year with a caterpillar cake, but I never received another birthday cake of any kind when I went to live with Granny. In fact, she barely acknowledged the day at all. I remember tugging at her apron the year after as I danced on the spot, already dressed for school, and excited to tell her that I was a big six years old today. She stopped boiling whatever was in her pot and turned to look at me for only a few moments, her eyes grey and detached, cold even, and then she turned back to the stove without saying a single word. I shuffled out of her sight, tears streaming silently down my face, and I knew then that this day, my special day, would never be the same.

Everything had changed, and I hated it. I hated my new house; I hated my new dull and dark room; I hated my new school and so I refused to make friends. I even hated that I no longer had something as simple as a nickname; no more Keeks. She was gone now thanks to Granny. She addressed me as Karly and Karly only. To her the pet's name that my mum had gifted me was childish and un-lady like. Most of all though, above everything that had changed so suddenly in my life, the thing I hated the most. was her.

Fresh tears gather painfully in my eyes at the memory of being back in my little pink bedroom, looking up at my parents and their smiling faces filled with so much love and adoration, and so I do what I always do; lock the memory back in its box, furious with myself for bringing it out in the first place.

My phone buzzes again, refusing to be ignored, and I reach over and tug the charger from the bottom, tossing it carelessly away as I enter my password, allowing my sleepy and now damp eyes to adjust to the bright attack of the screen.

Happy Birthday Beautiful x

My stomach flips wildly at the sight of his name. This is a surprise. It's been about four months since we last spoke, and I knew I would hear from him at some point today; I just didn't expect it to be so early.

I won't ask him where he's been or why he left, there's never any point. I learnt that cruel and harsh lesson after the first couple of times he vanished. The very first time though, that was something else. The pain was surreal. I felt like my heart had been brutally ripped from my chest by his bare hands. Even the pain I felt as a child when I lost both my parents didn't compare to the ache his absence left.

Everything was fine between us – more than fine until suddenly it wasn't. His name stopped appearing online, my messages failed to send, and his number was always out of use. A constant churning ache lodged deep inside my stomach yearned for him every single day. I began to doubt everything and anything. Did I do something wrong? Had I said something to upset him? Is he testing me to make sure that I'm good enough? There was also that gut wrenching worry that something had happened to him, that he'd been hurt or involved in an accident. Everything was out of my control; I was completely helpless.

He couldn't have left me on purpose. We had plans – big plans. With only a couple of weeks to go before his big move to Glasgow from London, we'd been discussing the silly things like what size television we would get and what colours we'd paint our rooms, when out of nowhere, my big, beautiful dream of a life together morphed into my very own living nightmare. I mentally tortured myself, searching for the answers that only he could give me, and I cried myself to sleep every night in the first few weeks after his disappearance.

After six long difficult months had passed, just when life without him almost started to become that bit more bearable, he returned to me, with carefully constructed excuses ready in his hands. Although I was extremely hurt at the realisation that he had in fact made the decision to leave me willingly, and admittedly quite sceptical, I quickly realised that whatever his reasons were for leaving me high and dry, they didn't actually matter now he'd chosen to come back to me. He was no longer a ghost.

Foolishly, I allowed myself to dive headfirst back into the whirlpool of our relationship, falling for him harder than I thought possible, much deeper than before – and then it happened again, and again, and again.

His erratic behaviour formed a solid pattern over the years, and I had no choice but to accept it. Ultimately, he was the one with the power and always would be, and so now I accept when it happens. I simply go with the flow, because I know now that this is just what he does and inevitably will always happen until he is ready. Whenever the possibility of a committed and stable life together edges closer to reality, instead of getting excited, I prepare myself for what is about to come.

I'm not stupid though. Of course, I confronted him about his vanishing acts when they were in their infancy, but he always had an answer ready to keep me pacified. He had multiple reasons why it wasn't possible for us to be together just yet. Sometimes a few of his more brutally honest answers included there being another girl in his life, someone closer to home, and although I was practically turning emerald green with jealousy at the obscene idea of him being with someone other than me, I confidently knew that they would just be there to pass the time; just something to do until we could finally be together properly. I didn't however expect his current fling to go that one step further, but unfortunately it did. Another outrageous inconvenience spiralling its web attempting to keep us apart. I had to keep reminding myself that she was temporary because I'm forever.

One thing is a certainty though, it doesn't matter how many times he tries to leave, he always comes crawling back. It might be a week, a month, or even a year, but he and I both know that our relationship is special. There is an undeniably solid connection that binds us together. That thing you always see in those cliché, predictable romcoms and wonder if it could really be possible for two human beings to feel so strongly for one another. Let me tell you, it is possible, because that's what we have.

I was only a few months shy of eighteen when I stumbled across his profile online. I was scrolling through one of my many social media accounts on my laptop after work one night when I noticed that I had a new friend or follower request, whatever they were called back then. I knew the minute I saw his picture: his beautiful face, his thick dark hair, his perfectly tanned skin that looked flawless under his white T-shirt. His perfect white teeth glistened as he bit his bottom lip slightly in a seductively charming grin. He was the one for me, I just knew it, and if I'd learnt one thing from life, it's that it's far too short and dull to not go after what you want.

He replied to the first message I left on his picture almost instantly, and we spoke for a little while in the comments section before exchanging instant messenger usernames. We could talk more freely and privately there.

By the end of the week, after messaging back-and-forth each night, I found myself racing home from work every night thereafter to check if he was online, desperate to get my fix. He was all I thought about and I was completely hooked on him like an addict to heroin, and although it's been an ongoing saga for ten long years now, rehab has never been an option for me.

JACOB

URGH, THAT FUCKING alarm. I groan grumpily as its angry siren forces me awake from a good night's sleep. On a normal day I would press the snooze button on my phone and try to chase a few more minutes of sleep before I really needed to get up for work – but not today. The little calendar icon beneath my thumb tells me that it's July seventeenth, but I already know what day it is, and I don't need a reminder or an alert for this one, it's deep-rooted in my memory.

The fact that I remember what day it is, doesn't mean I'm proclaiming to be a hopeless romantic or anything. Far from it actually, I'm just a normal bloke. I definitely don't remember every birthday or anniversary, especially ones I'm really supposed to, but I've just never been able to forget hers.

In between all the flirtation and banter, she told me about her parents' car accident, which would have left her completely alone had it not been for her grandmother. However, from what I know of her, she didn't care much for Karly; seen her as more of an inconvenience, actually. A constant reminder of the daughter she'd lost.

Her birthday was never something that was acknowledged, just swept under the carpet. Business as usual. How horrible that must have been for a kid; never receiving a present or even just blowing out candles on a bloody birthday cake. It made me feel sad, like really sad. My childhood was the polar opposite to hers. It was warm and loving and every year I had a big fuss made over me despite the fact I had two older brothers. Something else she never had. It stirred something unfamiliar inside of me, something beyond just sex chat and exposing pictures. Maybe that's where it changed for us. I began to feel protective of her, and when she finally caved and told me her date of birth, I made a promise to myself that I would always remember it, and I still do.

I gently peel back the thick duvet and slowly dip my legs out of the bed, careful not to nudge Lauren as she sleeps soundly beside me. As I pad my way down the hall to the main bathroom, I check the time on my phone – 07.11. Perfect. I know her routine well and so she'll be getting up for work shortly.

I close the door quietly behind me and reach inside the glass cubicle to turn on the shower, switching the jets from medium to full power. Perching myself on the edge of the bath as I allow the steam to fill the room, I mull over what I'm about to do. It's been a while since I last messaged her and she hasn't bothered to try to get in touch with me either, but then again, she wouldn't, not any more. She used to though, at the start. I'd blocked her number in an attempt to get rid, but almost every day a new email would arrive, begging me to talk to her. It was for the best that I didn't reply to those, and so I never did, even when I really wanted to.

I think it's been around three or four months since I last made a quick exit. A long time away from her, but not the longest I've ever cut contact for. I'm slightly annoyed at myself for relapsing, I was doing so well focusing on my job and spending time with Lauren, who has fairly recently become Mrs Cruthers, but I just can't find it in me to ignore her; not today.

My bare foot taps nervously as I run a hand through my hair, staring down at the empty text box on my screen, foolishly debating with myself if this will finally be the year where I don't do it, where I stay away. A waste of time really because of course, I decide that it's not, so fuck it, here we go.

Happy Birthday Beautiful x

CHAPTER TWO

KARLY

After spending a little extra time in bed this morning eagerly responding to his messages, I got up, went for a shower, dressed myself impeccably as always, and arrived at work with some time spare to grab a quick coffee from the pop-up Costa in Central Station before meeting my first client.

On the train journey into the city this morning, I blanked out all the grumpy and impatient commuters and allowed myself to drift into a soothing daydream of my ideal birthday morning; what it should be like.

I pictured my breathtakingly handsome Jacob waltzing through our bedroom door, a tray full of all my favourite things balanced perfectly in his manly hands; a stack of warm fluffy pancakes with a little tub of melted chocolate for spreading, my favourite pink mug with beautifully painted eyelashes filled with a freshly brewed caramel latte from our household coffee machine, not forgetting the extra two shots of syrup, making it sickly sweet because of course, he knows that's just how I like it.

There might even be a single white rose delicately placed next to an envelope with my name on it, taken from a huge bouquet still waiting for me to discover elsewhere in our perfect little home. I guess it's silly to call it a daydream really, because it's much more than that. It's an insight into our future, like a premonition. What a lovely morning this has turned out to be after all I think, as I check my lippy in the mirror before heading down to the shop floor.

I think perhaps I spoke a bit too soon. My second client of the morning has been a bit of a handful to say the least. It's so bloody frustrating when you get one like that: stuck up rich older women that think they know everything, but really don't have a clue or else they wouldn't have hired me in the first place.

I spent a copious amount of time rummaging through the busy rails for a suitable pair of tailored trousers that were described to me as bright fuchsia pink – but not too pink. She tried on five extremely similar pairs, that were all completely wrong in her opinion, before finally settling on the very first pair I'd presented to her that she'd now decided were perfect after all.

Despite any difficult clients I get, I absolutely love my job. I wasn't quite sure what I wanted to be when I was growing up. The other kids at school all seemed to have big dreams, especially the girls. Optimistic ambitions of becoming a pop star or an actress with only a few with more realistic options like a vet or a doctor. Me, though, I didn't have a clue. Granny didn't work, and I suppose she didn't need to because she was already filthy rich thanks to the money my grandad left her when he died. I never met him as he died before I was born, but from what I know about him, money was never a problem. Mum and Dad weren't dependent on anyone else though, at least not that I know of. They both worked long hours every day, so we weren't poor by any means, but there was no snobbery in our house. We were just a normal little family and had they still been around I might have been more career driven, but not having a hard-working role model to look up to left me a little lost in terms of career prospects.

One thing I did know though was that I always enjoyed fashion, and for as long as I can remember I've had a strong eye for finding the perfect outfit to suit any occasion – probably because I had a lot of practice of choosing my own while growing up since Granny wasn't in the least bit interested. She bought me new items when I took a stretch or my shoes were looking a bit scuffed, but there was never anything special about them. With the little I had, I taught myself how to pair the same top with different bottoms or the same dress, but with the sleeves chopped off. It gave me peace in a dark place, proof that I could be independent too by doing something I was actually good at.

I started working in a busy department store on Argyle Street on the weekends when I was just sixteen and desperate to leave school. It wasn't because I was bad at school, far from it, but I didn't have many friends there and wanted to reinvent myself. I no longer wanted to be known as the girl whose parents died, the girl who never had someone show up to school plays, the girl who ate her lunch in the corner by herself.

I worked hard in my first job, replenishing stock, chatting to customers in the fitting rooms and in general showing a fresh eagerness to learn, and so it wasn't long before I was offered full-time hours. I was over the moon and could finally leave school once and for all. No more bunking off and wandering around the shops in the cold. I loved working; I felt so grown up and nobody looked at me with pity.

I did everything I could to climb my way up the career ladder, proudly bagging promotion after promotion. It was only when Granny passed away that I decided to try my hand at something else. I could work in any concession department you put me in, but now that I had a taste for it, I craved more and more independence.

I applied for a Personal Shopper position within the same department store and was offered the job on the spot during my interview, naturally of course. Although I still worked inside the same store, it was not for one specific company and instead of a healthy managerial wage, I only earned the big bucks if my own client base was high. Minimum wage was all I received as a base which sucked to begin with, but the right person could earn a shit load more with the commission structure, which I inevitably did.

It wasn't a massive risk really though. If things hadn't worked out in my new venture and I wasn't making much money, it didn't matter now that I'd inherited plenty of Granny's money to fall back on. Even though she had no other living relatives, and I was her only grandchild, I was still positively stunned to find that she'd left me that lavishly oversized house of hers, which I sold instantly to buy something of my own. Something much smaller, better suited to just one person, less pretentious, less hollow. I settled on a little flat just outside the city centre that was close enough to everything I would ever need without having to drive a car – a life decision I made at an early age.

My little flat only cost a fraction of the money her house was worth and so I squandered some of what was leftover on designer clothes and expensive jewellery, paired with plenty of shoes and chic handbags of course. Any girl in my position would have. I wasn't entirely reckless though. I still have a healthy bundle tucked away for when Jacob finally asks me to move to London to be with him. I'll need to be able to pay my own way; I don't expect anyone to look after me, I never have.

Fortunately, but not surprisingly, things worked out in my favour, which meant I had both Granny's money and plenty of my own. I'm extremely successful and I have a constant flow of social media influencers and local celebrities requesting my services. My diary is full to the brim for at least the next four months and I also have a healthy waiting list for any rare, cancelled appointments which means most of my days are exactly like this one – jam packed with barely any time to grab something to eat throughout the day.

I usually enjoy being so busy, I thrive off my popularity, but now that I have Jacob's attention again, I really wish I wasn't at work today at all. Maybe I should have taken a holiday so I had more time to speak to him, but then again how could I have known he would message me so early? His message might not have arrived until later tonight.

As always, he is his usual charming and cock-sure self that I have to admit, I absolutely adore. He mocks some of the words I use; Scottish slang that's foreign to a Londoner, and it makes me laugh. It's comforting to know that he's missed me just as much as I've missed him. Not that he's told me, but I can tell for myself by how quickly he's replying to each message.

The thing I don't tell most people, not that there is much to tell anyway, is that I've never met Jacob in the flesh. I try not to let it bother me too much. It's a bit annoying of course, but not enough to stop this thing between us.

I've heard all the theatrical horror stories of people pretending to be someone they're not; using fake pictures to lure naïve people into their dark lair, all the while having an ulterior motive. Those stories are scary, I've watched the TV show *Catfish* just like the rest of us, but that would never happen to me, I'm much too smart to fall for anything like that. And anyway, I've seen plenty of pictures of him over the years to know that he is who he says he is. He would never lie to me.

The fact that we've never met and still have such a strong connection speaks for itself. It's beautiful really, and I believe that I know him on a more intimate level than anyone else because of this. I'm not blinded by a touch of his hand or the taste of his kiss. What I feel is pure and authentic.

I understand that some people might have an unsavoury opinion on our relationship if they knew, and I know what they would say – that I can't possibly love someone I've never met – but I assure you that you can, and I do. I tell Jacob everything; stories from my shitty childhood, my likes and dislikes, my bad habits – I even tell him about my nightmares. All the normal things you would discuss with a partner, no different to anyone else, and by confiding in someone for as many years as we have about all these personal things, it's inevitable you grow close. The only way we could get any closer is if it were in person.

The main reason we've never met properly is that we live at opposite ends of the country; me being Scotland and him being London. Not that it's ever been an issue for me. Nothing as minor as postcodes could convince me not to be with him. It really isn't even that far either. People have successful long-distance relationships all the time. I would drop everything quicker than a hot curling iron to catch that flight to London if he asked me to.

I might have even broken my own rule and learnt to drive for him. It would only have been a matter of waiting for the word go, and I would have readily driven the 8-9 hours if he had asked me to. Thinking about it, I probably still would.

The thing with him though is that there has always been some sort of heavy resistance. A dead weight that you just can't seem to budge no matter how hard you push or pull. Each time I urged him to set a date for us to meet up, the more he would pull away and serve me up another lame excuse.

A problem with his kidneys – that's what he told me the very first time. He had a job lined up in Glasgow at some fancy hotel doing electrical work before he went AWOL. It was perfect really; we wanted to be together, and he happened to have this amazing opportunity to work in the city of Glasgow with me set in motion and ready to go. When he came back to me after those six long months, he couldn't apologise more. Apparently, he was taken into hospital as a matter of urgency and kept in for some time, resulting in him missing his opportunity to work in Scotland – and in return be with me. That was just the first time though. I don't know if I believe all the excuses that followed after that as some were a bit far-fetched, but I do think that one was genuine.

There have been times where we've almost come close. I've travelled to London for work on several occasions and it could have been so easy for us to meet. But even then, he had an excuse for every failed attempt.

After a few years of the same, he met her, and I upped the ante, desperately needing to get to him before things went too far between them and so I pushed harder than ever before. I even pretended that there was a possibility of me moving to London for work permanently, meaning there would be no further issues with distance, no more excuses to be made. I know I shouldn't have lied, but he needed to realise that he didn't have a future with another girl, I was his future. Job or no job, I would have moved down south anyway and then found new employment. He would have been none the wiser. It really doesn't matter that I told a little white lie now though, he disappeared into another one of his episodes shortly after I told him and never mentioned it again when he returned.

As I'm twirling a strand of my freshly coloured mocha hair around my finger, waiting patiently for my customer to emerge from the brightly lit changing room, my phone starts to buzz in the back pocket of my favourite figure-hugging black skinny jeans. I pull it out to see Hannah's name lighting up my screen. I quickly silence the call and type a quick text.

Can't talk right now at work. What's up? X

I could have taken the call, but I'm slightly pissed that it's taken her this long to message me. She replies almost instantly.

Your Birthday is what's up! Happy Birthday Bestie! See you at seven for some tequila! X

I check the time – 15.13. Just under three hours till I'm out of here. I consider messaging her back and telling her I already have plans and that she was far too late to spring a visit on me, but that would have been a lie, and she would have known that I wouldn't be keen to spend my birthday evening with anyone else. Besides, I don't fancy sitting in by myself tonight now, not after the fun day I've had with Jacob. I'm in relatively good spirits, but she deserves to stew for a little while. I choose not to reply just quite yet and slide my phone back in my pocket, painting a bright smile on my face as my client's dressing room curtain swishes open.

CHAPTER THREE

I try my best to pander to my highly intoxicated best friend, but she seems to be enjoying my birthday more than I am.

'Come on, Karly! Just one more shot! I promise it will be the last one!' she wails at the top of her lungs. Her speech is slurred, and she bangs her lanky, pale leg off the corner of my white oak coffee table at least a handful of times. I say lanky, but she's only about 5 ft 3, not much more than myself at just over 5 ft, but she's always had these beautiful thin long legs that people would absolutely kill for. Maybe not tall enough to be a professional model, but definitely photo worthy.

She's recently had her long fiery red hair chopped from her waist to shoulder length. A bold move from her, but one that definitely paid off as it highlights her milky skin and bright blue eyes.

We are complete opposites in terms of appearance, and I like that where she is slim and pale, I'm curvaceous and partial to a good spray tan. There has never been any competition with us when it has come to men. They seem to prefer one type to another, so there has always been plenty for both of us to entertain.

I watch her dancing around with her arms in the air to an old school R&B playlist from her Spotify; her hair slick with sweat as it sticks to her forehead. She's singing all the wrong words and I don't know why, but it irritates me hugely.

My jaw feels a bit achy; I can't stop yawning. I don't mean to be rude, but it's been quite an exhausting night trying simultaneously to keep up with Jacob's texts, while feigning interest as she's harped on and on about her latest failed relationship. Her disastrous love life is always a topic of conversation, and after a while it has become extremely mundane. I know why she constantly has problems with the men she dates – she's too clingy and much too quick. As soon as she starts dating, she gets overly attached, and it doesn't take long to scare the guy off. She doesn't need to do this, she's beautiful, and if she just played things a bit cooler, she might actually stand a chance.

I used to try to explain this to her delicate, but she always seemed pathetically wounded by what I had to say before turning defensive and using my own relationship with Jacob as a sharp weapon against me. I eventually stopped trying to help her out and to this day her bunny boiler tendencies have remained the same.

As the night drags on, I simply don't have any energy left to stay up and dance with her any more. My head feels fuzzy from the home-made cocktails we concocted from whatever liqueur we found in my kitchen cupboard and what appears to be three-quarters of a bottle of tequila. I slump down onto my couch and melt into its cushions.

I know I really shouldn't, but I can't resist the urge to look her up on Facebook. It's niggling inside me, gnawing away at my curiosity, desperate to get out. Hannah's phone is sitting next to me and so I pick it up and enter her passcode – which is her birthday and oh so predictable. I reason that if I look her up on Hannah's Facebook account, it won't matter if my finger slips and accidentally hits something it shouldn't because she has no idea who I am, never mind who Hannah is. My mind jolts back to a time of panic where I made that clumsy mistake once before. It was some time last year when I was looking at her pictures and to be honest it's so easily done. One minute your thumb is hovering over the phone and instead of scrolling down, you've hit the like button. I quickly rectified my mistake, and nothing ever came of it, so I don't think she noticed. It didn't stop the anxiety I had waiting for Jacob to call and ask me what I was playing at, and so I'm more careful these days.

My siren red gel painted nails are a blur beneath me as I slowly type in the search bar – the name I hate the most. The screen fills with a list of people to choose from, but I know that she is always the fourth option down. There she is with her lusciously dark shiny hair draped gently around her shoulders as she smiles widely at the camera. She's wearing a pair of black distressed denim shorts with a plain grey T-shirt tucked in; a black western style belt with silver buckles pulls in her already tiny waist. Her legs look tanned, but it's not natural because I know from previous searches that she hasn't been on any holidays recently. Her bronzed arm is stretched behind her as she clutches on to a male hand – his hand, but that's the only part of him in this picture.

Her privacy settings are terrible, I can browse through all her recently uploaded pictures so easily, but I never allow myself to land on one of her dressed in white. That's something I can never bring myself to explore.

Scrolling through her status updates, I can't help but roll my eyes at how boring she seems. What excitement does he get from her? It isn't until I lift another shot of tequila to my lips that I notice that she posted only three minutes ago.

Lauren Cruthers: *2 days to go until a week in the sunshine with the girls! Tenerife, here we come! #Girlstrip*

My head feels so heavy as I stare at the screen, but I still understand perfectly what this means. She's going away – and she's going without him. As the opportunity races through my mind, I scramble to my feet and push past Hannah roughly as I head towards my bedroom. Her phone falls to the floor out of my now lazy hand.

I need to find it, oh god I need to find it quick. My diary, where the fuck is my diary? I know I left it in here somewhere. My head is pounding from adrenaline mixed with tequila. I don't need to look for long; I see it almost instantly, sitting on my dressing table staring right at me, as if a bright light has highlighted its desirability. I snatch it up and frantically flick through the crisp pages to find where I'd last jotted down how many holidays I had left to take from work.

I slump to the floor with a loud thud, allowing my head to lull backwards against my bed. The room spins as I shut my eyes and the black and gold striped book falls into my lap. My lip curls upwards in satisfaction. I have seven days remaining.

JACOB

HER TEXTS HAVE been all over the place tonight. She's quite obviously been drinking, and I wonder who she's with? I suppose I never truthfully know what she's up to. She could be with anyone for all I know. She doesn't tend to lie to me though. She's many things; impulsive, mischievous, and sometimes a little dangerous, but one thing I'll give her credit for is that she is painfully honest. She is also by no means stupid. She understands the boundaries to stay within if she wants to continue speaking to me.

I'm not being cruel you know. If anything, I'm the one who has it hard here. I put my relationship, my marriage, at risk every time we speak, but it's all under control. I've made sure that we only text when I'm at work or home alone. Admittedly, that hasn't always been the case. There have been a few times when I've sent a quick message to Karly when Lauren was sitting right next to me on our sofa. I know that's a shit head move but sometimes I just can't help myself. It's exciting.

Over the years, Karly has continued to push and push the idea of us meeting up, even more so when she found out about Lauren. I've considered it a few times; who wouldn't? I mean she's fucking gorgeous, but I've always stood my ground. That causes issues of its own, the rejection I mean. She doesn't like when I do that. In fact, thinking about it, sometimes she has a real fucking attitude problem that betrays her attractiveness.

Nothing to worry about though, it's not like she can do anything wild and reckless. She doesn't even know where I live, so I don't ever need to worry about her turning up at my door like some sort of psychopath. I've always been careful with that type of information, even telling her a completely different town from the one I actually live in. Shit, that would be a right mess if she got hold of my address, wouldn't it? Can you imagine?

I rattle out a few words and press the send button on my phone.

What are you wearing? X

This time she doesn't reply instantly, which is strange. I stare at the screen blankly for a minute or so. Still nothing. Surely, she's not going to leave me hanging? Our texts have been pretty flirty all day, which usually leads to things heating up a notch as the night goes on. A few compromising pictures are usually exchanged and sometimes even an explicitly filthy phone call.

She can't be doing much, she doesn't even like celebrating her birthday for fuck's sake. Frustrated, I shove my phone inside the pocket of my grey jogging bottoms and pick up the remote control that's fallen onto the carpet. Scanning through the sports channels, I become more and more agitated at her lack of response. I hate that she has this effect on me. I'm not used to being kept waiting; I like to be in control.

I find myself wondering what I can do to grab her attention. What I could send her to pull her back to me. I yank the phone back out of my pocket and open my stored photos, searching for any that I might have previously taken that would send the ball back into my court.

Suddenly, *K* pops up on my screen.

Something's came up, babe, night x

I stare at the screen in pure disbelief. She's kidding, right? What the fuck could be so important that's taken her away from me. Is it some other bloke? Has she invited some random geezer round for a night of fun? My stomach churns at the thought of someone else touching her, their grubby hands groping her curves. I know I don't have a right to be jealous, but I am.

Furious at her I decide to turn the television off and retire to bed. Heading upstairs, the warm scent of amber fills my nose, which only heightens as I gently push open the white wooden door to our bedroom. A candle glows gently on the window ledge and I blow it out as I walk past. Lauren has fallen asleep with a book still firmly attached to her hands. I slide it out gently and place it on the bedside table next to her.

She looks beautiful; even with her dark hair splayed messily across the pillow and her mouth hanging slightly open. I should forget all about Karly once and for all tonight and climb into bed next to my wife – where I should be, but I just can't help myself. I reach into my pocket and take my phone back out and slide open her name.

Make it up to me tomorrow night, babe x

CHAPTER FOUR

KARLY

The past two days have passed me by in an absolute blur. It took an unreasonable amount of time to successfully persuade management to grant me a week's holiday at such short notice. In my opinion, they were just flexing their muscles, showing me who was boss by flaunting their power. Reminding me that there is still a hierarchy that demands to be obeyed.

Whatever they were doing, it was pretty pointless. If they'd said no, it wouldn't have mattered one bit, because I was taking a week off with or without their permission.

I'd contacted all my clients who were scheduled for an appointment and explained to them that sadly there had been a death in the family, a complete shock, and therefore I would need to take some time off. I didn't feel too bad about lying because everyone in my family was already dead; it's not like I would be jinxing anything. A death in your family is an excuse that cannot be disputed no matter how disgruntled you are, and so they were all more than happy to rearrange.

The man next to me erupts into some sort of coughing fit, bringing me back to the here and now. Sitting in Edinburgh Airport, I realise I've been clutching the printed flight ticket a little too tightly in my hand and it's started to rip at the edges. I tend to clench my fists painfully tight when I'm nervous; it allows my face to remain impassive during difficult situations because the tension is directed elsewhere. I don't know why I didn't just save an e-copy of my ticket onto my phone. Perhaps holding the ticket physically in my hands makes everything all the more real. Something solid, not virtual or electronic.

Sitting across from me is a family of five. Mum is cradling her chubby legged baby girl, at least I think it's a girl, and Dad is engrossed in today's paper. Their other two furiously loud and frustrating brats are pretending to be aeroplanes in the middle of the two rows, zooming up and down, up and down. The noise is driving me mad when I'm trying my best to stay calm, and I can't understand the thought process in allowing the sheer chaos their offspring are causing.

I try my best to ignore them, turning my attention to other commuters waiting patiently to travel. Airports are full of all different types of people: bigwigs on their way to an important meeting, happy holiday makers eager to relax before a long and compact journey, groups of boisterous teenagers ready to fling away their dignity on a popular party island, regular travellers who use flight as their means of transport to work on a weekly basis. Regardless of who they are or where they're going, I doubt they want to be disturbed by furiously loud and uncontrollable children.

Enough is enough. My attempts are futile and so I decide to take a walk through the departure lounge, hoping it will also pass some time. There aren't many shops at this airport, which is disappointing, especially with it being in Scotland's capital. The ones that are here are ridiculously overpriced but still claim to offer you substantial discounts from the high street prices.

Dissatisfied by what I've seen so far, I retreat through Duty Free and browse the aisles lazily. Picking up different delicately shaped bottles of perfume. Spritzing a couple on to those flimsy strips of white paper. Some smell nauseatingly sweet and others have too many citrus notes for my liking. The mixture tickles the inside of my nose, threatening to erupt into a series of explosive sneezes.

I wonder what fragrance Jacob's plaything wears. I don't tend to stray from my favourite Thierry Mugler scent, but maybe I should treat myself to something new. After all, this is a special occasion. I try a couple more out and decide on an exquisitely shaped purple bottle; a seductive rich scent with notes of fresh roses and peonies combined with the dark sensuality of amber. Stella McCartney – my favourite by far. As it lingers on my wrist, I embrace the air of confidence it gifts me, something I need in abundance right now.

I stroll back to the waiting area in the departure lounge and I notice that my gate has now been displayed on the big screen attached to the white pillar. Other travellers have started to notice their newly announced gate too and have hastily begun to pick up their belongings – and their children – before starting to make their brisk way to boarding point. I always wonder why some people are in such a rush to get to their gate so early. The plane isn't likely to leave without them, especially if they're here in plenty of time. These are the same maddening people who insist on forming a lengthy queue and end up standing in the same spot for at least an extra thirty minutes longer than necessary.

I follow the crowd of eager passengers at a snail's pace and even pause to take a quick look at my reflection in a shop window. I'm happy with my choice of travel outfit; a pair of light blue skinny jeans that hug my bum perfectly, an oversized white shirt with a singular leopard print pocket that looks pristine against my tan, and a pair of brown and white sandals with multi-coloured fringes. I give my shiny dark hair a quick ruffle, injecting some extra volume into the roots and check my teeth for any red lipstick marks. I'm satisfied that my appearance expertly disguises the angst I'm feeling inside. I don't look nervous, but I am and I feel a world away from the girl who borders on cocky rather than confident. The only thing that lets me down physically are my hands that are trembling by my side. I'm not entirely sure if my shakes are purely from nerves or too much coffee – perhaps a mixture of both; coffee always gives me the jitters.

My phone vibrates quickly in my hand and two messages ping through simultaneously.

The first text is from Hannah.

Please be careful! It's not too late to change your mind! Xxx

I exhale slowly, releasing the small puffs of anger that she has roused within me. I need her support, not her concern. I want to scald her for not being more positive, but I close the message without replying. I'd only say something out of anger that I would later regret.

I met Hannah during my first year working at the department store. She was a sales assistant in one of the concession departments too when I became a Personal Shopper. She was always keen to strike up a conversation with me when I was searching for a client's outfit. I started to drop by more often, during breaks and rare gaps in my diary, and she would fill me in on any outrageous gossip like who's getting the sack or who's been caught shagging who. That kind of stuff. It was refreshingly nice to have someone to talk to, and she made me laugh.

I realised she didn't have many friends outside of work either, and so naturally, a strong friendship blossomed between us. It doesn't bother me only having one real friend; I found out very quickly that I didn't really need any more. Hannah is more than enough drama for me to handle, but that suits me fine having her all to myself. Nobody to come between us, nobody to divert her attention from me.

I'm not embarrassed or anything, why should I be? But I was reluctant at first to tell her about Jacob. I guess I was a little scared that she might mock me if she didn't understand the depth of our relationship, but I didn't have a choice. She kept quizzing me; always asking why I wasn't interested in anyone from the store when there were plenty of fit guys in the menswear department. And when we'd go out clubbing, she couldn't understand why I wouldn't give anyone who approached me a chance. So yeah, I had to tell her that someone else held my heart and had done for a long, long time.

She was understandably shocked at first, which I totally expected, but she didn't laugh at me or tell me I was stupid. Instead, she seemed a little excited by it. She told me it was like some sort of modern-day fairy tale and wanted to know absolutely everything. I was so taken aback by her readiness to accept my unusual situation that I spilled the beans on everything, start to present. It even felt like a weight had been lifted off my shoulders at being able to talk to someone so freely about my feelings and having them totally understand me. She asked me frequently what the latest on our situation was and always had my back when Jacob ghosted me, turning up at my flat with face masks, tequila, and king-size bars of chocolate. I think she gets a thrill from the wildness of it, and sometimes I think she might even be a little jealous that she doesn't have a Jacob of her own.

The second text is from Jacob.

Oi, are you playing hard to get today? X

I smile, he's cute when he's needy. I much prefer it when he's chasing me instead of the other way around. I take a quick snap of the runway from the glass window in front of me and add a quick message.

Speak soon x

A little while later I'm standing outside the terminal, grateful for the chance to stretch my stiff and achy legs. The budget airline I flew with was basic, so there wasn't much leg room. A light breeze gently blows through my hair, but it's not cold by any means. As the heat from the summer sun penetrates my skin, a similar warmth runs through me from the three miniature bottles of rose wine I necked on the plane. I only planned on ordering one to calm my nerves, but I soon needed more to distract me from the two bimbos sitting beside me. God, I wish they did single seats on a plane. I don't imagine they were much older than eighteen – possibly nineteen, but they were highly excitable; like two new puppies being taken for their first walk. I lost count of the number of times the high-pitched Barbie wannabe next to me banged into my shoulder as she posed for selfie after selfie. She did apologise the first few times, but after a while the little bottles of vodka she was starting to collect seemed to dull her manners.

I listened into their conversations discreetly as they batted around catty comments about the friends that couldn't join them, and I started to feel a little bad for not messaging Hannah back. I suppose she was just being nice. They reminded me to be grateful for only having one best friend. I never need to worry about bitching or betrayals with her.

I drag my case along the road to the designated bus stop where the shuttle bus has already arrived to take me to my hotel. The wheels rattle furiously against the concrete and loose gravel. I don't think there'll be many drop-offs because there aren't many people waiting to get on. I give the pleasant driver my case and thank him politely before climbing the four steep steps onto the bus. I choose a window seat near the middle of the carriage, putting my handbag down on the aisle seat beside me, hoping it deters anyone from sitting next to me. The air smells slightly stale, a mixture of sweat and humidity.

I turn my phone back to normal from aeroplane mode and send Hannah a quick message to let her know that I've landed safely and then take my earphones from my bag and pop them in gently, waiting for them to connect wirelessly to my phone.

I put together a very impressive powerful women playlist on Spotify before I left, and I need it right now to keep me going. There's something to be said for listening to music that encourages your mood. When I'm sad, sometimes I listen to Lana Del Ray and bawl my eyes out for no other reason than to release the angst inside me. The style of her music and the tone of her voice allow you to really feel the turmoil inside you, allowing you the freedom to release. As Beyoncé starts to holler in my eardrums, I close my eyes and rest my head back against the chair and let out a deep breath. Not long now I tell myself, not long now.

CHAPTER FIVE

My accommodation for the week is basic, but clean. The double bed is firm, and the sheets are a blank slate of white with a single gold trim embroidered across the middle. The white paint on the wardrobe doors could do with a freshen up and the bedside table has seen better days, but they'll do. I could have chosen the posh hotel that I'd seen online, I have the money after all, but it wouldn't have been close enough to the action.

I take my time unpacking my things and hang each item of clothing up on the flimsy metal hangers that the hotel has provided me with. From the bedroom, two sliding doors lead me out onto a wide balcony that you can also access from identical glass doors in the living room area. Normally I would have taken this opportunity to take a few snaps with the picturesque view behind me, selecting the best filter on my favourite one and adding a few additional touches before uploading it to social media. I would then have sent it on to Jacob too if we were in contact at the time because he doesn't have Facebook or anything like that so he doesn't get to see what I'm up to, but this time I can't do that. I can't risk him recognising where I am.

Once I'd fully unpacked, I changed into something more comfortable and pottered around for a while. Now sitting on the balcony, the backs of my bare legs sticking to the cheap white plastic chair, I peer down at the world below me. I enjoy watching people when they don't realise that they're being observed. Some walk around with a permanent frown, others smile as they read something on their phone and some laugh at a joke they've just been told, only to turn their head and roll their eyes. You can tell a lot about a person from how they act when they're unaware of judgement.

My stomach slightly grumbles, and I check the time. It's too early for dinner, but too late for lunch, which leaves me wondering what I should do now. Unable to sit still for any longer, I slide my dainty feet into a pair of black flip-flops that look cute against my ruby red painted toenails. I grab my purse and oversized black sunglasses from the table in the dining area and make my way downstairs to the hotel bar. It's busy, but there's still a few tables left for me to pick from, so I choose a vacant one at the far corner of the bar.

The extremely handsome waiter with thick dark hair and large chocolate button eyes puts my raspberry margarita down gently on a fresh cardboard beer mat. His gaze lingers a little longer than necessary on my bare legs before walking away smiling. I enjoy the attention, I can't lie, not to mention the view of his ass as he walks away.

I pull my sunglasses from the top of my head and push them over my eyes, allowing me to observe the others around me with invisible eyes.

41

I notice an adorable older couple sitting across from one another, sharing a bottle of red wine while holding hands in the middle of the table. She's laughing at something he's just said, and he looks extremely pleased with himself that he is still able to make his wife laugh so wholeheartedly after however many years they've been together. I appreciate elderly couples like them, the ones who still gift each other small tokens of affection. An age where people fought hard to make their relationships work instead of tossing them aside in hope of something better. I wonder if Mum and Dad would have turned out the same; I imagine they would have. They were always very affectionate towards each other; holding hands while they sat on the couch to watch telly. Dad used to always kiss Mum on the forehead when they hugged, and I'd watch in awe at my two beautiful heroes.

I continue to watch them for a few moments longer, enjoying an insight into what Jacob and I are still to become. It excites me, knowing we still have so much left to look forward to.

My gaze drifts to an attractive man, early thirties I would say, sitting by himself and tapping away on his iPad. A full icy Corona with a slice of lime in its mouth sits beside him and I can't help but notice that there's no glass of wine or cocktail accompanying it, suggesting he's here alone. He is dressed smartly in a short-sleeved white shirt with a few buttons left open at the collar exposing his smooth neck. The material hugs his muscular arms perfectly and the fashion critic in me can't help herself examine further as my eyes flow down his navy chino shorts that he's paired with similar coloured Ralph Lauren loafers. His hair isn't blonde, but not quite dark enough to be brunette, which is why I'm surprised I even noticed him, I always go for dark-haired men. I drink him in, impressed by his taste, and I smile discreetly in approval. The invisible stench of wealth oozes from him. He definitely has a bob or two in the bank that's for sure.

Had this situation been back home, I imagine he would have approached me after I flirted from afar, flashing him my sexiest smile that says I'd be happy to indulge him. He would have asked me if he could join me for a drink and because it would have been rude of me to turn such a handsome man away, I would say yes and he would take a seat beside me, not across from me. We would spend the night flirting back and forward and depending on what qualities he possessed, the more similar to Jacob's the better, it would then be entirely up to me whether I accepted his invite to accompany him home. I rarely invite men back to mine. My flat is my sanctuary, my peace. A place with no memories of heartbreak and abandonment. When I go home with anyone, I know that I'm in control. I'm the one who leaves in the morning before they wake up. They never get the chance to leave me. Tonight though, I don't smile at him and I don't even attempt to catch his eye, because I'm not here for him; he would only be a distraction.

An hour or so later, after sampling a few fruity cocktails from the happy hour menu, I decide to wander outside of the hotel; stretch my legs and find somewhere to grab a pizza to take back to my room. A bit of dinner and a good night's sleep will set me up for tomorrow's activities. I lift my belongings and shimmy my way through the busy tables, noting a few new faces that have joined the bar. I press the round button at the elevator to take me down to street level and casually flick through my Instagram feed when laughter explodes from the metal doors. The smell of perfume attacks my senses as they spill out one by one; their large cases dragging behind them. 'Sorry, babe!' one squeals as she bangs heavily into me and nearly knocks me off my feet. The noise reminds me of a wild pack of hyenas that I'd seen on a wildlife documentary not so long ago.

When I think that all of them have finally emptied the lift and am now safe to continue my journey, I take a step forward to enter but am surprised that there is one final girl left to exit. As she emerges from the doors, she pulls her sunglasses from her face. My feet refuse to lift from the ground, I try to run; I try to break free, but I'm stuck in the moment as I watch her shuffle to catch-up with her friends. I didn't expect to see her until tomorrow. I feel now a wave of heat rush through my face, my stomach doing somersaults. I've seen plenty of pictures of her before, I knew what she looked like but I'm star-struck viewing her up close. I'm a rabbit caught in headlights. Seeing her in person is so different from viewing her life through a screen.

JACOB

'DO YOU HAVE everything?' I ask her. She's running her fingers through her hair while looking in the bedroom mirror for self-validation. Her bulging suitcase is waiting by the door ready for me to lift downstairs.

'I think so,' she replies. 'I'm sure one of the girls will have whatever I need if I've forgotten anything.' She seems a bit tense, flustered almost, as she pushes her hair up and down at the roots – I don't really know what she's doing there to be honest.

She's been a bit off with me recently, and I don't know why, but it's been really fucking annoying. I wish women would just tell you what's wrong with them when you ask them outright, you know? I'm not a bloody mind reader.

'Last chance to change your mind, babe.' I tease. 'You could always just stay here with me.'

She pauses and puts down the red lipstick that she was holding firmly in her hand and turns on her heels to face me.

'Do you not want me to go?' she asks.

I'm just messing with her of course, but I know that if I really did want her to stay, she would. I quickly fill the gap before she changes her mind. 'I'm just messing, you doughnut. I'll miss you that's all.' She doesn't reply. Instead, she stares up at me blankly, her eyes starting to fill with fresh tears. She is tiny in comparison to my 6 ft stature. Maybe I've been unfair to her by joking around. This is her first time away from me since we got married, she's bound to be a little apprehensive, and let's be honest, who would want to leave me, anyway? She turns her back on me quickly, realising that I've noticed her damp eyes and so I step towards her and pull her into me, wrapping my arms around her petite waist. I'm not lying to her, I will miss her, but I must admit there is a little part of me – OK a big part – that's giddy with anticipation.

To be honest, I can't fucking wait for a full week to have some fun of my own without anyone looking over my shoulder. Reminiscent of my bachelor lifestyle; a week of bliss.

Her pretty blonde friend picks her up in a taxi about forty minutes later and after I've waved her off to Gatwick Airport, the first thing that I do is head to the fridge and pull out an ice-cold beer. I'm not usually into blondes, but her best mate is hard not to appreciate. She's a little firecracker too, a pocket rocket Barbie. Completely different to my wife.

Excitement pulses through me as the fizzy liquid slides down my throat. I send my brother a quick message asking him if he fancies a few beers down the pub and then I scroll my thumb through my contact list until I land on Karly. I wonder what she's doing right now.

CHAPTER SIX

KARLY

Finally, the tightness in my legs starts to ease, I'm able to lift my foot and so I rush inside the elevator, waiting for what feels like an eternity for the heavy metal doors to close and help me in my escape to safety. I struggle to shake the image of her face; her natural beauty, her perfectly plump lips, and her pale but glowing skin. She is much prettier in person than I ever gave her credit for, and strikingly so.

She wore a black playsuit that hugged her petite body, paired with a pair of wedge heels. I noticed the presumably expensive gold hoops which hung from her ears. Something unsettled me about this. Her outfit was very well put together. That wasn't the problem, it just reminded me of what I wore to a friend's barbecue last summer. I didn't like the similarity; it made me feel uncomfortable, actually. I'm understandably agitated by this whole situation, not to mention pissed at how stunning she looked, but what I'm feeling is something more, something eerie. I'm unnerved by Jacob's selection of females because there is no denying that there are infinite similarities between us. Her figure, her dark hair, her sparkly eyes that reel you in. If I was to take a guess, I'd say she'd probably be around my height too without those fucking heels on.

There is absolutely no way I'm going to be able to stomach anything to eat now, so instead I head back to my room. I swipe my key card at the door, but it doesn't register right away, and I grow even more flustered as I wave the plastic card around a few more times, begging it to grant me access. The door finally opens, and I burst straight through the living room area to the balcony doors, flinging them open with more force than intended and flinching at the sound of them thudding against the wall. I peer down at the pool, frantically scanning over stacked sunbeds and the remainder of today's bikini bodies, but I can't see her now – I can't see any of them.

I rest my hands on the metal railing and close my eyes. The raw heat it has gathered burns my fingertips and I allow it to do so; a welcome distraction from the anxiety whirling around inside me. I pray that she didn't see me. She didn't flinch at the sight of me, so that's a good sign. I take deep breaths in through my mouth and exhale through my nose until I find some comfort in the realisation that she doesn't know who I am, and slowly the chaos inside me starts to ease.

The next morning, I wake to the sound of plastic beds being dragged instead of lifted across the ground as the battle for the best sunspot commences. I stretch my arms above my head and yawn. I barely slept last night. My mind was racing frantically, unable to slow down, conjuring self-doubt and bad thoughts, one after the other. I feel groggy and I realise that the cocktails I consumed yesterday won't have helped any.

I run my fingers through my hair, loosening the tugs that have formed from thrashing against the pillow. I don't know what time it is, but I suppose I should get up, anyway. I throw back the light-weighted bed sheet and shuffle over to the edge of the mattress, lowering my legs, and letting the soles of my bare feet adjust to the cool temperature of the tiles.

My first stop is the kitchen. After pulling a bottle of ice-cold water from the fridge, I take a few deep gulps and make my way out to the balcony and rest my arms on the railing. It holds a different temperature from yesterday, soothing rather than menacing. I turn to pull over one of the chairs, but the morning dew has gently landed on the surface of the table and each of the plastic seats, so I remain standing.

I realise that a bunch of beds have congregated to the left-hand side of the pool. Each of them has a different coloured towel placed delicately on top, and I'm positive they all belong to females. A blonde-haired girl appears, and I recognise her from yesterday. She throws down a fluorescent yellow beach bag beside one of the beds and then disappears from my eye line once again.

My eyes hop over the other beds, searching for an empty space. This habit of getting up before the crack of dawn to bag the best spot on a bed seems to be a tradition that cannot be broken regardless of your destination. To my luck I see the perfect gap directly across the pool from where the girls have gathered. That will do me just fine.

I watch as the rest of the group appears like marching ants and place their belongings beside their chosen beds. When they're satisfied, they make their way out of the hotel, taking the stairs this time instead of the lift. I count their heads as they walk away. They are one head short.

With the coast now clear, I grab my own beach towel from my room and quickly run down the four flights of stairs which leads me to the pool. I struggle to catch my breath and my heart pounds deeply as it desperately pleads to burst from my chest. The bed I want is still empty and I quickly throw my pink and white striped towel on top. A woman behind me tuts and clucks like an annoying hen, quite clearly annoyed that I've disturbed her peace and quiet. I turn on my heels, ready to head back to my room and as I walk past her, I flip her the finger and smile widely as she winces in horror.

I stare down at two bandeau bikinis that I've pulled from the bedside drawer and thrown onto the bed. One set is canary yellow with delicate little white flowers. The other is a plain design but completely in your face shade of neon orange. Normally, the attention-grabbing orange set would have been my first choice, but I don't want to stand out for the wrong reasons. I want them to notice me, acknowledge me – but not in a threatening way.

I pull off my pyjamas and toss them in the direction of the chair that sits redundant in the corner of the room. I slip my legs into my bikini bottoms and tighten the toggles at my hips before clipping the bandeau at my front and then shimmying it round to the back. I'm useless when it comes to fastening a bra too, I have to do it the cheat's way.

I stand facing the mirror and pinch the loose skin at my stomach and groan. I wish I'd lost a few pounds before coming here. It would have made me feel better about myself, but there was no time; everything happened at lightning speed. I grab my barrel brush from the dresser and unwrap the plain white cotton scrunchie from the handle. Tipping my head upside down, I give my thick hair a quick ruffle before scraping it up onto the top of my head in an attempt at a messy bun. It's not quite right though, perhaps a little too neat, so I pull a few strands of hair astray from either side of my ears and twist them gently around my fingers, letting them fall into a slight curl.

I take my make-up bag into the dimly lit bathroom and take out a cheap black Kohl eyeliner and mascara set that I found at the bottom of a drawer back home. I run the pencil along the inside of my bottom lid and gently smudge it with my index finger, creating a make-up artist's worst nightmare. I then apply four coats of mascara to each eye, making sure that there'll be enough cheap product there for it to successfully melt and drip when appropriately lubricated. I opt for no foundation or concealer today, allowing my freckles and the dark purple bags under my eyes some freedom. Maybe it wasn't such a bad thing that I got such a shit night's sleep after all.

A sharp laugh escapes my throat. I can't believe just how awful I look. There is absolutely no way I would ever be seen in public like this back home. No dewy glow, no statement lip, and definitely no contour, I'm quite possibly horrific, and yet I can't help but smile because I know I've created a masterpiece.

I head back into the bedroom and pull my straw bucket bag from the wardrobe and throw in my key card, a bottle of factor 15 sun cream and my phone. I also chuck in my headphones at the last minute. I don't plan on using them because I want to be able to hear all their conversations, but I'll take them down with me just in case.

I tug a long white crochet kimono off one of the hangers and slide it on before grabbing my oversized black sunglasses from the bedside table. I push my feet into my flip-flops and take one final glance in the mirror. It's show time, baby.

At pool level, I drop my bag onto the hot red concrete tiles and adjust the position of my sun bed so that it's lying completely flat. I take my spot cross-legged in the middle of my towel, gently removing my kimono, careful not to poke any additional holes in the crochet.

On the other side of the pool, the girls have returned from their morning walk and now occupy their spots. A skinny girl with fiery auburn hair tied up in a high ponytail applies thick cold splodges of cream to her friend's back. She cackles brashly as the other girl squirms beneath her icy touch. My heart twitches slightly at the thought of my own red head back home. I guess I kind of miss her.

Two of the other girls lie next to each other on their front, their bikini tops unclasped to avoid those pesky unwanted tan lines, and I can see the remnants of freshly applied oil glistening on their skin. The last bed however remains empty – her bed, and I wonder where she is.

An hour passes as I wait patiently for her to arrive. My skin has begun to soak up the beautiful morning sun and a drop of sweat trickles down my back. Even though she has not yet surfaced, I decide that enough time has passed for me to set the ball rolling. I retrieve my phone from my bag and slowly begin to scroll through my Instagram feed. My aim here is to create the illusion that I'm fixated on a rather long-winded message that I've just received. I feign confusion, disbelief, and pain as I start to hunch my shoulders and imitate quiet puppy like whimpering noises, forcing my chest to rise up and down. I drop my phone suddenly between my legs and theatrically throw my head into my hands. I push my fingertips under the rim of my glasses and drag my fingers over my eyes, smudging my black mascara that will now have started to dissolve in the heat. I pull my fingers down my face, painting black streaks across my cheeks like distressed war markings. I carry on with this facade of despair for a couple more minutes and then lift my head, positive that I'll see someone from the group making their way over to me. To my horror, all I see is an elderly couple peering over in my direction and whispering to each other. They also don't make any attempt to get their wrinkly old bodies up from their beds.

Behind the privacy of my dark shades, I glare furiously at my targeted audience. Only one of them is looking over at me, but she quickly turns her head, fearful that I might catch her. I'm positively miffed. Why have none of the others shown any interest? I know they can hear me, there isn't that much distance between us, and they can definitely see me. What a bunch of bitches! I was so confident that this was going to work; I had every faith. It was simple. A fool proof plan. All I had to do was pretend to be visibly distressed and surely one of those girls would feel the urge to do something, want to help. Surely a poor girl sitting by herself, clearly upset would be enough to encourage anyone to make their way over. I was supposed to let them comfort me, let them befriend me, and then I would have had an in – but nobody has budged. So much for fucking girl power.

I swing my legs off my bed and slide on my flip-flops, pausing for a minute before springing to my feet and briskly making my way over to the pool bar.

'Hi,' I say to the barman with the crisp tight white T-shirt and slick jet-black hair. 'One tequila sunrise.' He smiles at me despite my rudeness and then starts to flex his muscles by tossing some bottles in the air before pouring the ingredients into a gun metal cocktail shaker.

'Oh, and don't hold back on the tequila!' I snap.

I drum my fingers loudly on the bar as I wait for my drink, furious that things haven't gone to plan. Why did nobody react? What has gone so wrong here? I just don't understand. I didn't expect the full group to stand to attention like soldiers, but I at least hoped one or even two of them would have taken bait.

When he's finished his little performance, I thank the bar man and take the cool plastic cup in my hand, reaching for a straw but then deciding against it. I take a few large gulps while standing at the bar and let the tangy liquid slide down my throat, wincing as I begin my walk back to my bed. Wow, as requested, he really didn't hold back on the tequila. Another few large gulps and my drink is no more. I crush the plastic cup in my hands and crawl on to the bed, flopping down on my front and resting my head on my arms now folded at the top of the bed. I'm frustrated – yes; confused – most definitely; but beaten – not by any means. I decide to try again this afternoon. I close my eyes tightly and allow myself to drift off to the sound of Spanish music playing softly in the distance.

CHAPTER SEVEN

A heavy splash wakens me; a couple of drops of water landing on my arm. I check the time – 4 p.m., shit! I've slept much longer than I intended to. I push on to my hands and force myself to kneel up. My arms ache from being left dormant in one position for too long, and a hot itching sensation brews between my shoulder blades. Carrying on all the way down to the bottom of my back. I wince as I try to move, my skin feeling tight. I realise that I never applied sun cream before I fell asleep. I groan quietly. This has not been a good day.

All four girls are sitting upright and chatting among themselves. They remind me of little plastic ducks you find at one of the stalls in a carnival; all of them lined up, waiting to be hooked in an attempt to win a prize. I'll hook one of you.

For the second time today, I pick up my phone and pretend to study the screen. It burns in the palm of my hand. Like me, it's also fallen victim to overheating from lying carelessly in the sun, and the instant sharpness of pain assists me in producing genuine tears. I spot a little red number one next to my message icon. It's Hannah, asking how things are going while adding that it's still not too late to change my mind and get a flight home. In the same message she seems to come to her senses, realising that there isn't much chance of that ever happening and so suggests that if I'm adamant on staying then why not try to find a new man of my dreams while I'm here? Someone fresh and exciting; someone without so much baggage. Or even just a holiday romance she quips. This girl! Doesn't she get it? This isn't something I can just walk away from. I've never been able to. I ignore her message and take a long, deep breath and pretend to cry once again. This time though, I'm a little louder, a little uglier, and a little more desperate. I pause briefly between sobs, listening for movement, but I hear nothing. No scraping of beds as they're quickly pushed to the side, no heavy footsteps as they rush towards me – nothing. It doesn't take long for my tears to become genuine, but not because I'm sad. No, not sad at all. I'm full of pure rage; it overpowers me, causing my whole body to tremble. They are ruining everything, and I've had enough.

I reach below my bed for my bag, ready to pack up my things and head upstairs, but I'm startled by a cool soft hand landing delicately on my shoulder. As I look up, she takes a seat on the empty bed beside me. She takes my hand in hers and gently clasps her other over the top, scooting in closer to me so that her knees are grazing mine.

'Sorry, I don't mean to be nosey,' she starts. Her voice was surprisingly delicate for a typical Essex accent. Not as raw as some of her friends' voices. 'I've been pottering in and out of my balcony today, trying to catch whatever sun I can as I've not been feeling too good and I couldn't help notice you.'

I realise I'm holding my breath and force myself to exhale. She continues, 'I couldn't bear watching you any longer, and you don't need to tell me what's wrong, but are you OK?'

I study her face. Up close, she really is quite simply beautiful. The bridge of her nose has started to freckle from the kiss of the sun and even without a hint of make-up she has a natural radiance about her. She doesn't look sick to me. With my free hand placed between my legs, I discreetly pinch a bit of loose flesh from the inside of my thigh, coaxing fresh tears to my eyes. I gently slide my hand out from under hers and slowly push my dark glasses up onto the top of my head. I hope my eyes look puffy.

'I'm so sorry, I didn't mean to disturb you.' I stammer. 'It's my boyfriend. He, eh, he told me he didn't want to be with me any more – a day before we were due to come on this holiday. I've tried to speak to him today, but he doesn't want to know.'

I let a few loud sobs escape my throat for good measure before continuing. 'I didn't know what to do, so I came on this stupid holiday by myself and now everything is just a mess.'

Who would have thought that she would have been the most decent of the pack? I hadn't planned for things to go this way. This is what I planned to tell one of her friends, hoping they would take pity on me and invite me to join them, but she has gifted me a new opportunity – an even better one.

She looks at me thoughtfully with kind blue eyes. 'Oh, you poor thing!' she gasps. 'Don't worry, babe, you won't be spending another day here alone. I'll look after you. Oh, and I'm Lauren by the way.'

JACOB

LAUREN PHONED A day later than expected to say she'd arrived at her hotel safely. I asked why I hadn't heard from her when she landed, or even at all for the entire first day, and she told me that she hasn't been feeling very well spent her first day cooped up in her apartment. I don't think it's anything serious, it's probably been travel sickness; she suffers quite badly from that.

A shiver runs through me.

Whatever it is, I just hope she's not fucking pregnant.

I've only just become a husband, I'm not ready to become a dad for fuck's sake.

I was a bit surprised when she told me about the new friend she's made, it's not like her group of friends to welcome a stray. Doesn't matter either way to me mind you, as long as she is able to get out and about and start enjoying herself.

Since that phone call I've barely heard from her, and in all honesty, it's been peaceful as fuck. Sometimes I just need some space to myself. There's nothing wrong with me, it's just this whole marriage thing is still new to me; I no longer have the freedom that I was so accustomed to.

I'd say I'm what most girls call their type. What is it they say? Tall, dark, and handsome. At 6 ft 2, with thick dark hair, subtle olive toned skin – due to my Italian heritage – and a wide cheeky smile, I had my pick of girls at any pub or club I went to. They were as disposable to me as the rubber I used with them; I had no use for the same one twice. That all changed when I met Lauren though. I decided to try my hand at a serious relationship and even remained – what do they call it – monogamous. Well, kind of. A few slip-ups here and there don't really count. Not if they don't mean anything. Lauren was something special though, someone worth investing my time in, trying my best to be a good guy for.

Strangely, I also haven't heard much from Karly. She sent me a quick snap yesterday of what looked like an airport, but she didn't reply when I asked her where she was off to. I'm slightly pissed off at the lack of communication from her. This is the perfect time for us to talk without having to worry if anyone might see my phone. She would usually beg for my undivided attention, so it's weird that she's missing out.

She's likely to be on one of her work trips, I know she sometimes needs to travel to different parts of the country for fashion events and brand promotions. On one occasion she flew to London to help style some models or something for the launch of a new boutique store. She was only about an hour's drive from me. I knew what was coming. She ever so gently, bless her heart, broached the subject of going for a coffee at the hotel she was staying at. No strings attached she said, nothing will happen between us she said. As if I believed that. She might have believed that she was dangling the carrot ever so delicately, but nothing about Karly's approaches were delicate. Her hints were always as subtle as being whacked with a sledgehammer.

Now I'm not gonna lie to you, I did consider it. It was tempting of course. Fuck, everything about her is tempting, but I couldn't bring myself to go through with it. I sent her a brief and blunt text about twenty minutes before I was due to arrive, turned the car around, and went back home to Lauren. I ain't stupid, and neither is she. We both know deep down that it might start with coffee but would indefinitely end up somewhere much more dangerous. The chemistry between us is electric, I know it would only intensify in person and I would absolutely cave to my primal instincts. It's women like her that are the downfall of men like me; men who want to be decent, but she's not the only one. I've encountered many manipulative women in my time.

My phone buzzes in my back pocket and I reach behind to retrieve it. I check the name that pops up on my screen and my lip curves upwards in smug satisfaction.

Ah, there you are.

CHAPTER EIGHT

KARLY

I'm waiting for Lauren to arrive at the pool bar when I get another text from Jacob. I completely forgot to reply to his previous message with everything that has been going on. I usually reply to his messages instantly, I can't help myself, but recently I've been slower than usual. I realise that without actually meaning to, I'm giving him a taste of his own medicine by keeping him waiting. A bit of well-deserved pay back I'd say. I smile down at the screen. He's so not used to this, it's new to him, and now he's shamelessly double texting. He knows fine well that I won't be able to resist a second message though. He is very clever; I'll give him that.

I didn't know what to wear tonight, a struggle that's extremely foreign to me. I know how to dress myself well. I mean, it is my job, so I know what suits me and what doesn't. It pained me to abandon that skill even if it was only for one week. Tonight though, all my usual instincts were thrown right out the window. I had to think differently; look at myself as merely an understudy rather than the leading lady. I needed to look fragile – a damsel in distress as they say, therefore bold colours and heavy accessories just wouldn't do. No girl who was at her lowest ebb would dress so flamboyantly, and so I opted for a simple pair of light blue skinny jeans, a white chiffon camisole, and a pair of flat white sandals with brown tweed straps. Very demure; a stereotypical plain Jane, and God, I fucking hate it.

When doing my make-up, I applied a thin layer of nude lipstick and a quick whip of mascara, leaving the rest of my face completely bare. I also washed my hair and straightened it within an inch of its life so that it looked limp and lifeless but was at least clean. I pray that the humidity gives me a wide berth and doesn't attack until after dinner if it really needs to.

She told me to meet her here at 7 p.m. and much to my annoyance she's now ten minutes late. I was hesitant at first when she earlier suggested that we go for some dinner together tonight, just me and her, after all I didn't expect to engage in a dance with the devil right away.

'What about your friends?' I asked her, but she told me not to worry about them. I did find it a bit peculiar that she chose to break away from her group instead of simply inviting me out with them. Maybe she didn't want to add to my angst by introducing me to a large group of fresh faces when I was quite clearly already very distraught. Kind of sweet, I guess.

I hear the click of her solid wedge heels as they approach me from behind.

'So sorry I'm late!' she exclaims. 'Had a mare with my hair tonight.'

I stare at her bemused because she's obviously lying. It doesn't look like she's had any sort of nightmare whatsoever.

She's dressed in a striking blood-red jumpsuit with a thin black belt wrapped around her tiny waist and her hair sits around her smooth shoulders in thick loose curls. She has a full face of make-up on, including a matte red lipstick that compliments her outfit perfectly.

I glare at her some more, completely bewildered. She looks fucking amazing, there is no doubt about that, but something doesn't sit right with me. I rack my brain trying to pluck the answer from my memory when it hits me. That outfit, that hairstyle; it all looks far too similar to a picture of myself I recently posted on my Instagram. I think the only difference between that picture and Lauren standing in front of me right now is that she isn't wearing any earrings. She may as well have. She could be my doppelgänger. I let a sharp snort escape me. I've gathered by now that Jacob has a type, but could he be taking things a bit further? Could he be suggesting outfits to Lauren that resemble mine? I wonder if he is trying to mould her into a second-rate version of me. I can't understand why though, especially when he knows he could have the real thing.

'Is everything OK?' she questions, her brow furrowed with concern.

I snap myself back to reality as quick as possible and blurt out a weak ass excuse of simply being in awe of how lovely she looks. She laps the compliment up, cackling loudly as she throws her head back. Damn – not even a smudge of red lipstick on her teeth.

She chose a loosely Moroccan styled restaurant for dinner. The brown tables with satin red tablecloths sit intimately together, each one placed directly under a rustic dimly lit shade. A soft mist sprays lightly over people eating their dinner, refreshing their skin with gentle droplets of what I assume is water, as they devour their delicious looking meals.

I order first, picking skewered chicken breast accompanied by mixed peppers with a dish of peppercorn sauce, and she orders exactly the same. I wonder if she copied me or if she genuinely has the same taste in food. I smile inwardly; yet another similarity between us.

I tactfully start to build the blocks of our friendship, asking her all about herself: where she comes from and what she likes and dislikes in life. Normal chit chat, nothing out of the ordinary when you meet someone new. She tells me that she lives with her husband who she married just six months ago, in a little town just outside of Essex. Apparently, it rests only a street away from a stunning sea view; something she and her husband absolutely adore. I allow her to continue speaking, but I don't really hear what she's saying because it suddenly dawns on me that the only detail that I don't know about Jacob is his address.

She tells me that she owns her own hair salon on the high street and that it's called *Lauren, With Love*. How terribly tacky, I thought. How vain you must be to splash your name across your own shop front. I hope my face didn't show my repulsion too much, but to be honest I've always had a problem stopping my thoughts from escaping via my face. She delights in telling me all about her husband, Jacob; a

THE LIES SHE TOLD

handsome electrician from Battersea who she self-proclaims is her soul mate. I ask her how they first met, because I genuinely don't know the answer, and she tells me that they met in a bar in the City Centre of London in the evening. She boasts that he was with his friends and she was with hers. She played hard to get, but he was persistent. It made me feel sick to my stomach, and it churned as I tried to digest both the dinner and her words. She's living the absolute fucking dream, isn't she? The life I should be living. It isn't fair.

She continues to ramble, as if she enjoys the sound of her own voice. Although they've only been married for less than a year, they've been together for four. I try to feign interest; I already know these details, I've asked Jacob before, and hearing them pour from her mouth is not something I'm particularly enjoying. I need to pretend though, I must or else I might give something away.

At the end of our meal, the waitress approaches us armed with a tray of two glasses filled with a beige liquid and a couple of ice cubes; complimentary drinks that tasted like a cheap imitation of Baileys. As I neck the last of mine, she eventually finishes talking about herself and broaches the subject of my 'breakup'.

'So, tell me' – she starts – 'how can any man not want to come on holiday with a gorgeous girl like you?'

I tell her the story I've practised over and over in my head; using small snippets of truth among a mesh of lies. I told her that my boyfriend (I called him Mark) and I'd been together for ten years and things had recently become a little strained. I tell her that I've been dropping hints for him to finally take things to the next level, but that he was just so strangely reluctant to move forward. I tell her that I felt rejected and insecure, and I grew to become suspicious of where he was going and who he was talking to. I explain that I was convinced there was another girl in his life, but that I tried so hard to keep telling myself that I was being silly. I mean, he loved me – how could he try to replace me?

She sat quietly, her body frozen like a statue, and was completely fixated on every word that left my mouth. On a whim, I decided to spice things up a little and threw in a little something extra about a note being left on the bedside table just a day before our holiday saying that he needed some time to himself to think things through, and then as if by magic, he was gone, and I didn't know where he was. Sounds familiar, right? I couldn't resist. Being the professional that I am, I manage to conjure up a few tears on cue, and she speedily rises from her wicker chair embarrassingly, almost tipping it over, and lunges forwards to grab me. She envelopes me in a tighter than life embrace, and I know here and now that I have her. Hook, line, and sinker – this was too easy.

After dinner we take our time strolling past the countless bars and restaurants, weaving in and out of the clutches of zesty seasonal workers desperate to pull you in to successfully up their commission. We decided that we'll make a little detour before heading back to the hotel after all. We climb a steep set of stairs that leads us to the entrance of a snazzy rooftop cocktail bar. She excuses herself and heads to the toilet and so I take the liberty of ordering us two Long Island Iced Teas and a shot of tequila each.

A table overlooking the strip lies vacant, so I pop our drinks down quickly before anyone else has the chance to grab it. It's extremely lively down below us, and I wonder if I would be able to spot any of her friends. Surely, they would all be out enjoying themselves. Maybe she'd ask them to join us and introduce me, but I don't see any of them.

When she returns from the toilet, we chat comfortably about the usual girly things: make-up, hair, and trashy TV shows as we sip on our cocktails. Conversation is easy with her, there are no awkward silences and I hate to admit it, but I genuinely find her quite funny. I didn't ever expect to like anything about her, but it was difficult to avoid. Despite this, I still watch with pure pleasure when her face twists horribly and morphs into something quite unflattering as the sharpness of the tequila reaches the back of her throat.

I nip to the loo and when I come back, I'm surprised to see that she has just about finished her tall icy drink that was definitely more than half full when I'd left the table. I look at her intensely, studying her face for any signs of confession that she'd maybe knocked it with a clumsy arm and toppled it over, or even chucked it away because it was too strong for her, but there was absolutely nothing in her face to suggest any guilt.

Her large sapphire eyes now look a little glossy, and I notice that she is starting to slur some of her words, and she keeps forgetting where she is in the middle of sentences. She confesses how happy she is to have met me and tells me that under no circumstances am I allowed to spend this holiday by myself. A small part of me feels flattered that someone is being so nice to me, with no agenda or ulterior motive other than becoming my friend.

My original plan was never to personally befriend her. I was going to form a friendship with one of the other girls; drop subtle hints over a period of time about a boy I knew and wait for the penny to drop and realisation to kick in that low and behold, her friend's husband had a big secret – and even bigger explaining to do. It would have caused absolute chaos among the group and threw a right spanner in the works for Lauren's perfect relationship. But hey, these things happen and I have a different plan now, one that's going to work out quite nicely.

As we walk back to our hotel after an enjoyable evening, I notice that her legs are faltering, and I can't help but laugh. She looks at me questioningly and joins in on what she thinks is a funny joke; two drunk girls stumbling home after a wild night out. The difference between us though is that I'm not stumbling. My night has been calculated and perfectly controlled, not wild. Oh, Lauren. Poor, sweet, naïve Lauren. How easy it was for me to get you so drunk tonight. I wonder if you will make a habit of this. Who knows what you might do?

JACOB

Are you enjoying yourself? X

Absolutely x

It's been quiet without you x

Are you there?????

Yeah, I'm here! X

Have you been busy? I haven't heard much from you x

Very! Something ... UNEXPECTED cropped up that's had all my attention – Sorry! X

That's OK, babe, anything important? X

You could say that x

What do you mean? X

Oi, what's with all the secrecy? X

You know me, babe. I like to keep you on your toes x

CHAPTER NINE

'Come up here! Dance with me!' I shout over the mixture of laughter and loud music.

She shakes her head and laughs politely, but I'm not taking no for an answer. I slither down from the sticky bar and my skirt hitches up a notch too far, exposing a slice of white lace between my legs, provoking a group of leering men to wolf whistle from their table, and so I flash them a smile. I'm not embarrassed, and they're only human.

I'd left her sitting at the tall round table in the middle of the room. She was starting to bore me, and I needed to release some pent-up energy. I desperately wanted to dance, and she couldn't stop me. She doesn't make the decisions any more, like she'd initially done at the start of our time together – I do. I discreetly eased my way into a position of power, allowing her to take the lead for the first couple of days, but then I flourished before her eyes, transforming into a confident and headstrong butterfly. I think she believes that she is the sole reason that all traces of my heartache have now disappeared. That our friendship is what coaxed me out of my tormented cage, and now I'm running free.

I take the glass from her hand and put it down on the table. 'Lauren, listen to me, there is no point sitting here on your todd with a sour face when you could be having the time of your life dancing on a bar, *Coyote Ugly* style – now get up!' I demand.

I yank her to her feet a little too roughly, and she purses her lips and mouths the word ouch, but I don't think she actually said it aloud; it's too loud in here to tell. She's a little wobbly, a result of the copious amount of alcohol I've expertly plied her with all evening. I position her in front of me and guide her through the crowd, maintaining a tight grip on her waist, leading her straight past the group of rowdy men and prop her up at the front of the bar. If she's not going to willingly have any fun, then I need to get her ready. You know, loosen her up a bit.

I order us three shots of tequila each and line hers up in front of her. From the corner of my eye, I notice one of our avid admirers from the whistling table. He's fixated on Lauren and I know that look; lustful and mischievous.

I divert my attention back to Lauren, and she looks at me warily, silently begging me for reassurance as she slowly takes the first shot glass in her hand. I push the bottom of the glass upwards towards her mouth.

'Go on then,' I urge, watching her carefully, making sure all three of her shots are swallowed one after the other.

When she is finished, I quickly neck mine and push our empty glasses aside. There's a reason I always choose tequila over sambuca; it's because I know how much I can tolerate with tequila. I know my limits; I know when it starts to affect my judgement. I realised that Lauren didn't possess that same superpower.

I hoist myself back onto the bar and stand towering over her, my hand stretched out for her to take. She looks up at me weakly pathetic and hesitant, but I keep my arm firmly out and she quickly realises that she has no other choice but to place her clammy hand in mine and join me.

I enjoy the rush of heat that the shots have given me. The bass drums through my entire body, vibrating through my veins as I dance without care; my hair swinging from side to side. The handsome stranger from the corner of the room is still staring at Lauren, who is still completely shell-shocked at finding herself standing on a bar in front of an extremely busy pub. She looks awkward and evidently unsure of what to do with herself, and so I grab her hands and push them up into the air, keeping hold of them tightly as I force her to dance with me. Her body begins to loosen off a little from its rigid disposition and she slowly starts to sway to the beat of the music, following the rhythm and allowing her body to fold into mine seductively. The wolf whistles have returned in full swing and she's laughing now, genuinely enjoying the attention that we are getting. She is no longer timid; she is as free and fluid as the alcohol swimming through her blood stream and to be honest, I'm a little proud of her.

A few other girls have taken our lead and joined us on the bar, clearly jealous of the fun we're having. I was initially annoyed by their presence because we were having such a good time together just the two of us. So much so that I almost forgot what I still had to do. They

73

have started to mingle between us, wanting to get in on the action that's attracting so much attention. I entertain it for a short while before tearing my hand away from one of the girls' tight grip when I notice that Lauren is now at the other end of the bar. She looks beautiful and blissfully unaware of anyone else around her. She won't even notice that I'm gone and so I shimmy my way towards the end of the bar and jump down, landing only a couple of feet away from our group of admirers.

Upon closer inspection, I realise that every single one of them is attractive and eager for attention. I introduce myself to a couple of them, noticing pale stripes of skin where wedding bands have lived earlier that day but seem to have been stolen by night. The guy I need doesn't have a white line or a solid band resting on his left hand. I slide my way over to him and place my hand on his chest. It's firm, and the heat is radiating from him – even through his white T-shirt. I whisper into his ear and his grin widens. He says his goodbyes to his mates, and they all thud him on the back approvingly as he walks away with me, leaving behind an eruption of whoops and cheers.

I take his hand and he follows me over to the bar where I tug at Lauren's ankle. She crouches down to meet my face and I notice a few beads of sweat have gathered on her top lip. I release my prey's hand and brush them away with my thumb, smoothing her hair with my other hand.

'Come on, babe, we're going for a walk,' I tell her.

Like an obedient child, she doesn't resist or plead for us to stay. She doesn't even ask who my new gentleman friend is. Instead, she jumps down from the bar confidently and far more agile than how she got up there. I look at her amused, wondering how she managed to do that so easily without my help.

I dig my toes into the damp sand as a cool breeze whips through my hair. The sea glistens beautifully as the moon reflects off its body. A couple of feet away, Lauren and Scouser Jack, who I abducted earlier from his mates' stag do, are deep in conversation. I study her face carefully as she laughs enthusiastically at whatever he's telling her. They seem to have forgotten that I'm even here, and if this wasn't going so fucking perfectly, I'd think it actually a little rude.

She lifts her hand, and a bolt of excitement ripples through me as she gently strokes his arm. I knew he was the one as soon as I saw him. Although his hair is shorter and a much deeper shade of dark than Jacob's, he has undebatable similarities to my favourite Londoners face. His dark eyes shine brightly when he laughs, and his smile sends shivers down my spine. He is without a doubt the most similar man to Jacob that I've ever come across in my life. How could Lauren not find him attractive when he looked so much like her husband? It would be impossible.

I notice that the drinks I encouraged them to take from the bar are almost empty. I asked the bartender to add three extra shots of vodka into Lauren's previously ordered double.

Where is Jacob in Lauren's mind right now? Is he even there at all? She is incredibly lucky to even call herself his wife and yet here she is with me, flinging herself at handsome Jack. I wonder if she has ever done anything like this before. I hadn't previously considered that possibility, something I hadn't considered, which makes this all the more exciting. I decide that I'm done playing gooseberry now. It's time that we all head back to our hotel.

The security guard shushes us for being too loud, but we ignore him. The three of us burst through my apartment door and I pull Lauren away from Jack's clutches and into my bedroom. We both fall backwards onto my bed, giggling like schoolgirls. I turn on my side to face her. Those mesmerising long and wispy eyelashes flutter as she struggles to stay awake. I push her roughly, but she simply bounces back against my hand. Fuck's sake. I pinch a bit of loose skin on her arm, carving a deep crescent with my nail, but still, she doesn't stir. I realise that I might have taken things a bit too far; given her too much to drink. Her mascara has smudged drastically, and strands of her hair are plastered to her damp forehead. I sit up and stare down at her venomously. You stupid, stupid bitch. Why couldn't you just do what I needed you to this one fucking time?

I scoot off the bed and walk round to where her head lies limp, pushing my arms underneath hers and tugging her upright. She's slumped against my chest, her head lulling to one side. I use all my body weight to balance her as I lift her arms above her head and pull at her white sundress, sliding it up and over her head. I drop her limp body back down, leaving her vulnerable and exposed in only her underwear. I stand back and observe her lying there, wondering what it is that she has that I don't. She isn't perfect; she has visible flaws: light white stretch marks on her outer thighs that have developed over time with her curves, and a shadow of a scar above her hip that looks like a stab wound. A darkness creeps into my brain, daring me to imagine the unimaginable. I wonder what her body would look like if it suffered trauma and pain. A sharp rip of a warm knife across her stomach that exposed her organs, or even just blistering third-degree burns from boiling hot water if it was poured over her legs. Would he still want her then?

The rumbling of items being thrown around from the kitchen startles me from my trance, and I'm fired back to the present. I peer outside the bedroom door to find Jack with his head in the fridge.

'Jack … Jack,' I whisper, beckoning him over, encouraging him to enter the bedroom. He staggers towards the door, bouncing off the metal handle and grimacing in pain as he pushes past me. 'Here, lie down next to Lauren. She asked me to get you.'

I gesture towards the bed where Lauren is lying unconscious and blissfully unaware.

My heart skips a beat as he flashes that beautiful dazzling pearly white smile, even with his eyes lazy from the alcohol. He pulls his T-shirt off, revealing his deliciously tanned torso. He struggles with his belt and the buttons of his jeans, only managing to unclasp the first one. I give him a helping hand and undo the other two and then yank his jeans down to his knees. He flops on to the bed beside his sleeping beauty, nuzzling his head against her neck and wrapping an arm around her waist.

I stand there and watch as his eyes begin to close, and his breathing becomes heavy as he drifts into a sleep of his own. So, tonight didn't quite work out like I'd hoped, but let's face it who's really going to believe that it didn't. Nobody will listen to what two irresponsible drunks have to say. I quickly dart into the living room and grab my bag that I dropped to the floor on the way in. I pull my phone out and re-enter the bedroom. I look at the scene in front of me through the square screen; their two bodies intertwined, half naked and exhausted from a wild night of passion. My lips curl upwards forming a wickedly satisfied smile. I take two pictures and then leave the room.

CHAPTER TEN

THREE WEEKS LATER

The gym is hot and sticky today; the air con is broken. The sound of wild feet pounding the treadmills accompanies the clatter of heavy weights as they slam to the floor. The machine says that I've been running for twenty-three minutes and I'm exhausted. I don't particularly like doing cardio but running is a vice for me. It allows me to break free from my mind, even if only for a little while.

My phone starts to rattle inside the cup holder of my machine. Lauren's name stares at me, begging for acceptance. This is the fourth time she has tried phoning me today, and it's only 10 a.m. on a Sunday morning. Over the past few weeks, my phone has been blowing up with texts and several long-winded phone calls; going over and over the same details of what happened while we were in Tenerife.

The girl is a hot mess. She's paranoid that Jacob will find out about her little fling, and even though I've told her about a million times, she still insists on questioning the details of that night. It doesn't matter how many times she asks me; my version of the truth will remain the same, and yet she still clings on to something out of her reach. She desperately seeks any fresh words of reassurance that I'm willing to give her, but she's wasting her time.

When my phone shows no sign of piping down, I decide that I've probably tortured her enough for today by ignoring her calls, and I surrender to this one.

'Hey, Lauren, what's up?'

I press the big red emergency stop button on my machine and hop to the side of the runner, wiping my damp forehead with my arm. Her voice is weary, and it makes me smile.

'I'm going out of my mind here, babe. I don't think I can handle this anymore. Do you think I should just come clean?'

She's crumbling perfectly, little by little as each day goes on. Her guilt dragging her into a thick dark cloud of insanity. I could tell her to confess to Jacob; convince her that the best option for her now is to come clean about that night. I could tell her that she shouldn't leave a single detail out, as she'd only get caught in another lie. Before I have a chance to respond, she interrupts my train of thought.

'None of the girls are speaking to me. They are still pissed at me for blowing them off on our holiday, and obviously I can't tell them what happened. I just feel so alone.'

I take a slug of water from my plastic bottle as I head for the gym's exit. As I step outside, the cold wind stings my flush face. I change my mind about telling her to confess. I've found a new seed to plant, and it doesn't take long for a flower to blossom.

'I'm sorry about your friends, Lauren, that's really shite from them. If I lived closer, you know I would be there for you.'

I pause, allowing the intention behind my words to develop.

'Babe, I know how busy you are with work, and it's mega short notice – I get it, but do you fancy coming down here for a few days?'

Hah, bingo! I don't say a word, forcing her to do nothing but wait patiently for my answer. I hear each shallow breath she takes, and it thrills me. I use these few precious moments to revel in the idea of her needing me so badly. Nobody ever really needs me.

Fed up waiting, desperate for an answer, her voice sounds again in my ear. 'Please,' she begs. 'I could really do with a good friend right now.'

She is putty in my hand. Who would have thought that the poor girl she met that afternoon in the Canary Islands would assume the role of the comforter now? That weak, pathetic soul who was so desperate for help, for friendship. Me, that's who. No, actually, not thought – knew. I sigh ever so dramatically and clear my throat.

'I shouldn't really take any more time off work. I'll probably get into a shit load of trouble for cancelling clients at such short notice.'

She doesn't reply. The line is silent.

'Awk, listen, it's fine. I'll sort something out. See if I can get a cheap flight down this week. How does that sound?'

She squeals, a piercing shriek assaulting my ears.

'Thanks so much! Thank you! Thank you! Babe, you're a lifesaver. I really don't know what I would do without you.'

I cover my mouth with my hand, hoping I'm successfully masking the gentle laughter that has started to escape my throat. I cough hard, regaining composure before I continue our conversation.

'Hey, what are friends for, right?'

I end the call before she can say anything else. I can't believe this is working out so well. A hell of a way to find out where he lives, but a fool proof one, nonetheless.

I don't have any holidays left to take, I used them all up on my last-minute getaway to Tenerife. I expected her to invite me to visit at some point, but I hadn't planned on it being so soon. I thought she might have kept in touch throughout the rest of the summer and even over the Christmas period. When the New Year arrived, so would a clean slate of annual leave and I would have been able to take as much time off as I wanted. The idea of waiting didn't bother me. I've waited this long already, haven't I?

It only takes me a couple of minutes after ending our call to make an executive decision that will nip this trivial issue right in the bud. I don't need to ask anyone if I can take additional time off, and it doesn't matter one bit if the last-minute cancellations I'm about to make will annoy my clients. None of it matters any more – because why would it when I won't be coming back.

Later that day I phone Lauren back to let her know that I'll be able to come down to visit after all. As soon as tomorrow if she wanted me to. She is ecstatic, and eager to help in any way she can. She doesn't ask how I managed to get time off at such short notice, and I'm extremely grateful for her ignorance. I tell her that I can only stay until

Thursday and would need to fly home that night, but it seems to be more than good enough for her. She asks for my email address for some weird reason, but I give her it anyway and we say our goodbyes. About half an hour later, she pings me over details of a flight that she has already booked and paid for.

The flight leaves from Edinburgh Airport early tomorrow morning and arrives at Southend-on-Sea, returning on the latest flight on Thursday night. I had to google the area because I expected to be flying into Gatwick or Stansted Airport. Jacob had never mentioned Southend to me before.

During our phone call, Lauren had insisted that I stay in her guest room and I took my time to carefully weigh up my options. If I accepted her generous offer, Jacob would recognise me the minute I'm introduced as her friend from holiday. I would look bat shit crazy; turning up at his house and pretending to be someone I wasn't. Even armed with the photos of Lauren's betrayal, he would see me as nothing more than a liar and in turn might not believe me when I tell him about her fling. That's a whole lot of drama I want to avoid, so I must be smart about this and bide my time appropriately. I'm so close now to getting what I want, I have to tread carefully and so I book my own accommodation, settling on a quirky boutique hotel with a beautiful seafront view, not too far from the airport. I treat myself to a deluxe suite with all the trimmings for the duration of fourteen nights instead of three as Lauren expects. I reckon by day three of my visit Jacob will be well informed of his wife's little mishap, and I'll still need somewhere to stay as I watch the drama unfold.

He will undoubtedly demand that she leaves their home, paving the way for me to make my grand entrance. I imagine he'll text or call me almost immediately, desperate to tell me all about it. I'll act surprised of course, and it will be nothing but pure coincidence that I'm in the area for work at the exact same time he needs a shoulder to cry on. I'll be that shoulder for him, but not for too long. He will quickly realise that his marriage to Lauren was a mistake, a sham, and it should always have been me. When he inevitably asks me to stay – I will.

Now that the flights and my hotel are sorted, I only have a couple of things left to do. I won't be rude, I'll be as professional as I can about this and instead of ghosting the store, I type out a short but informative email to my boss. I thank her for the experience but explain that I won't be returning to work at the store tomorrow – or ever. I don't bother with much of an explanation; I don't feel the need to. After I press send, I add the recipient address to my block list. Knowing her, she'll probably try to send me back a long-winded, unpleasant, and completely irrelevant reply, but that will be a waste of her time, not mine.

Time is moving at the speed of light and I still need to pack and sort out a few loose ends, but there's one more person I need to speak to first.

JACOB

THINGS HAVE BEEN a bit strange since Lauren got back from her trip. She seems distant, as if her mind is somewhere else, and every time that I go to touch her, she recoils abruptly as if the contact scalds her. I've even caught her staring blankly at me a few times when I've been watching telly or typing a text. I don't know if I've done something to piss her off, but I swear she looks like she is ready to let rip at me for something. But she never does.

On top of that, she's been working a lot of late nights at the salon, and when she eventually does come home, she heads straight for bed, barely saying a word.

I've also noticed that none of her friends have been round to visit. Not even her best friend Georgia, which is definitely a sign that something is wrong here. I've started to really panic thinking about what it could be. Did something happen when they were away? Have they fallen out? The idea seems impossible; they're very close, but then again, the two of them are very fiery. Spending all that time together without a rest period is bound to initiate a few squabbles.

I might just be overthinking all this, but there's just something niggling away at me; telling me that something isn't right.

Another change to the norm is the amount of time Lauren's been spending on her phone. It's like the stupid thing's fucking glued to her hand. She refuses to put it down for even a minute when I'm around. When I ask who she's speaking to, she tells me that it's nobody, just Zara – the new friend she made in Tenerife. I don't know much about her except that Lauren found her crying by the pool one day. Apparently, she'd just broken up with her boyfriend and Lauren took her under her wing. I've always admired her compassion for others, one of the many reasons I fell for her in the first place. She always put me first, before her friends and even before herself. My feelings were all that mattered to her. That's why I'm finding it so bloody difficult to understand why I'm being shunned right now.

When I did ask more about her, she told me that the two of them were extremely similar in a multitude of ways. They dressed similar; they enjoyed the same food and liked to dance to the same music. She joked that they probably have the same taste in men too. I asked what she looked like as although she claims they spent a lot of time together. No pictures of this mysterious stranger have been uploaded to her Facebook account. A weird one I thought, considering how well they seem to have bonded.

She described her as being petite, around 5 ft (the same height as her) and having long dark hair – also the same colour as hers. She seemed to take pleasure in telling me all about her, as if she had a crush or something. She couldn't believe that a girl so naturally beautiful and warm could be treated so poorly by any man. I didn't know what to say to that to be honest with you. I'm not in any position to judge how any man treats a female. I've never proclaimed to be a saint myself.

There isn't any harm in her having a new friend, especially if they get on as well as she says they do. I just find it strange that it seems to be the only thing she's bothered about right now. I must admit, from what she's told me about her they do sound quite alike. I still don't have a picture or anything to go by, but personality-wise, she sounds exactly my type.

Standing barefoot in only a pair of white boxers, I pour myself a glass of cold water from the kitchen tap and check the time. It's just gone ten o'clock and I have five-a-side football at eleven on Sundays. Better get my arse in gear. I take a drink of my water and listen to the muffled sound of chatter coming from upstairs. Unless Lauren has taken up talking to herself now too, I'm guessing that she's on the phone to someone. That, or someone's found their way into my house without me knowing. I stay still, trying not to make any noise so I can listen in to what she's saying, but it's no use, her voice is far too faint and so I give up.

While she's occupied, I may as well use my free minutes to text Karly. She looked hot as hell in her gym clothes this morning; every curve of her body hugged perfectly in black sportswear. I deleted her picture quickly after, careful as always not to leave any traces of her behind. My phone slips from my hand, narrowly missing the marbled floor as I snatch it up just in time. It was the sound of Lauren plunging down the stairs and into the kitchen like an angry elephant that startled me.

'Morning, babe, can I get you anything?' I ask with a smile.

She grins at me menacingly, like a wild beast ready to attack. What the fuck have I done now?

'No, thank you, I'm fine,' she replies as she grabs a cereal bar from the cupboard and pops it in the handbag that dangles over her shoulder. 'Just in case I forget, Zara called, she's going to be working in the city this week, so I'll probably be out and about quite a bit.'

She rests her hand on our glass dining table and glares at me, waiting for a response; searching my face for something I'm not quite sure of.

'Err, OK.' Is all I manage to say.

She flees the kitchen before I even realise that the conversation is over. What the hell was that about? She seemed angry, but for what reason? Surely, she is happy that she'll be seeing her new friend as she's the only one she gives a shit about recently. I shake my head and rub my eyes with the heel of my hands. I don't have time to figure this out right now. I gulp the last of my water and place the glass in the sink before heading upstairs. I should be worried about Lauren and her newly discovered mood swings, but I have another thought at the front of my mind instead. If Zara is going to be in town, will I get to meet her?

CHAPTER ELEVEN

KARLY

The air is thick with tension as Hannah and I sit across the table from one another. I chose her favourite coffee shop as our meet up spot and even managed to bag her favourite corner table with a private view of the street outside. Since I told her about my move, approximately eleven minutes ago, she's barely said a word to me and I'm positively fizzing at her attitude, not to mention her blatant lack of support.

I bet Lauren would have been supportive if she was in Hannah's position. Why can't she be more like her? Obviously, I couldn't tell her the truth, not after the way she reacted to me going to Tenerife. Instead, I told her that I'd applied for a highly sought-after job a few months back that involved working closely with some footballer's wife on a permanent basis. The 'job' was of course in London, but it had completely slipped my mind because I didn't believe in a million years that I would be fortunate enough to be offered such a prestigious opportunity. I mean, hundreds of people must have applied. Why would I tell her about something I never expected to happen?

Anyway, I expressed that I know it seemed a bit sudden, but I had no other option as there was only one condition between me and my dream job and that was that I had to start immediately.

She stares moodily down at her untouched coffee that she may as well have ordered as an iced version because I guarantee it will be frozen by now. She refuses to meet my eyes as I speak at her rather than to her, and I can't quite believe that she's acting like such a little brat. I get that this isn't entirely true, but if I had been offered a position like this, it would have been a terrific opportunity for me. Not many people get the chance to work with a celebrity, and it wasn't that unbelievable – I'm fucking good at what I do. Isn't your best friend supposed to support you in everything you do? They are supposed to celebrate your success with you and egg you on to be the absolute best version of yourself.

The silence between us now is so deafening that for a minute I genuinely wonder if there could be something wrong with her hearing. She hasn't said one word. Not even the faintest hint of a measly smile or the twitching of a petted lip. My ever so short temper begins to flare like a fireball ready to launch; my chest beginning to tighten. I try to rack my brain. What exactly is her problem here? Is she upset that I'm moving away? Or is she just simply riddled with jealousy? I actually think it might be the latter. She never had the same ambition to go get what she wanted as I did, but still always expected the benefits. It's the same in all aspects of her life: work, love – in anything really. I refuse to say another word here until she chooses to break the uncomfortable silence. I'm fearful for the venom that could explode from my mouth.

The waitress pops down a fresh caramel latte in front of me. I didn't bother ordering Hannah another just so she could waste more of my money. As I lift the cup to my lips, a fucking miracle happens.

'So, what are you going to do about your flat then?'

I almost choke on her words. Is that really all she's fucking bothered about, my stupid flat? She has always adored my little palace; calls it her second home and spends most of her time there, even when I'm not home, but I just can't believe that's what she is so upset about here.

Although mortified, I take a deep breath as I sit my cup back down without taking a drink and decide to try to cut her some slack. I know she's desperate to escape from the clutches of her family home. Her parents are strict and old, not forgetting senile. Their early signs of Alzheimer's means that they forget how old Hannah really is. They treat her like a child and not the hot tempered, twenty-seven-year-old fiery red-haired siren that she is. I have to admit though, it's always been a little hard for me to sympathise with her. She could have done something about it for herself. Created a life of her own years ago, one where she was happy. But again, it was her own sulky lack of ambition that failed her.

Fortunately for Hannah, and being the excellent friend that I am, I'd already decided not to sell my flat right away for two reasons. Let's be honest, it would have been completely irresponsible of me to uproot my entire life to London without keeping a back-up plan in place. Secondly, I know that Lauren might want to get away for a while after Jacob kicks her to the curb and the flat would be perfect for her. I'm sure she'd love it and would be grateful for the respite. Until then, I would let Hannah hang there for as long as she could.

I take a sip of my coffee, savouring the sweetness of the sticky caramel that had dribbled onto the rim and then rest my cup back down on the burnt oak table.

'Well, I was thinking you might like to move in and look after it for me – if you wanted to, I mean.'

I watch her face change shape into something more familiar and much more like my best friend. Her previous scowl melting as she realises that she has landed on her feet here. I'm aware that this corroborates everything I say about her expecting things to just be given to her, but I am a good friend to her and know that she needs this.

The muggy, tense air begins to clear as she starts to chat more freely now, appropriately asking me more questions about my new job and where I'll be staying. It's taken her getting something she benefits from for her to be happy for me. Ridiculous really. I manage to think on my feet quickly to create solid and believable answers for all her questions. I think I might have preferred it when she'd forgotten how to speak.

I don't make a habit of lying to Hannah. She's usually the only person I'm completely honest with – about everything – but I know that she'd try her best to stop me if she knew what I was really doing, and I really can't be bothered with that. I know I'm doing the right thing for me here. Well, for us – Jacob and me. That's why when she asks me to answer her next question honestly, I lie straight to her face, and don't feel the slightest bit guilty about it.

'I promise you. This has nothing to do with Jacob, or even Lauren for that matter. You were right all along – it's time for me to move on. I only wish I'd listened to you sooner. You have my word. Jacob is no good for me.'

She gives me a single nod, which I take as a silent understanding that I'm telling her the truth. She wouldn't think otherwise because I've never lied to her before. If anything, throughout our entire friendship I've been a little too honest when it comes to delivering a message. I'm blunt with my words, I know this, but I mean well in what I say. When the dust has settled in London after the upcoming chaos, and things are as they should be once and for all, I'll tell her the truth and apologise sincerely for lying to her. She'll forgive me, I know it. We've been friends for far too long to hold grudges. Our friendship has developed so strongly over the years that I no longer see her as just a friend, but family. She's the only family I have and for all her faults, I do love her. And anyway, by then she'll be able to see how happy Jacob and I are together, just like I always told her we would be, and she'll admit that she was wrong and understand that I did the right thing. Until then, though, it's imperative that she doesn't know the truth.

I sit cross-legged on the shaggy pink rug in the middle of my bedroom, staring at the largest sized suitcase I have. It's now full to the brim with my favourite shoes, clothes, and accessories; everything I just couldn't do without. It would have been impossible for me to take everything I own in one go. I have clothes spilling out of every cupboard and drawer available, and that doesn't include the vacuum-packed bags I've stored away under my bed. If I get there and realise that there is something that I desperately need, I'll just ask Hannah to post it to me. Now that I've fully packed and am ready to leave tomorrow, I feel a little unsure of what to do with myself. An unexpected pang of sadness encourages my eyes to water as I take in my surroundings: my cosy bed, my shabby chic dresser, and my perfectly pleated curtains. I jump up from the floor and grab my empty wine glass, taking it into the kitchen to refill with sweet rose wine.

My eyes scan over every item I see in here too, acknowledging everything I've worked hard for. It might have been Granny's money that helped me with the foundations, but I built my empire entirely on my own. I put my heart and soul into every detail; choosing every scented candle to match the mood of each room, every patterned strip of silver wallpaper hanging on my feature wall, right down to the perfect shade of white oak furniture. I've never been unhappy here, but there has always been a part of me missing. I wasn't supposed to be on my own in this flat. Both of our clothes were supposed to hang in the matching his and her wardrobes that I bought, and two empty wine glasses were supposed to be abandoned in the living room from the night before. The empty dresser at the left-hand side of my bed should have been full of his socks and boxers. Even his soggy towel was supposed to be lying at the foot of the shower for me to collect and wash. I wouldn't have had to give up my job or travel so far away from my best friend. I take a gulp of the tangy mixed fruit liquid and sigh.

With real love comes great sacrifice and choosing to abandon my perfect little bubble is mine. It's strange to think that very soon my life here will be nothing but a distant memory.

CHAPTER TWELVE

I'd initially planned to go back to bed for a couple of hours when I arrived at my hotel this morning. I didn't sleep much last night, and I wasn't looking my best because of it. Dark shadows circle my blood-shot eyes, and no amount of concealer was helping me out here. To make matters worse, when my flight landed, I turned my phone back on to find Lauren had already sent me a text with plans for our first day together. In the end, I didn't have time to shut my eyes for more than half an hour before I needed to get a move on, and it made me feel worse than I did before.

Her great idea for today was to attend 'High Tea'. That's what they call it down here, not afternoon tea like we do back home. She called it a gift, from her to me; just to say thanks again for coming to her rescue at such short notice. It might not have been an expensive pair of shoes or my favourite perfume, but it was a really nice gesture.

I've begun a turbulent battle in my head in regard to my feelings towards Lauren. I don't hate her; definitely not. In fact, I've come to realise that I don't even dislike her. I'm actually quite fond of her. Sometimes it's quite easy to get lost in the realms of our newfound friendship because we genuinely get along so well. I've never had another best friend – only Hannah, but Lauren seems to appreciate me in a way that Hannah never does, and quite frankly it's refreshing.

I know that I haven't known her very long, but in this short space of time that she has been in my life, I've enjoyed most of it. I've loved having someone reply to my messages almost immediately; day or night, and I've loved being someone's go-to person. The person that springs to your mind first in your time of need. I've never been anybody's first choice, not really. Sure, I've always been invited on work nights out and things like that, but it's always been out of courtesy, not necessity. Sometimes I even think Hannah only hangs out with me when she doesn't have better plans or somewhere else to go to distract herself from her family.

My head spins at all these different thoughts whooshing through my brain. I don't know how to feel. I shouldn't be feeling this way at all. Lauren isn't my friend. She's Jacob's wife. The niggling nauseating feeling I have sucks me right back down to earth like a filthy leech as a familiar knot forms in the pit of my stomach. It's that same feeling that gives me the strength and encouragement I need to carry on with what I came here to do; and it wasn't to make friends.

A couple of short hours later I find myself sitting in a busy tearoom in the middle of Soho, London. The large magnolia walls are filled with framed pictures of iconic celebrities that include the likes of Frank Sinatra and Marilyn Monroe. Behind the service counter, a shimmering golden wall has been carefully speckled with glitter set to grab your attention. The furthest away wall is also a bit different. That one is dedicated purely to colourful illustrations and photographs of vintage transport. My favourite is the hand painted one of old but classic motorbikes; lined up in a row outside a shop front. They are among friends of a kind, none of them out of place or unwanted. It's beautiful.

The temperature has started to gently rise now that it's after mid-day and so I remove my black leather jacket and fiddle with the intricate gold coins hanging from the chain around my neck; making sure they're sitting as they should be. I keep my hands above the table and clasp them gently in an attempt to stop myself clenching them into painfully tight fists in my lap.

Once again, I find myself waiting patiently for her to arrive. She's eight minutes late. Punctuality doesn't seem to be Lauren's strong suit. The waiter has brought over a beautiful little pot of freshly made tea and so I pour myself a cup while I wait for her to arrive. The strong brew fills my nose as I drop two white sugar cubes into the little white porcelain cup followed by a generous amount of milk – 'builder's tea', some people call it.

I feel nervous as hell sitting here by myself. I feel way out of my comfort zone. Other customers appear oblivious to the empty seat across from me, but I'm convinced that someone is laughing at me for sitting here on my own. Maybe they think I've been stood up. I look around me cautiously, desperate to find an unfamiliar face staring at me, just to prove that I'm not going mad. There isn't one though. Nobody is interested in me from what I can see. Well, at least not inside the tearoom. I just can't shake this feeling that someone, somewhere is watching me. Could someone be watching me from outside? I have a perfect view of the busy street outside and nobody is acting oddly or out of sorts. I don't recognise anybody, but then why would I? I rack my brain as I struggle to remember the name for something like this. I read it in a book once; the name behind an irrational fear of someone watching you. As hard as I try, I'm unable to grasp it, so I try to laugh off this feeling of unease as I shake my head and take a small sip of sweet tea.

A further infuriating five minutes later, the door swings open and a sharp gust of wind blows some napkins from the tables closest to the door on to the floor. She spots me almost instantly and I watch her intensely, as if she is moving in slow motion. As she approaches me, her smile widens. I cock my head to the side in curiosity. She looks different today. Her hair is tied up in a sleek ponytail and a pair of silver hoops hang from her earlobes. Her outfit is admirable; faded black skinny jeans paired with a plain white top and a silver studded black leather jacket similar to my own.

Sometimes when I see her, I'm still taken aback by how much she reminds me of myself. But that's not what's chilling here. That's not why goosebumps have started to bubble on my arms. I push my chair back and stand up so that I can greet her properly, just like normal friends would. I notice that she's wearing a new perfume. It smells muskier than her usual scent and I think I recognise it, but I can't be sure. The annoying thing about perfume is that sometimes two people can wear the exact same scent, and yet it smells entirely different on their skin. It might or might not be the same as mine, but it does definitely hold some sort of resemblance to the one I purchased at the airport before going to Tenerife.

As she drapes her jacket over the back of her chair, I notice that she is sporting large dark purple circles of her very own that hang lazily under her eyes.

'You look amazing!' I tell her.

It was only a little white lie. Sure, her outfit is perfect, and her hair looks quirky, but her face is the problem here – it's haggard. She looks weak, completely exhausted, and definitely not as bubbly as when I first met her. She shakes her head, brushing off my compliment. She's not stupid, she knows that she looks rough around the edges, but I'm sure she's grateful for the compliment, anyway. That's what a good friend would do, right?

'I'm so glad you're here, Zee.'

She calls me that now. My new super cool nickname gifted to me after introducing myself as Zara.

I've only ever had one nickname, and I haven't heard that for a long time. My mum's voice echoes in my head. A memory of us playing hide and seek forces itself to the forefront of my mind. I can hear her calling for me. 'Where are you, Keeks? I'm coming to find you my beautiful girl!' It hurts to think about, and I crush the image in my mind's fist as quickly as I can.

I smile at her weakly, but still kindly as she glances at my half-empty cup of tea and so she picks up the white pot and pours me a new one – before herself. She is so nice to me. All these little things she does, these small tokens of affection are what complicates this whole situation.

However, as pleasant as all this is, I can't ignore the irony of the situation we are in right now. No longer am I the one in need of saving. The roles have been flipped on their heads, and I'm the hero of the story now. I've come to rescue her from the hell she's putting herself through. I'm the one she chose, and this time I find myself reaching across the table and taking her hand in mine, the exact same way she'd taken mine the first day we met.

Our tea has actually been quite fun. We split the generous variety of delicious miniature cakes in two so that we could both enjoy the same ones and drank our way through three or four pots of tea. I knew my motive for being here today is not the same as hers, but I found myself wondering if there was any way I could save a piece of this little unexpected friendship when everything comes to light. I'm not entirely mad for thinking this. She has said herself that she is lucky to have me, and I suppose I sort of feel the same way about her now too.

Guilt isn't usually a feeling I experience often. I don't offer promises to people, so if I do happen to let anyone down, that's their problem – not mine. I definitely didn't expect to feel guilty about this. It's not that I'm changing my mind about wanting to be with Jacob, it's just that I didn't expect to find myself caring about his bloody wife so much. She wasn't even supposed to be likeable, not to me anyway. I expected her to be plain and boring, someone who lived their life completely vanilla. No flashy colourful aura, just boring old black and white, and yet she seems to hold all the same vibrant crayons as me.

I know that I need to try much harder to push these feelings to the side. It's absolutely vital that I don't allow my emotions to get the better of me. To remind myself why I came here, I pull my phone from my bag and unlock it quickly; opening my photos and clicking on one of Jacob. My Jacob. His beautiful face is exactly what I need to see. My heart flutters, his gaze grabs hold of my heart and refuses to let go. When I look back up at Lauren, she is innocently taking a sip of her tea and my blood boils to the point of blistering heat. You are still in my way right now. You've always been in the way.

CHAPTER THIRTEEN

I twist my hair into a tight bun and secure it on the top of my head with a scrunchie and then take a seat at the dressing table. I squeeze a drop of creamy cleanser onto a white cotton pad and circle it around my face in smooth motions as my make-up from today disappears without much effort. I stare at my reflection in the large oval shaped mirror and let out a heavy sigh. I make a conscious effort to relax my shoulders and unclench my jaw as I release the abundance of tension that has been trapped inside me since arriving here this morning. I don't know how to feel right now. There's a part of me that feels intoxicated, and yet I haven't had a single drop of alcohol. It's my messy head that's the problem; heavy with conflict, buzzing around my brain like a swarm of angry bees desperate to find their source of honey before it's too late.

After we had finished up with tea, we took a stroll through the streets of London, weaving in and out of the high paced crowds as we popped into a handful of busy stores for a leisurely browse. Before I knew it, a few more hours had passed us by, and I found myself being invited back to her house to share a bottle of wine. I politely declined, claiming that I was completely worn out from my early flight and then all the walking around. I didn't particularly want to part ways with her to sit in an empty hotel room by myself, but I couldn't exactly go to her house if he could be there. And I couldn't ask if he would be because that would sound too weird. I'm still not entirely sure, but I thought I saw the faintest of eye rolls when I turned her down; as if she was annoyed at me for it. I'm tired and probably overthinking things, so it's more than likely that I'm mistaken. She's been nothing but nice to me for as long as I've known her. That has no reason to change now.

She was quite persistent though, which in itself was a little strange, and because she wasn't ready to accept defeat, she insisted that we therefore pick things up tomorrow instead. She explained that she had to work in the morning for a couple of hours but could take the afternoon off so that we could spend more quality time together. This type of behaviour is so foreign to me. Plenty of men have been desperate to spend time with me, but never females. She even asked if I would like to pop round to her salon before she finished so that she could pamper me with a complimentary bouncy blow. Never one to turn down the opportunity to look my best, I obviously accepted. I still have plenty of time left for what I came here to do. I don't see any harm in taking some time for myself.

Lying flat on my back in the middle of the bed, my eyes are open, but I can't see a thing. The thick blackout curtains have won their battle against the moonlit sky. I don't know what time it is, but I've been lying in the same position for a while now. I just can't shake

Lauren from my mind. Her perfect and uncomplicated life is about to begin its dizzy descent into a tumulus spiral, and she is blissfully unaware. Everything she has will be taken away from her, but then again, it will be rightfully given to me. I should feel happy that this is finally happening. Excited, even triumphant, but right now I don't feel any of those things.

My legs kick furiously in a bout of frustration. She's wormed her way into a piece of my heart that I didn't know existed. A place that has lain dormant for as long as I can remember. A single tear slides down my right cheek and I bat it away. I can only hope that she'll forgive me in time. I don't expect her to be particularly thrilled when Jacob and I get together. I don't even expect her to ever love the two of us together, but she could grow to accept it, especially if I mean so much to her.

She is lucky, really, because she is so beautiful. With her kind bright eyes and smooth sallow skin, she has nothing to worry about, and I know in my heart that it won't be long before the right man snaps her up. Maybe I could even help her find someone. Sign her up to a few dating apps, encourage her to go speed dating and be her wing woman when we frequent pubs and clubs. She'll find someone that she was supposed to be with from the start, and then there'll be no reason why we can't stay the best of friends. The first hurdle is going to be the hardest, but when we get over that, everything will work out as it should. I just need her to understand that it's not her life I'm stealing – she stole mine, and all I'm doing is taking it back.

The gentle chirping of birds between the trees and subtle splashes of waves hitting rocks in the distance are the only sounds I hear as I wake up early in this unfamiliar bed. There's no sound of chatter from the room next door, and I can't hear any busy footsteps in the hallway. I'm groggy and cranky from my disturbed sleep, but as I start to come round, I begin to feel slight flutters of excitement for the day ahead. Today will be our last full day together. The last day where our friendship is pure and untainted, and I want to make the most of it.

The hot pulses of water from the shower help waken my limbs, and I'm starting to feel a little fresher as each minute passes. I turn the knob back to an upright position as the water comes to a halt and slide open the cubicle door, grabbing the fluffy white towel from the hook and stepping out onto the bathmat. I wrap the towel around my chest and twist each side into each other to secure it in place.

I take my time as I apply my make-up. First smoothing moisturiser over my face before applying my primer and swirling a brush around my most expensive cream foundation then painting it gently onto my face. I make sure that it's blended perfectly at my hair and jawline. I apply a dark shade of brown powder to the crease of my eyelids and then add a pop of gold shimmer onto the base before adding a slick coat of smoky black liner.

There's no point in wasting time styling my hair seeing as it will soon be getting washed, but I still wish it looked a little better than it does. These Essex girls are renowned for their immaculate appearance; I've seen all the reality TV shows, and I don't want to stick out like a sore thumb. I decide that my best option is to pile my hair into a neat bun on the top of my head, knowing that when it's pulled away from my face, my eyes appear much bigger and brighter.

The weather today is dry and pleasant, so I open my suitcase and take out a little yellow sundress that sits just above the knee, that I pair with chunky black biker boots with silver studs and of course, my favourite leather jacket. My legs are still ever so slightly bronzed from the Tenerife sun so there is no need to apply fake tan today and yet I still do. I smother a healthy amount of instant tan onto my legs and hold my dress up as I wait for it to dry. Why is it your legs always seem paler than the top half of your body?

Now ready, I grab my bag, my room key and my phone and make my way down to the hotel's restaurant. I'm not really that hungry – nerves I think – but I make myself a cup of sweet coffee and pinch a pain au chocolat that has been left over from the breakfast buffet. I wrap it in a napkin and shove it in my bag for later on.

I swither at the door, realising that something doesn't feel right; something's missing. I turn on my heels and dart back upstairs to my room and head directly for the dresser, picking up the crimson red lipstick that almost escaped me. I twirl the black tube delicately between my fingers, considering that it might be too much for a daytime look. Sod it, I decide. I don't care if it's too much, I always look great wearing it and more importantly feel more confident under its armour and so I smooth it over my lips, puckering them in the mirror in admiration. Now I'm ready.

Her salon sits on the corner of a long street, positioned perfectly at the end of a row of little boutique shops and busy local cafes. Its shopfront is white and glossy, with two large sized windows with frosted panels so that you're only able to catch a glimpse of customer heads and not their bodies. I look down at the Google maps app that's open on my phone but there really isn't any need to; I've definitely found the right place without a doubt. The signage itself is bold and vibrant; neon pink writing illuminating the name *Lauren, With Love.* I take a deep breath to steady myself before I give the glass door a gentle push. The sound of busy hairdryers erupts instantly, and you can just about make out that the radio is on in the background. The smell of peroxide, mixed with the subtle burning of hot hair is prominent, but expected, and yet I still manage to notice a subtle floral aroma that floats gently around the room among the chaos of scents, creating a calm and relaxing ambience.

I straighten the bottom of my dress and adjust the strap of my handbag back onto my shoulder and wait patiently at the desk for the receptionist with muted lilac hair to lift her head from her phone and acknowledge me.

'Can I help you?' Her tone clipped and somewhat unfriendly, and I'm a little startled by her abruptness.

'Hello, yeah, I'm here to see Lauren,' I say. My own Glaswegian accent feels out of place and doesn't ring true in my ears, and I force a painfully polite smile.

She stares at me, a look of bemusement and disgust as if I've just spoken to her in a foreign language, and then licks her thumb and flicks open a few pages of the diary sitting in front of her. She shakes her head as if to say that I'm lying and I'm just chancing my luck in the hope that there has been a cancellation.

'Do you actually have an appointment?' she spits.

'Yes ... I mean, well no, not an appointment exactly,' I stutter. What the fuck is wrong with me? Why am I so affected by this little Trollip's attitude? I'm the customer here. She should be falling over herself to help me. I straighten myself up, ready to give her a mouthful of abuse when I hear my now second favourite voice in the world.

'Zeeeeeee!' Lauren's voice squeals from behind me. 'Thanks, Becky. Zara's here to see me, aren't you, babe? I must have forgotten to pop it in the diary. No harm done though, right?'

She links her arm in mines and the sulky receptionist now seems to have had a personality transplant all in the space of two seconds as she beams brightly at her boss; a stark contrast from the look she'd just given me a few moments before. I decide that it's not worth the hassle arguing with her now. The little minion is irrelevant to me now that Lauren has found me.

She pulls at my jacket, sliding it off my arms, and hangs it up on the gunmetal coat stand. I wait for her to hand me over to one of her assistants, but she doesn't. Instead, she insists on washing my hair herself as she ushers me over to the row of ceramic basins. I notice a few bewildered glances passed back-and-forth among the rest of the staff as she wraps a black cape around my body before directing me to sit. It must be a very rare occurrence for the owner of the salon to carry out such a basic task.

The water is scalding hot, and her nails bite into my scalp as she massages the fruity scented shampoo into my roots. I don't say anything to her, even though it kills. She really must be out of touch with the whole hair washing process, which isn't surprising I guess if she has people to do it for her. Next, she quickly applies some conditioner and then rinses my hair clean almost immediately. She didn't leave it on for very long, and I'm annoyed because it's going to tug a lot more than usual when she comes to brush it. At home, I try to leave it on for at least 4-5 minutes before rinsing it off.

A sharp bolt of fresh pain interrupts my train of thought as the back of my head cracks against the sink. I let out a sharp yelp, but she doesn't seem to notice and continues to pull and jerk roughly at my wet hair. Maybe she didn't hear me over the sound of the shower or the roar of hairdryers. I know she'd have stopped if she'd thought she'd hurt me. I really wish she'd just let one of the others wash my hair. This was starting to feel like I was being tortured rather than pampered.

When she's finished with me at the basin, she wraps a towel around my head and directs me towards a black chair at the end of the row. As she attempts to comb out the knots, she makes a few tutting noises and tells me that it would do me good to chop a couple of inches off the length. It's taken forever for my hair to grow this long, without the need for hair extensions, so I thank her, but tell her that I'm fine with how it is. It wouldn't have been this tuggy if she'd just fucking used conditioner like a normal person. She doesn't say anything in return, and I feel her touch becoming less patient on my head as she drags the comb from my scalp down to the ends, tearing out any knots she meets on the way. I think she might for the first time be annoyed with me. I can tell by her silence and I feel bad for being so ungrateful.

I was lucky enough for her to free up some time to give me a free blow dry, and now she's offering to spend additional time trimming my hair too. I quickly change my mind, realising that I'm being rude.

'Actually, I could do with a trim now that you mention it. But only a trim, OK?' I plead.

'Of course! Don't worry, you're in good hands, babe!'

I study her face in the mirror as she concentrates, sectioning my wet hair between her fingers. She takes the first chop confidently. Fuck! That's way more than just a bit off the ends. My eyes begin to water as she continues to hack wildly. Who does she think she is, fucking Edward Scissorhands? I'm terrified of how short it's going to look when it's finally dried. Everyone knows that it bounces up a couple of inches further when it is.

I should have just said no, why didn't I say no?

She seems completely oblivious to my angst and doesn't say much as she works away. She just carries on, not a care in the world. She takes her time to dry my now sharp and short hair; sectioning it with big barrel brushes that will create an end result of big and bouncy curls, although who knows how big and bouncy, they're going to be now that she has butchered me.

'Ta-daa! All done, babe!' she gloats.

The end result is horrifying. I ignore her gaze as she searches my face, waiting patiently for me to deliver praise. Was she fucking mad?

I wasn't exactly going to pat her on the back for this, was I? I wanted to scream at her. Slap her. Do anything I could to punish her for not sticking to what we had agreed, but there was little point now. I can't turn back time.

The damage is done.

I shuffle over to the pink crushed velvet sofa next to the door where I sit fizzing with rage as I wait for Lauren to collect her things from the staff room. I pull my bag onto my lap and unzip it carefully and discretely so that nobody around me is able to see inside. I hold the photograph of Lauren and Jack between my fingertips as my hand shakes furiously. I try to extract comfort from my weapon.

She has ruined me today, made me look a fool, and now I can't wait to return the favour.

CHAPTER FOURTEEN

A couple of attractive men walk towards us and I hang my head quickly; completely mortified to be seen without my luscious long locks. She notices though and asks what's wrong so tell her I thought I'd felt a drop of rain. She crooks her neck to look up at the bright blue sky, searching for a cloud that's nowhere to be seen and her brows furrow in confusion. We chose to sit outside the coffee shop because of the nice weather. Our table is positioned directly under the warm glow of the sun. I could have and should have come up with a much better excuse than that.

Her red nails poke out from her open toe sandals as she sits with one leg gently draped over the other sipping an iced latte through a straw. Her dark hair is styled poker straight today, which is unusual as it's normally curled slightly at the ends. She has on a plain black T-shirt that's tucked into a pair of high waisted stone washed blue jeans with an expensive designer belt wrapped around her waist. I wish she didn't look so effortlessly beautiful, especially right now that I'm sat here looking like such a fucking train wreck.

She releases the straw from her dazzling white teeth before she speaks.

'I have the house to myself for a bit. Fancy coming over?'

I'd expected her to invite me to hers again, seeing as I refused yesterday, and so today, I'm more prepared. I don't need to worry about concocting an excuse this time because she's just told me that Jacob won't be at home.

'Sounds good to me,' I say. It pains me to smile at her. I'm so angry at her for what she has just done to me, but I need to get over that, and quick. I'm finally going to see where my Jacob lives. Where he speaks to me so gently in a hushed but husky voice down during our late-night phone calls, where he undresses after a long day at work, exposing his beautiful, tanned body and climbs into bed. I'm going to see all the places where although he is with her, he is thinking of me. I've waited so long for this that I feel my insides tremble with sparks of excitement as they sprout wildly through my entire body. I grab my bag and push away from the table. My bad mood about my hair is slowly but surely beginning to fade as my heart is filled with something much more thrilling.

The blood pounds in my ears as I make my way up the red cobbled path behind her. She unlocks a tall wooden gate and I notice that we are entering the house from what appears to be the back door rather than the front. I wonder why that is. Some people do that though I suppose, don't they? She strides up to the door and pushes her key inside the lock and twists firmly to the right. The door to my future life swings open. I wonder if she realises how lucky she is, and just how good she has had it for so long.

I hesitate before stepping over the threshold, wanting to capture every detail of my surroundings. The garden is half grass, half concrete, and a freshly painted sage hut perches perfectly at the bottom right corner. The space is wide and inviting, perfect for hosting parties and gatherings. I can imagine it filled with Jacob's friends and family, all laughing and joking – maybe standing by a barbecue as Hannah and I sip rose wine and watch them cook a variety of burgers and sausages. It feels so real, like it's meant to be. I can almost smell the meat sizzling away in the air.

I smile and step inside, closing the door gently behind me, aware that my fingerprints are now merging with where his have been. Suddenly I struggle to remember how to breathe. The room spins and jerks out of control, and I have to close my eyes to steady myself before I fall over. I can't believe I'm finally here.

The back door that I've just entered has led us directly into the kitchen, and I allow my eyes time to float over the scene before me. I've seen some of these items before; the chrome silver kettle, the black marble worktops, a rack of grey and white mugs stacked neatly beside the microwave. All little insignificant things that I've seen in the background of pictures that didn't mean much to me before but now feel so familiar experiencing them in person.

She ushers me through an alcove towards her grand living room, and I pause to slide off my boots before I go any further. I don't want to leave any marks on my soon to be carpet. My bare feet land on the plush grey pile that's ultra-soft between my toes; like stepping onto a precious cloud. A grey but almost charcoal coloured couch beautifully accessorised with plump dusky pink feather cushions sits against the wall to my right-hand side; directly across from a huge silver framed television that has been hung carefully on to the wall. I can see him lying there, his arm stretched above his head as he flicks between channels while texting me – thinking of me – wanting me.

Believe it or not, I hadn't originally planned to enter the house while Lauren still lived here. I intended to find out her address by accepting an invitation to hers. I was going to ask for the address that I should tell the Uber driver, without any intention of actually showing up as expected. Instead, I was going to wait till it was late at night, when the street was dark and asleep. That's when I would have taken the trip over and slid the envelope containing those incriminating photographs through their letter box for an early morning surprise. I would have addressed it directly to him and when he opened it, chaos would explode throughout the entire house and I would be far enough away from the scene, back in the safety of my hotel room, completely detached from any roots of blame. Naturally, she'd have questioned where it came from and if Lauren did have the audacity to accuse me, I would act completely affronted and steer the blame towards any one of her friends that dare I remind her, were also on that trip. Hell, it might even have been Jack. For all she knows he could have been some sort of crazy psychopath who tracked her down. The most important thing is that Jacob would be none the wiser of the true identity of the sender and would never in a million years suspect it was my doing.

'Don't be shy, sit down and make yourself comfortable.' Her voice startles me as she unnecessarily puffs one of the cushions for me. She asks if I would like a glass of wine, I guess one won't hurt. My gaze hops over every object in the room. A grey, white, and muted pink colour scheme is consistent throughout and it feels homely rather than clinical. I like it actually, but I'll still need to change it to something new. Something we both like when we make it our own.

A picture frame in the corner of the room catches my eye and a heavy brick starts to take shape in the pit of my stomach; conjuring dark, nauseating envy where only happiness should be. I can't tear my eyes away from it. This is something I never wanted to see; have tried to avoid seeing for as long as I can remember. Him in a dazzling black suit, her in a figure-hugging white dress with a long fishtail. Both of them hand in hand as their other overlaps as they hold a knife over a three-tiered wedding cake. Bile rises to the back of my throat and I swallow it back down and wince. This is wrong, all fucking wrong. This should be my home – mine and his – not hers.

She returns from the kitchen with two glasses and a bottle of rose wine, politely filling my glass before her own and handing it to me with a wide smile. I can't stand the sight of her right now, and it's excruciating to pretend. My blood bubbles beneath my skin, scorching my skin in anger. I want to snatch the bottle from her hand, lift it to the sky and then send it soaring down towards her; enjoying the explosion as it smashes against her skull. I want her to feel pain. I want her to feel all the same suffering I've had to endure on a daily basis for ten long fucking years.

Desperate for a minute to gather myself before I do anything too impulsive, I ask permission to use her bathroom and she gives me directions to the main one upstairs, explaining that the tap is faulty in her downstairs toilet. I take the same carpeted grey steps two at a time, hurdling my way to safety. As I reach the top of the stairs, I exhale sharply as if I've been holding my breath under water for far too long. I can see that the door to the bathroom in front of me is wide open, unable to be missed. I pause before entering, now finding myself frozen to the spot as a new idea springs to the forefront of my mind. I take one small step further towards the bathroom and then reach out and pull the door over very slowly; careful not to close it completely, but just enough to create the illusion that it's occupied.

I creep along the hallway, praying that there are no loose or squeaky floorboards that might cause Lauren to suspect I'm not where I'm supposed to be. I give each door a gentle nudge until I find the one that I'm looking for. A king-size bed with a dramatically tall black suede headboard rests in the centre of the room on top of a thick pile of cream carpet. At either side of the bed there is a black bedside table, and the sheets are made-up to perfection. I tiptoe further into the room, closer now than I ever thought possible. I allow my fingers to skim over the soft satin milk white sheet; the same sheet he sleeps under. Pure pleasure dances around my stomach, waltzing through my veins.

The silver watch that he always wears on his right wrist sits on the left-hand side table beside a half-empty glass of water. This must be his side of the bed. I tear my hand away from the comfort of his bed and find it drifting towards the glass. My finger traces the rim ever so gently. Round and round it goes, exactly where his mouth has been, and I close my eyes as I appreciate the connection. I don't know how long the glass has been there, but I don't care. My hand trembles as I lift it to my lips and take a sip, knowing that we now have shared something physical – even if it is something as simple as water.

Oh. Shit. I realise that I've left a smudge of red lipstick and so I lick my thumb and rub away the evidence of my mouth's presence. I wonder if he'll take another drink from this glass before it has been washed. Will he taste me? Will he be able to feel how close we are? I almost can't contain my excitement at the thought. I sit the glass back down quietly and then scoop up his watch, circling the cool metal inside of its face with my thumb. I think of it pressed against his wrist, touching his beautiful skin, the skin I've not been about to touch yet. I carefully wrap it around my own wrist and fasten the clip, but it hangs loosely demonstrating the difference in size between us. Far, far too big, and yet it still feels like a perfect fit.

The sound of footsteps beginning their ascent up the stairs jolts my attention, and then I hear her call my name.

'Zee, are you OK?'

Fuck, fuck, fuck. I must have lost track of time. My legs won't budge, my eyes are now fixated on the door, waiting for her to appear and ask what the hell I'm doing in her bedroom. What do I do here? I have nowhere to hide, and what excuse could I possibly have that would make her finding me in their bedroom any less weird or creepy? My throat is bone dry with fear. I'm unable to conjure any words to make the situation better, and my heart thuds wildly against my chest.

119

I bite down hard on my bottom lip, still glued to the spot, waiting for the devastating blow, when a phone starts to ring from downstairs. I hear her stop abruptly in her tracks and register the jog back down the steps towards the sound that just saved my life. I release a sigh of relief, but toxic adrenalin has been ignited deep within me and I realise that I'm shaking beyond control – but not just from the fear of being caught. Touching his things, being so close to him; all of it has lit a burning fire of desire, and I don't want to lose this feeling of exhilaration. I want more of it. I want all of it – all of him. She has to go.

I quickly make my way back to the bathroom where I should have been and give the toilet a quick flush, hoping that she'll hear it downstairs. I run the tap for a couple of seconds and dip my wrists under the icy cold water to soothe my nerves. I turn off the tap and grip the edge of the ceramic, my fingers still trembling against its base. I quickly yank open a couple of plastic drawers, searching for something – anything – I could use, but nothing fits. As I look down, I realise that Jacob's watch is still dangling from my tiny wrist. I slide it off without needing to unclasp it and push it deep inside the pocket of my leather jacket. What if I didn't forget to take his watch off? What if it was a sign? A sign that he is with me right now; directing me, encouraging me, pushing me to do what needs to be done. I realise I haven't tried the mirrored cabinet above the sink, and so I raise my shaky hand and give the handle a gentle pull. It swings open easily, narrowly missing my head. I peer inside and it's like the heavens have opened above. It's perfect. It's so fucking perfect. The watch was the first sign. This is the second. I know he wants me to do this.

I tiptoe my way down the staircase, my hand skimming the white banister, and then slowly enter the living room that leads me back into the kitchen. She has her back to me and is talking quietly on the phone; completely unaware that I'm behind her. My grip tightens around the smooth set of silver cosmetic scissors that burn in my palm of my hand and I feel powerful and confident. As I creep closer, the urge to raise my hand high and then plunge the sharp point through the side of her neck is overwhelming; like it was always meant to be.

This will all be over in a matter of minutes. All I need to do is take a couple more steps towards her and thrust my weapon into her pale skin as many times as it takes. Jacob won't find her until he returns from work, but it will be too late. She'll have bled to death before anyone is able to discover and rescue her. This is almost like a twisted fairy tale; the ones they don't show on kids' channels and yet they should, because the princess is always victorious in getting what she desires.

I see the scene in my mind's eye; her beautiful bright kitchen decorated with menacing spatters of raw blood. I take one single step forward, closer, much closer. She still doesn't turn around. She still doesn't know that I'm here. I take my second step, my right arm now extended ready to launch its attack. I close my eyes tight, scrunching them to the point of pain.

'Please forgive me,' I whisper, as my arm falls through the air.

CHAPTER FIFTEEN

The burst of the front door opening and then slamming shut grabs both of our attention. She spins on her heels and lets out a piercing yelp at the sight of me lurking behind her. She drops her phone onto the marble tiled kitchen floor, and I wince at the crack.

'Shit, Zee! You scared the life out of me there, babe!' She laughs.

I don't laugh with her. In fact, I don't do anything – I can't. I'm unable to force even the simplest of smiles because the power struggle between us has now once again see-sawed, and I'm now the one up in the air with my legs dangling below me, much too far away from the ground and definitely in immediate danger. My right arm is pinned tightly against my lower back, the scissors biting into my palm. Stay still, I tell myself. Don't let her see behind you.

'Please forgive you, for what?' she asks perplexed.

I hear a deep and husky cough echo from afar as another door is now opened and then closed, but she doesn't seem phased in the slightest. She doesn't flinch, she doesn't call out for whoever just came through the door – which means it's someone who is free to come in and out as they please. Someone who lives here too. Oh shit, oh shit, oh shit. I desperately need my feet to move, but they're frozen stiff under some wicked and torturous spell. I need to find a way out of here – and fast. My previous plan of attack on Lauren must be abandoned because I can't risk it now, there isn't enough time to do what needs to be done and escape.

'Lauren, I'm really sorry I have to run.' I gasp as I manage to free myself from paralysation and push my feet into my boots that are still lying on the floor, still careful not to remove my right hand from the bottom of my back.

I snatch my bag from the table on the way past, whipping it open and discretely dispensing inside the scissors that are now slick with sweat due to my nervous perspiration. I fumble to find the words, but somehow, I do.

'The manager of my hotel just called. There's been a flood – from one of the rooms, and it's … pouring into the landing.'

It wasn't the most believable of excuses, and I kicked myself as soon as it escaped my lips, but I had to say something, anything to allow me to break free of this bear trap I've found myself in. I notice the flush of the downstairs toilet and give myself a shake. I don't have the time to stand here worrying if it was believable or not.

'OK … but you're sweating. Are you OK?'

She steps towards me, offering me comfort, but before she can touch me, I've dodged her grasp. I swing open the back door and flee from the garden before she is able to stop me, and then I run. I run faster than I've ever run before. I'm catapulting myself to I don't know where, just anywhere other than that house.

A few people curse as I push them out of my way, but I ignore them and keep going. My heart constricts painfully. It starts to attack me brutally from within; my own body betraying me, firing sharp and crippling pains through my chest. My legs start to fail me as I'm forced to slow down and eventually, I let them come to an inevitable halt. I don't need to run anymore, I'm far enough away I'm sure, but I beg them to just keep going and my head is so fucking heavy. The street before me starts to spin wildly out of control and my mouth begins to water. Oh crap. I dart round the side of a house, stumbling into a dark and grimy lane, and lurch forward, throwing up nothing but black coffee and bile. The back of my throat burns raw with the acidity of my stomach's contents. Tears stream from my eyes as my body convulses like something out of *The Exorcist*. When there is eventually nothing left to erect from my stomach, I wipe my mouth with the back of my hand and smooth down my damp and sweaty hair. My legs give way underneath me as I fall back against the wall behind me and stare up at the bright blue sky. Right now, I don't have a clue where I am, but I know that I'm safe.

I take out my phone and open my Uber app, allowing it a couple of seconds to find my current location and I'm so grateful for technology at this moment in time because without it, there is no way I would have been able to find my way out of here for myself. I glance around me as I struggle to catch my breath. Wherever I've ended up seems to be quite isolated; rough, almost. A few houses that I can see in the distance have boarded-up windows and aged for sale signs in their unkempt front gardens. Breathe. All I need to do here is breathe.

I'm not in danger any more. I'm OK. I repeat this over and over in my head until my need for fight – or in my case – flight mode begins to slowly but surely fade away. A couple of minutes later my car arrives and I hop inside, melting into the safety of its soft leather seats.

Back in my room, I stripped bare as soon as I got through the door and took a long hot shower in an attempt to freshen myself up, but it was no use. My nerves were still fraught. I surrendered to the chaos and slumped to the bottom of the shower, lying in the foetal position as the water bounced off my fragile skin. I desperately tried to piece together how it all went so horribly wrong, but my efforts were futile, and so all I could do was lay there until I found the strength to move.

Now that I've forced myself back to life, I find myself pacing back and forwards. Again, and again and again. Still racking my brain for whatever it is that I'm missing here. There has to be something, I've been so careful. How did this happen? Where was the pivotal moment where things took a sharp turn? Think, Karly, think. OK, she told me that he was working late, I'm sure of it because I would never have agreed to go back to hers if I thought for one minute he'd be there. That's it! That stupid, dozy, idiotic little cow must have got things mixed up. She's not heard him right, or she's been mixed up with another day. She ruined it, that's what she's done, and what's worse – he fucking ruined it too.

A loud blood-curdling howl escapes me. I was so close to ending all this, and now I'm right back at the start. A losing streak in our game of Snakes and Ladders. Everything has changed now though, of course. I can't go back to simply posting the photograph through his door. No, no, no, that just won't cut it now. More than ever before I am highly aware of the extreme lengths that I'm quite clearly prepared to go to now, in order to make sure I get what is rightfully mine.

I can't just post fucking photos. No chance. It's not even solid proof, not really. Just two people who've drunk too much and passed out next to each other. She could easily worm her slimy way out of that. I was naïve to think that would work in the first place. My fists clench painfully at my side. Another maddening scream escapes me. If only she really had slept with him. I could have filmed the whole thing on my phone and had real ammunition to work with. I might not even have needed to send it to Jacob, I could have blackmailed her into leaving him, forcing her to do so without causing her any harm. But she had to fuck things up, didn't she? She had to force my arm. She only has herself to blame here. This is not my doing.

I was stupid to think that I could keep both of them. My feelings for each of them would constantly engage in a vicious battle with one another, and the one that came up trumps would be him – every time. It always will be. Everything is going to be OK. When she's gone, I expect that he'll be upset to begin with, it's only natural, but that will fade over time. Time is a healer and all that shit, and when it does, and his grief subsides, I'll be there waiting.

My stomach growls angrily. It craves food but is still extremely unsettled from my little, embarrassingly public, vomiting spree earlier on. I perch on the edge of my bed, my elbows balancing on my knees as they jut up and down. I've changed into a pair of black leggings and threw on an off the shoulder jumper that shows just a sliver of my black underwear on my left shoulder. I need to figure out how I can get back into that house. Just me and her though, no interruptions this time. Minutes later, as if she has read my mind, a text from Lauren arrives.

Babe, really worried about you. Hope everything is OK? X

I study it carefully, mulling over my response, but before I can figure out a reply, she sends another.

J has gone back out for the night, probs won't be home till well after we've gone to bed if you fancy a sleepover? X

It's another sign. I'm sure of it. I'm doing what needs to be done, no doubt about it. Things are starting to escalate and yes, much quicker and entirely differently than originally planned, but I don't see a point in wasting anymore time now. I know for certain what I need to do now, and tonight I'll strike while the iron is still hot. Come tomorrow morning, everything will be perfect.

CHAPTER SIXTEEN

An hour or so later Lauren picks me up from a busy pub, just around the corner from my hotel. I couldn't fight my hunger anymore and decided to wait for her there while I ordered a strong drink and something off the snack menu to pick at. I didn't bother to try to make myself up. What was the point anymore?

I wait for her to offer to help me with my suitcase, but she doesn't. She stands with her back against the driver's door, chewing gum and staring into space. So, I pop the boot and fling my case inside myself. When I slam it shut, she makes a smart-ass remark about the amount of stuff I must have with me for only a few days to need a suitcase that big. I grit my teeth and force my lips to remain tightly shut and do my very best to smile back at her. I mimic a small and disingenuous laugh to break the silence. We will see who is really laughing soon, won't we, Lauren?

On the journey to her house, I listen to her ramble on and on about Jacob, and how he was acting so odd when he arrived home.

'I was sure he was working late, but I guess I just got mixed up. Anyway, it doesn't matter now because he definitely won't be home to disturb our little girls' night, babe.'

She's acting differently than normal. I can't really explain it; there's just something odd about the way she's speaking. She doesn't seem to be taking breaths between her sentences and keeps wittering on about the most pointless things. I notice that her voice has definitely gone up an octave or two; it's even more of an annoying trill now than it was before. She delights in telling me that she has gone to the trouble of making up the guest bedroom for me, which is strange because I saw it earlier today when I was snooping, and it was already made. I can't question her on that though, because then she'd know I wasn't where I was supposed to be, so I let her continue to spout some more shit about how I'm welcome to have a nice bubble bath while she cooks our dinner. My stomach twists at the thought. I feel sick at the thought of more food entering my tender stomach, I don't know how I'll be able to eat a full meal.

'You're so lucky that none of your things were damaged, Zee,' she tells me.

I nod in agreement. 'Yes, very lucky indeed.' I'm about to respond further, embellish some more bits to make my story more believable but the song that comes on her playlist next takes my breath away.

Baby girl you know my situation, and sometimes I know you get impatient.

It's our song. Mine and his. The one that whenever we hear it, we think of each other no matter where we are. She's still talking, but I don't hear a word she's saying. The Fabolous song has me under its spell; the way it always does. All I can think of is him and the pictures he sends me when he plays this song in his own car. He knows it will provoke a reaction from me, because he knows me too well. I quickly swipe a tear away from my eye before she notices and turn my head to gaze out the window. It feels so wrong to be sitting next to her while this is playing, but I have no choice but to sit and listen.

I can't leave you alone, and I know I'm living wrong – but I can't let you go. You're the one I want in my life, I already got a wife, can't leave you alone, and I know I'm living wrong – but I can't let you go.

JACOB

I FINISHED A job earlier than I thought today. Thinking it would be a nice idea to ditch the pub and head home and surprise Lauren by making her a romantic dinner in an attempt to shake her out of this bad mood of hers. I stopped at the shop around the corner from our house and bought all the ingredients needed to whip up her favourite pasta dish. I was convinced this was going to earn me major brownie points, and I was pleased with myself for thinking of the idea in the first place.

Desperate for the loo, I dump the bags onto the floor at the front door and unzip my old dirty grey hoodie that I wear to work most days and hang it over the end of the banister. I nip straight into the downstairs toilet before going through to the kitchen.

As I wash my hands and turn off the tap, I notice the sound of movement from deeper inside the house. Not just that though, it sounds like muffled voices. Who the fuck is in my house? I briskly make my way through the living room, bracing myself for the discovery of an intruder, but am surprised to find Lauren putting two wine glasses into the dishwasher.

'Oh, hey, babe. You're home early,' I say.

'Yeah, I wasn't too busy today so finished up early to spend some time with Zara.'

She looks flustered as she leans against the worktop, her fingers gripping the edge so hard her fingers are changing colour. What's wrong with her now, for fuck's sake?

'You just missed her actually,' she says tersely.

'Did I?' I reply. 'Where did she go, then?'

My interest was piqued now as a thousand voices in my head began to run wild. It's quite convenient that as soon as I arrived home, she disappeared. Something is way off here. The one thought that keeps pushing to the forefront of my mind is, what if this Zara wasn't actually a Zara after all? What if she never existed in the first place? Zara was just a blanket of disguise for who she's really been with?

I force myself to concentrate on the words spilling from her mouth; focusing on the lies she might be telling. I listen to the pace of her sentences. I watch her body language for any clues, but I'm not picking up on anything too alarming. At least not any more alarming than her current attitude towards me.

'Her hotel just phoned to say there had been a leak somewhere, and that they needed her to come back right away,' she explains calmly. I notice the colour fill her fingers again as she loosens her grip on the worktop.

'That's a shame,' I say. 'I hope none of her stuff is damaged.'

She sneers at me, and then an awkward silence fills the space between us. Am I supposed to say something here? What is she wanting from me? Eventually she turns and places a bottle of wine into the fridge with a loud bang. I just don't get this – any of it. What is she hiding, or dare I say it, who is she hiding? Rubbing my temples and exhaling loudly, I turn my back on her and make my way through the living room and head up the stairs. As I enter our bedroom, I come to an abrupt halt as I notice a foreign smell. It smells a bit too feminine to be cologne, but it doesn't smell like Lauren's usual perfume either; it's a bit muskier, a bit sexier actually. She has been wearing a new one since she got home right enough. Maybe it's that. Fuck, I hope it's that.

I look around the room carefully for any tell-tale signs of mischief, but nothing looks out of place. The bed is still made as neatly as it was this morning and the glass of water that I left at my arse from last night is still lying untouched. Would she have left it there if she was expecting company?

On Lauren's bedside table are the same pair of black earrings that were left there before she went on holiday, and even they don't look like they've been moved. I'm going fucking mad. I sit on the bed and then flop onto my back, feeling stupid for even considering my wife might be having an affair. After a few minutes of telling myself what a complete idiot I am, I bounce onto my feet and pull my sweaty T-shirt up and over my head. I undo my trousers and make my way into our En-suite bathroom for a shower. I reach for my wrist to unclasp my watch, but my skin is bare. I must have forgotten to put it on this morning.

I reach inside the cubicle and turn on the hot water, but something is still niggling away at me and I just can't put my finger on it. Gut instinct tells me to turn back on myself, take a second look. As I do, my stomach drops. My watch is missing.

CHAPTER SEVENTEEN

KARLY

W hen we arrive at the house for the second time today, we don't head in the direction of the back garden as we had done earlier. Instead, she parks in the driveway and leads us straight through the front door, grabbing my hand and pulling me straight up the stairs. She leads me into the bathroom and hands me a beautiful blush pink, silk bathrobe and two white fluffy towels and then whips out a fancy-looking bubble bath from the cabinet. I hold my breath, hoping that she doesn't notice that the scissors are missing and thankfully she doesn't, but even if she did, there is no reason for her to suspect that I would have them anyway – Why would I?

She leaves me to it and so I do as she insists and begin to run a bath. I perch on the edge of it as the water begins to fill and push my white tennis-style Vans off with my feet. I shrug off my leather jacket before chucking it into the corner. I cross my arms over my body and hike up my jumper, pulling it up and over my head, and then rise to my feet, peeling my leggings down over my bum, continuing down my thighs until they reach my feet and I gently step out of them, one foot at a time. I unclasp my black lace bra and then pull down my matching knickers and drop them into the puddle that's now my clothing. I take hold of the bottle of peony scented bubble bath and add a generous amount to the water and notice that my hands are a little shaky. I guess I feel slightly uncomfortable, standing here naked and exposed in the large unfamiliar bathroom.

As I wait for the tub to fill, I potter around; snooping through each drawer and basket, still waiting patiently for the hot water to rise to an acceptable level when I notice that the door is still slightly ajar. I quickly hop over and close it firmly, snubbing the lock tight. I don't know why I felt the need to do that. It's not like Lauren is going to burst in here while I'm in the bath. That would be a different level of friendship. Hannah and I aren't even there yet. The thought of Hannah makes me a little sad. I wonder if I should have told her everything; she could be helping me right now. But instead, I'm hurtling through this madness at what feels like a million miles per hour with nobody there to catch me if I fall.

I step one smooth leg into the deep bath as steam rises and fills the air with the wonderfully light floral aroma, then followed by the other now that I know the water isn't too hot. I slouch down and rest my head back against a soft, white bath pillow, stretching my tanned leg a little further to turn the tap off with the tip of my red painted toe. Big bouncy bubbles surround me like fluffy clouds gathering in the ever-changing sky, the scent of peonies soothing my frantic mind and I allow myself to close my eyes and sink further into the water; my hair splaying around my head like a mermaid. Ha – let's see what she thinks of me getting my hair wet for a second time today after all the effort she went to today to style it. I know she clocked the bun I'd piled on to the top of my head when I approached the car. She must be livid. I chuckle to myself as water fills my ears and muffles the sounds of her moving around downstairs.

A new smell has wormed its way into the comfortable little bubble I've created for myself, intruding into my personal space and disturbing my moments of serenity, forcing me to remove my head from the water. It smells herby – garlic, maybe? Whatever it is that she is cooking, it causes my stomach to release a ravenous growl. If I can smell whatever she is cooking this strongly, then I assume dinner is almost ready. I sigh in frustration. I guess I've spent enough time in the bath, anyway. My fingertips have started to prune in agreement. I slowly rise, feeling a little dizzy at the shock of emerging from the warmth of the water to sharp, cool air. I grab one of the towels she left me. The smaller one first and tip my head upside down and wrap my hair into a secure pile, towering high, before stepping out carefully onto a soft pom-pom style bathmat and wrapping the larger one around my body.

After dinner, I'll encourage Lauren to follow my lead and take a relaxing bath of her own. It shouldn't be too difficult to convince her. I'll insist on running it for her too, so she doesn't have to lift a finger and I'll tell her that it's simply a thank you for her hospitality. She would be extremely rude to refuse, and that just isn't Lauren. I imagine she'll question what I'll do with myself while she's in the tub and I'll insist on doing the washing up – it would only be fair seeing as she cooked.

She'll undress as I have done, climb into the bath and rest her pretty head against the same bath pillow that only minutes ago supported mine. And only when enough time has passed; when she is completely and utterly relaxed, will I creep in slowly, as silent as a mouse, and grab her throat, plunging her entire head deep into the hot water. I expect that she'll struggle under my grip, but we are around the same build – perhaps I'm even a little stronger, so I'll be the winner here as I watch in unclouded satisfaction as small bubbles escape from her nose while she tries desperately to clutch onto any air that she has remaining in her lungs. But there won't be much, and I'll hold her there for as long as it takes and stare into her eyes as I watch the life drain from her pupils.

Intoxicated by what is yet to come, I gleefully scoop up the bathrobe she left for me and unlock the bathroom door. I'm met with a welcoming cool breeze and my shins begin to goosebump. My damp feet leave little dainty marks as I pad my way down the hall and into the guest room that Lauren said I could stay in. From my bag I unpack a pair of long-sleeved white and pink striped pyjamas and lay them on the bed. I swither whether to get changed into them or wear the robe she has given me. It is very nice. Too nice to waste actually. I decide against wearing the pyjamas right now and instead I drop the towel to my feet and slide my arms into the gown, enjoying the soft brush of silk enveloping my body, caressing my skin.

Out of the corner of my eye, I notice a familiar purple bottle sitting on the bedside table. As I pick it up, I realise that it's the same perfume that I'd bought in the airport before going to Tenerife. It doesn't look like it has been used much, but it has definitely been spritzed a handful of times as the liquid doesn't quite reach the top. I look back at my pyjamas that are still sprawled on the bed and then down at the robe tied across my body. The shade of pink in the stripes is almost identical to the robe. My mind ticks away like a grandfather clock; piecing together a puzzle that I don't think I'm supposed to be a part of. My eyes dart back to the bottle of perfume – the same one as mine. Something doesn't feel right here, but I don't know why. I try my hardest to think back to each occasion we spent together, trying to merge together other peculiar similarities that I'd registered between us but so foolishly disregarded. Tick, tick, tick. I remember the vivid red jumpsuit she'd worn during our first dinner together, and how it was almost identical to mine. Tick, tick, tick. I think of her choice of food and drink, and how she always ordered the same as me throughout the entire trip. Tick, tick, tick. It's getting faster now, whatever it is, it's speeding up and about to arrive with a bang.

I have all the pieces and yet I can't quite complete the jigsaw. I keep trying. I knew Jacob had a specific type from the moment I saw her, because undeniably she looked like me with her thick dark hair, her pretty face, her petite figure accompanied by those seductive hourglass curves, but it isn't possible for her to know so much about me. How could she know what clothing I've worn or what brand of perfume I wear?

Has Jacob been so desperate to be with me that he has moulded Lauren into a diluted version of me? He could have taken note of the clothes I had on in the pictures I sent him and bought the same for Lauren. He could have asked me my favourite perfume out of curiosity, and I would have told him thinking nothing of it, for him to then go and buy Lauren the same just so he could smell my scent. He knows all my favourite food. I've told him things like that before. He could have ordered for Lauren when they were out for dinner, only he would be ordering my favourite dish and have encouraged her to go along with it. Although flattering, it's also quite horrifying to think that Jacob might be more obsessed with me than I originally thought. Or is it? Isn't this what I've always wanted, for him to be completely and utterly besotted with me?

I decide to head downstairs before drying my hair so that I can ask her discreetly if she has noticed any similarities between us. Perhaps she is oblivious to them, or maybe not, but either way I'm too curious not to ask. I travel down the stairs at speed and spin into the living room, but the fake smile I've painted widely on my face slowly melts away as an icy chill crawls over my skin, sending shivers up and down my arms, making the hairs on the back of my neck stand up. I edge further towards the kitchen; something doesn't feel right. When I finally see behind the concave that leads you fully into the kitchen my blood runs cold.

'How was your bath?' she asks with a great big smile spread across her face.

She's leaning against the worktop and twirls a glass of wine in her hand. She takes a sip.

'Please, take a seat,' she tells me.

But I can't move, I'm glued to the spot.

JACOB

LAUREN GESTURES TO the chair sitting directly across from me at the dining table, inviting our guest to sit down, but there is no sudden movement from behind me. I wonder why nobody is moving, so I spin round only to discover her standing there. What the fuck? My eyes dart quickly from my wife, to Karly, and back again. It took me a few seconds longer than it should have to register her face; a face that I've known for ten years, but never in my wildest dreams did I expect to see her standing in my house.

Lauren smiles as she takes a sip of wine from her glass. Neither of them is looking at me, and I don't understand what is happening here. Why is she in my house? No, how is she in my house? And how does she know my wife? How does she know where I live? I can't stop the flurry of questions racing through my head, but I try my best to keep my face composed, careful not to give anything away too prematurely.

'Zara, are you OK?'

My wife's voice snaps me back to the here and now. Did she just call her Zara? Who the fuck is Zara? The realisation suddenly hits me like a sledgehammer. She thinks that Karly ... Fucking hell, she thinks that Karly is Zara. I exhale deeply. OK, so she doesn't know who she really is – this might still be OK. All I need to do is get Karly by herself and speak to her, convince her not to do anything stupid.

Karly shuffles over to the table, dressed in what I think is Lauren's silk robe, and pulls out the chair and takes a seat, draping one of her bare legs over the other, exposing her upper thigh provocatively. I try not to stare as Lauren places a freshly poured glass of wine on a coaster in front of her and then makes her way over to me.

'This is my husband, Jacob.' Lauren introduces me, standing behind me with her hand gripped firmly on my shoulder.

Karly smiles at her, the corners of her mouth not quite reaching her eyes, and then turns her head to face me.

'Hi,' she says softly. 'I'm sure you've heard all about me.'

Her familiar Scottish accent sounds in my ears so much more vividly than over the phone, and it suddenly dawns on me that Lauren never told me Zara was Scottish. I just assumed she was English, but would it even have mattered? Scotland is a big country with loads of girls. Why would I suspect that it might have been Karly, my Karly, that she'd met? I wouldn't have. This isn't my fault.

Karly's eyes are now locked on mine as Lauren shuffles around the kitchen, preparing to serve us dinner. The kitchen is eerily silent even though there's a sporadic, loud clattering of plates and pots.

'Oh shoot! You must be wondering what's going on, Zee. I must have got mixed up again,' Lauren says. 'I was just so sure Jacob was heading out for the night.'

Karly finally tears her eyes away from mine to smile at Lauren in acknowledgement and then turns to face me once again.

'It's nice to finally meet you, Jacob.'

Wispy strands of dark hair escape from the towel that's balanced on top of her head and her face is make-up free; cute freckles dotting her skin. She really is as beautiful as I've always thought – perhaps more so in person, but she is still one crazy bitch that's for sure. How the fuck did she track down my wife, and why has she pretended to be her friend? I shake my head, annoyed at myself for asking such a stupid question because I know the answer, don't I? She's done this to get to me, of course.

Wait a minute. What did Lauren just say? Did she say I would be out tonight? Why would I be out when I went to the trouble of coming home early to surprise her? I was going to make dinner for the two of us; but she was adamant that she'd do it, but for the three of us instead.

'Are you all right, babe?' Lauren asks me. 'You've gone a bit pale, haven't you?' She giggles childishly as she walks towards the table with two plates in her hand, taking her place at the centre of the table, in between Karly and me, and stares down at the creamy pasta resting on our best dinner plates. She lets out a deep sigh. Out of nowhere, she raises her arms and then launches the plates of food on to the glass table with explosive force. The ceramic smashes as it hits the glass, shards of white plate fly through the air.

'Oh, what a shame,' she says calmly and then everything changes. 'Karly, would you mind helping me clear this mess up?'

PART TWO

CHAPTER EIGHTEEN

ONE YEAR EARLIER

LAUREN

'Hey, babe! You're home early,' I coo at Jacob as he enters the kitchen. I still love seeing him come home from work all dirty and rugged. Even now, after we've tied the knot, I still get butterflies when I see him standing in the home we created together.

'The job's done, why wouldn't I be home?' he snaps back with a scowl.

Woah, here we go again. He's been in a foul mood for days now. I've tried everything I could think of to snap him out of it: cooking his favourite meals, wearing new lingerie in the fiery shade of red that really gets him going, and even making sure his favourite programs are set to record if he wasn't going to be home in time. Nothing was working though, and to be quite honest, I'm growing frustrated.

He turns his back on me without saying anything else and exits the room, leaving behind the aftermath of his wrath as he makes his way through our living room and stomping dramatically loud as he climbs the stairs. A couple of minutes later, I hear the bathroom door slam shut and the power of the shower jets coming to life.

I try to shrug off his bad mood – for the umpteenth time - and decide to make my own way upstairs to collect his dirty work clothes. I always wash them for him when he gets home. As usual, they're lying on a heap in the middle of our bedroom floor, but I try not to let it bother me. I just don't see what's so hard about putting them in our actual laundry basket, but whatever, it's no big deal. I scoop them up in my arms and carry the bundle back down to the kitchen, dropping them onto the floor when an unexpected thud makes me jump. Shit, what was that?

My knees click as I crouch down to investigate the source of the noise. They always do that, ever since I was a little girl. I used to love gymnastics and dancing, anything that involved jumping about really, and I guess it's taken its toll on my joints. I rifle through his clothes, his designated grey work hoodie first and then his black work trousers when I find it; his phone that's still in his trouser pocket. The screen illuminates as it springs to life beneath the touch of my fingers. I let out a sigh of relief, grateful that it's not cracked or scratched. I cringe at the thought of his beloved phone being damaged, I can only imagine how deeper into his bad mood that would have pushed him. Sometimes I think he loves that thing more than me.

I must have swiped something by accident with my clumsy fingers because a list of his most recent notifications is in front of me, displaying several incoming messages from someone named 'K'.

That's strange. What does K mean? An unfamiliar feeling stirs inside me, a feeling I'm not used to, something unsettling. He doesn't have any mates whose name begins with the letter K. No Kyles or Kennys, or anyone else that I know of. Even if there was a friend that I hadn't met, why would he not save their full name? Why shorten it to just one singular letter? It seems like very odd behaviour.

The black phone in my hand silently mocks me. It's daring me to enter its password, just to have a quick scroll through the messages, nothing else. Just to put my mind at rest. I'm sure there is a reasonable explanation behind it.

I try a few sequences in a desperate attempt to crack his password: my birthday, his birthday, his mum's birthday, but nothing matches. My palms start to sweat; a mixture of irritation and panic at being caught snooping. I wipe them on my jeans as I juggle the phone between the two. The bright light of the sun has vanished from our kitchen window and has been replaced with a dark and gloomy cloud. It's as if nature is trying to tell me something isn't right. It is determined to eliminate any optimism I still have. I've never needed to use his phone before, well at least not without him unlocking it for me first. It's not strange that I don't know his password, I'm sure lots of couples don't share those kinds of things, but I can't help but think that there must be a horrible reason as to why his password is so secretive, so out of my reach.

I stand back up and begin pacing back-and-forth, racking my brain furiously, trying to think of what it could be. A few moments later, a light bulb flickered inside me. Oh you, doughnut. Of course! In my eyeline is a mug lying upside down on the dish drainer – his mug. His love of football is second to none, and I kick myself for not thinking of it to begin with. It's not secretive at all, at least not to anyone who knows him so well. In big blue numbers wrapped around the white mug is the year his favourite club was founded. It reads *Chelsea FC EST. 1905*. Although I'm pleased that I've realised what it is, I'm still a bit pissed that he has chosen a stupid footy team over something to do with me, or even us to use as his password, but I don't have time to spend stressing that right now. He could be down any minute.

My fingers are hesitant as they type in the digits, but when I do, his home screen rewards me by bursting into life and allowing me free rein. I pause before clicking on anything. Do I really want to be that type of wife who goes through her husband's phone? I've never suspected J of hiding anything from me before – he's never given me any reason to. I laugh nervously to myself. I'm being ridiculous, of course I am. K is probably just a guy from work or a bloke he's met down the local. He was probably in a rush to get home when he took his number and didn't have time to type in his full name. All very innocent, entirely explainable, and definitely nothing sinister; I scald myself for thinking the worst.

I place his phone down gently on the kitchen table ready to walk away and continue with my original task of doing his dirty washing, but a new vibration against the glass pulls me back to it. This time, without any hesitation I snatch the phone back into my hand, frantically unlocking it to discover a brand-new message from K. This time though, now that it's unlocked, I see a preview of the message splashed across the home screen. It burns my eyes.

I'll meet you at eight in the hotel bar. Head for the back of the room. You won't regret this, babe, I promise x

I grip my chest; my acrylics dig into my skin as they clutch in desperation of stopping my heart exploding into a million pieces, like a violent supernova in the depths of the universe. My universe. A pain unlike any I've ever felt before. I should have trusted my gut. I knew something was a bit off with the secret name and the sports related passcode. He would never have thought I would have guessed that. I never watch his stupid sports channels. But now, none of that even matters because I had good reason to be suspicious, didn't I? My dearest, darling husband is having an affair.

The grey clock on our kitchen wall seems to tick louder than ever now, like an angry cricket just ticking away relentlessly. The room is spinning, and my eyes are so out of focus, but I try to search for the time among the haze. I need to know how long I have left. It's a struggle, but I manage to see the outline of the small hand pointing at the number five. I steady my focus, rubbing my eyes hard until they begin to hurt, but eventually, I can see that it's five o'clock on the dot. Only three hours until eight o'clock. Three fucking hours until my husband stares me straight in my face with those big, beautiful eyes and lies to me.

I pull a chair away from the glass dining table and slump down onto it, my legs collapsing like jelly underneath me. The phone has locked itself in the absence of my touch, but I can't bring myself to unlock it again, not yet. I hit my forehead with the heel of my hand, trying to rouse up a solution or at least some sort of plan on how to handle this whole fucking shit-show of a situation. I consider storming upstairs and confronting Jacob right now, but something stops me. Something inside tells me to act smart about this; don't act on impulse. Think this through. Instead, I change my mind and decide to type in his code once again. I need to know all the facts before I take action here. I need to know everything. I open his messages and click on the last received one. His phone gives birth to a chain of messages. Ironic really, because in comparison, my life feels like it has just ended.

CHAPTER NINETEEN

Their conversation seems to have started this morning at 7.20, with no trace of discussion before this. I snort in disbelief at just how stupid he thinks I am. Something I've never been is stupid. I like to have a laugh, joke around a bit, get up to a bit of mischief, yeah, but never stupid. People often make the mistake of thinking I am though, and I let them, because that way I always have the upper hand. This is how I know that if he is meeting up with some tart tonight, then this quite obviously isn't the first time they've spoken. He has just gone to the effort of being careful enough to delete any of their older messages. He probably does this at the end of each day when they've finished chatting and he comes home to me. Not today though, no today is different, isn't it? It seems that today they were still in the midst of conversation, and that's why these messages are still here. Who's the stupid one now?

As uncomfortable as I know this is going to be, I start from the top, reading every single word very carefully, examining their dialogue in great detail. I flinch at how comfortable they are with one another, as if they're old friends – but with a twist. In one of their messages, this K, whoever she is, tells my husband how much she's looking forward to seeing him, and that she can't believe it's taken so long for it to happen. I pinch the bridge of my nose with my thumb and index finger as I try to understand. What does she mean by that? I'm confused as hell right now. Has he been having a fucking affair or not? Maybe he hasn't been physical with her yet, maybe he has been fighting it, trying hard not to give into temptation, but in terms of an emotional affair, it's all there in black and white. Just because there is a lack of physical contact between them doesn't make this any less hurtful – any less of a betrayal.

One text sent from him reads:

Yeah, only YOU would do that, you melt x

What the fuck. It really is as if they've known each other for years, but how could that even be possible? I've been here for years. I just can't wrap my head around what's going on. He doesn't have any female friends – I would have known – and he works with a bunch of sweaty old men every day. Where has she come from? This random little slag who has managed to grab my husband's attention and lured him away from the promise of his vows.

I glance up at the clock nervously. I know he could head down here any minute now. I tap the phone in the palm of my hand when suddenly my whole body comes to a halt. It's taken me much longer than it should have to realise exactly who this is. A cool tear slides gently down my cheek before a deep sob escapes my throat. I quickly cover my mouth with my hand, hoping that it wasn't loud enough for

Jacob to hear me from upstairs. The nerve of this guy. He's been mugging me right off from the beginning.

When Jacob and I first started dating, he took me to a snazzy little cocktail bar down a backstreet in London. He seemed distracted, and I was getting pissed off because his phone was buzzing constantly. Why ask me out and then have people blowing up your phone all night?

He kept glancing at the caller ID and then declining the call with a quick swoosh of his finger before finally placing the phone face down on our table and out of my sight. After an hour or so, I grew tired of the persistence of the calls and the effect they were having on our date. I felt like he had somewhere else to be. Maybe even someone else to be with and so I just asked him outright – who was it that needed to get in touch with him so fucking urgently and more importantly, why wasn't he answering? It was obviously someone he didn't want to talk to in front of me, that was for sure.

If it had just been a mate, surely, he would have picked up the phone and told them where he was and that would have been the end of it. I had every right to ask him who it was, because frankly he was wasting my time if he wanted to be elsewhere.

Although he was frustratingly reluctant to come clean at first, eventually he realised that I wasn't going to let it go. I was like a dog with a meaty bone, ravenous for the truth, and that's when he told me all about her.

Some years back, he had started chatting to a girl who had hounded him online and at first the two of them seemed to hit it off.

They flirted back-and-forth. He admitted using her for sex chat and a cheeky picture now, and that was the extent of it for him. Not for her though, she was a bit too clingy; talking about houses and marriage – even kids, and so he decided to cool things off. She was having none of it. She in her warped mind believed that they'd formed some sort of magical connection and wouldn't stop contacting him. He admitted that it was a strange one because it was a relationship of some sorts, but not a physical one; more a relationship of convenience on his part, just something to do when he was bored – but he could totally understand why she might have read into things differently, and that it's something he wasn't too proud of.

I admit at the time I was quite intrigued. I mean, have you ever heard the likes of this? It was mad. However, I couldn't ignore the fact that he was willing to open up to me about a horribly unflattering side of himself. It was one I didn't know, one where he disregarded girls' feelings for his own amusement and pleasure. It took guts for him to be so honest with me so early on in our relationship. I could have run a mile for all he knew. Plus, it didn't make any difference to me whatsoever, because I wasn't jealous in the slightest. If anything, I just wanted to know more and more about the whole thing. I felt kind of sorry for her.

I delved into as much as I possibly could; firing question after question at him and to his credit, he answered every single one. No – she wasn't a Catfish, and yes – he did find her attractive in spite of all the crazy that came with her. One important question that I really needed to know though was how long this had been going on for. My jaw almost hit the floor when he told me it was closer to ten years than five. Ten fucking years. Are you having me on? I was stunned and baffled – and so many other things all at the same time. How can you speak to someone for so long without ever having met with them in person? How could that be classed as a relationship? How could you possibly fall for a guy you had never even fucking met? And why the hell would you disrespect yourself so much that you allowed it to happen for ten fucking years? I just couldn't grasp it.

I didn't ask for it, because I didn't need it, but he offered me assurance that since dating me, he had no interest in entertaining her anymore and had been ignoring all her calls and messages, which is why she was blowing up his phone so much now. I was happy with that because I honestly didn't feel threatened by her in any way. How could I be? She wasn't real, not properly. She was virtual, not physical. She had never touched him, never held his hand, never kissed him, and definitely hadn't ever slept with him. Whatever she believed they had together was false; an illusion, because here he was with me and not her. If he wanted her, I mean really wanted her, he would have travelled to meet her – Scotland wasn't that far. She wasn't important to this beautiful man sitting across from me who was so openly declaring how much he was into me, not her. Anyway, she was quite clearly unhinged, I could tell that from a mile off, and after that night, there was no need for us to speak of her ever again.

I think back to that night now. How everything seemed so magical towards the end of the evening when there were no secrets between us anymore. I feel like such a fool for believing him. Was she ever really gone? Maybe she was. Or did he encourage her to return? Surely it wasn't him, it must have been her. I'm enough for him; he doesn't need attention from anyone else because I give him all mine. The harsh reality of the situation though is that he isn't ignoring her now, is he? It's worse actually, much worse. It looks like he has decided to go that extra mile after all and has agreed to take things one step further.

Ideas bat around my head like a furious tennis ball. Should I put his phone back in his pocket where I found it and pretend that I haven't seen their disgusting messages? I could keep my mouth shut; carry on as normal and hopefully he realises what a mistake he's making by himself. He might not even go.

My top lip twitches and I almost laugh out loud at the thought of even contemplating such an absurd idea – a weak and pathetic idea. No, that isn't me, that isn't how I do things. I'm not weak, and I'm not blind anymore. My eyes are wide open, and I can see everything clear as day. The ball is firmly in my court now, not theirs. If I can just contain my anger for a little while longer, plaster a pretty smile across my face when he tells me he is going out, then I can follow him when he goes to meet her tonight. If he wants entertainment, I can give him it in abundance. I'll happily intrude on their cosy little evening together and watch the colour drain from his gormless face as he realises that I know everything.

I can see it all playing out in my mind and it almost excites me. I know what will happen next. He is stupid but not completely, I'll give him some credit. He's smart enough to know that he has it too good here and he won't want to lose me. I'll make him grovel like a pathetic

155

whimpering puppy for my forgiveness and enjoy every second of it. I want to see him on his knees, begging me to take him back. I want to see tears fall from his eyes. I want to see him dismiss her in front of me, as if she is nothing more than a piece of shit on the bottom of his shoe.

I take a deep breath, wipe my cheeks dry as I push back out of the chair and crouch back down to the floor with a fresh clicking of my knees and pull his trousers from the pile of filthy clothes. I slide his phone back into his pocket for him to come and find after his shower. I bet he shits himself when he realises that I've collected his clothes and he hasn't deleted those messages. As I stare down at the floor, bracing myself for the performance of a lifetime, I hold my hand up in front of me. My tastefully oversized diamond engagement ring, accompanied by my freshly cleaned wedding band, glistens in the light of day that has returned to the kitchen. They sit perfectly on my left hand. I have something she doesn't, something she'll never have. I have him.

CHAPTER TWENTY

FIVE WEEKS EARLIER

Hannah Trainer likes your post.

That's odd. Do I know a Hannah Trainer? I pop another piece of milky chocolate into my mouth and click the view profile button. A pretty girl with fiery red hair and skin as pale as the moon stares back at me from her profile picture. I study her for a few moments, trying to place her, but I don't think I recognise her. I scroll through her news feed hoping that her face will come back to me, and that it will make sense as to how she has found her way on to my page, but more importantly, why she's been so deep in my profile that she's liked one of my posts from three months ago.

Maybe there is something familiar about her. She has bright wide oval shaped eyes, and her hair is pretty; not long, but not quite a bob either. Maybe she's visited the salon recently and has decided to check out its owner. Some people do that, don't they? They want to find out who's behind the brand. She might even just be looking to leave a good review about myself or one of my stylists, but it's still a bit strange that she hasn't used the salon's own Facebook page. I groan in realisation. Maybe she's looking to complain instead and is bypassing the middleman by seeking me out privately, going straight to the organ grinder and all that shit. But there is no bad review, and I don't have any messages from her, so in the end I decide that I'm wasting my time looking for something that isn't there. Not one post of abuse on her own timeline about my salon and there's nothing particularly special or significant about the rest of her posts.

About to put my phone back down and continue binge watching my favourite trashy reality TV show, I catch sight of her location at the top of her page: *Glasgow, United Kingdom*. Glasgow, as in Scotland? That's a bit far to come for a haircut, isn't it? So, she can't be a client then. How else has she stumbled upon my profile? I try to pull something from my brain, repeating the city over and over again. Glasgow, Glasgow, Glasgow. It's no use, I don't know anyone from Scotland. The use of the word Scotland however stirs a familiar heavy knot in my stomach, and I sit upright on my sofa as my insides begin to churn. I wish I hadn't scoffed so much chocolate now.

I click on her uploaded photos and swipe quickly through her pictures, desperately hoping that I don't find what I think I just might. I don't recognise her – that's a definite, but I'm worried that someone else is lurking in the shadows behind the profile of Hannah Trainer.

It only takes seven swipes for my worst possible fear to be confirmed. Standing in what appears to be someone's back garden; a freshly lit barbeque smoking in the background, I see you instantly. Perched on the grass, dressed in a cheap looking black playsuit with little frills. You smile brightly at the camera; your red lipstick perfectly painted on to your thick plump lips. Your black wedges balanced firmly on the green patch of grass instead of sinking into the ground. Hot acid rises to the back of my throat and I force myself to swallow it back down. The mere sight of you hits me like a tonne of bricks. I jump to my feet, not quite believing what I'm seeing and the glass of wine at my feet spills onto my grey carpet. I don't care though. I'll deal with that later. Fuck the carpet.

This cannot be happening. I checked his phone at every opportunity for months after the day I found those horrible messages and there was no further sign of you. No phone calls, no texts, no pictures – nothing.

To my surprise, he didn't go through with meeting up with you that night. I know this for sure because he spent the full night at home with me. Well, not the whole night exactly. Around twenty past seven, he told me he was popping out to the shop to get us some snacks for when we watched a film later. He told me I could pick while he was out and joked that I still probably wouldn't have made a decision by the time he got home. Obviously picking a film was the last thing on my mind, but I waved him off like the adoring little wife I am and waited a couple of minutes – just the perfect amount of time, before jumping into my own car and following him as I'd earlier planned to do.

I was careful to keep my distance but stay close enough to remain on his tail. I didn't know what hotel you were meeting at, so I couldn't afford to lose him. His pace started to slow from a sprint to a slow chug and I almost crashed into the rear of the car in front of me when out of nowhere, his car performed a swift U-turn and started to drive back the way we had just come. I panicked, thinking that he had seen me and that's why he had turned back, but I continued to follow him, anyway. I followed and watched him as he turned into the familiar streets of our area and I realised that he was heading towards the shops, like he had said he was going to. I swung the car around as fast as I could and put my foot down on the accelerator, flying back to the house before he arrived home and realised that I'd left the house. Ten minutes later, he returned with a plastic bag filled to the brim of all my favourite treats and a notoriously cheeky smile on his face.

I should have known he wouldn't have gone through with it, not really. For whatever reason, he had a change of heart before taking things that bit too far and I was flipping ecstatic. That night was different too. He didn't look at his phone once and I was so thrilled by the outcome that I decided it was best not to mention anything at all any more. Instead, I gifted him a second chance and tried as hard as I could to keep the secret hidden deep inside me.

As for you, I thought you must have taken his rejection well because there were no more messages or calls. I thought you'd left him alone for good and kept whatever dignity you had left. I was sure you were gone. You should have been gone.

My entire body rattles furiously, shivers crawling up and down my spine like little black ants in a hurry for crumbs. I don't need any confirmation from anybody; I already know in my gut that it was you who pressed the like button – not your friend Hannah. You probably don't even know that you've pressed something by mistake, alerting me to your unwelcome presence. You stupid cow. You've made a big mistake here, no – a huge mistake, actually. You see, after I read your messages, I'd tried my best to find you on social media, like any girl would have, but I was never able to find you. I didn't know your name, did I? Just the first letter, and he didn't have any girls on any of his friend lists on social media with a name beginning with the initial K. I gathered that you weren't connected on social media at all, which made finding you all the more fucking frustrating.

I didn't know much about you, just what he had told me and what I saw in your texts. You weren't from around here. You weren't even from the same country and you had told him that you had to fly from Edinburgh Airport and not Glasgow, which was closest to your home, and how it was a real inconvenience seeing as you didn't drive. Oh boo-hoo, poor fucking you.

I did, however, discover what you looked like. A couple of pictures were hidden among your disgustingly disrespectful messages, and much to my annoyance, you're actually extremely beautiful. In fact, you looked a little like me with your long dark hair and petite frame. I could tell that you looked after yourself too because your skin was flawless, right down to the precise shaping of your eyebrows.

Unfortunately, though, a picture wasn't enough to find you. Turns out you can't just drag a picture into Google, and it tells you everything about them. I'd watched the TV show *Catfish* plenty of times, I really did think it was that easy. I needed your name, though didn't I? And I was furious with myself for not asking Jacob this when he first told me about you. Why didn't I ask your name?

My finger now hovers over the tag that's attached to the picture. There you are, the girl from the messages, dancing smugly before my eyes. My thumb hovers over your name, taunting me. *Karly Winters*.

Funnily enough, it had never occurred to me before that you might try to look me up. Why would you? Surely, you wouldn't still be pining over a married man. That would be pretty pathetic. Are you that pathetic, Karly? Could you still be stalking him, hoping to find something to use against me, something to use in an attempt to lure him away from me? As angry as I am at you right now for your sheer lack of 'girl code', my anger swiftly diverts to my husband. There's only one way you could have found my page, and that's because of him. He must have told you, my name.

My pale cheeks flush as the blood rises to their surface in pure rage. What other details of our life has he overshared with you? What else has he told you about me? What information have you found out for yourself by checking up on me online? I need to know.

I log out of my Facebook account and type my own name in the search bar. I want to see what you see when you're lurking in the shadows of my life. The screen finishes loading, and I shake my head, extremely disappointed in myself for being so naïve. My privacy settings are weak – very, actually. All my posts are on full display for anyone to see, and so are my recently uploaded pictures. You have had a privileged spectator view of my life – and my marriage. I may as well have propped up a chair outside my front door and handed you a pair of fucking binoculars.

I scroll through my latest posts, deciphering if there is anything there that might have suggested a problem in my marriage, an inkling that something might be off between us which might have encouraged your most recent psychotic behaviour, but there's nothing. I like to keep my relationship fairly private, so there isn't much about Jacob on my profile apart from an album of our wedding pictures that were just too beautiful not to post.

As my thumb climbs back to the top of my page, I'm reminded that I recently posted about how excited I am for our annual girls' trip. We go somewhere different every year, leaving our boyfriends or husbands at home and letting our hair loose for a week. My best friend Georgia and I usually decide where the group will go and this year, we decided on Tenerife for a good knees-up.

My own words stare back at me, trying to tell me something important and eventually it comes to me; the realisation that I've given you a very special gift. For seven whole days Jacob will be home alone and my absence is a fantastic opportunity for you to run wild.

I try to calm my mind but thoughts of you anywhere near, never mind touching, my husband poisons my rationality. Would he invite you here – to our house? If he's lied to me with such blatant success before, how will I even know if you've been here? The only way for me to really get the answers I need is if I orchestrate this sordid affair myself. You know, goad you into it, assure you that there is absolutely no chance of me turning up, and that you will be safe.

I open a blank web browser and type in the name of our hotel, clicking on the images tab so that I have hundreds to choose from. I carefully select a few that specifically have the name of the hotel on the side of the building and then upload them to my Facebook. If you were to be invited here, and were to ask Jacob where I would be, for all I know he might tell you down to the last detail anyway seeing as he's clearly been so generous with the information about me that he has shared with you. If you decide to invade my privacy again, which I can almost guarantee that you will, then you will be able to match the information that Jacob has given you as reassurance to the pictures I've posted especially for you.

CHAPTER TWENTY-ONE

I watched him very closely on the days leading up to my girls' holiday. Each time his phone rang, I wondered if it was you. Each time his phone buzzed, I tried to catch a glimpse of your name on the caller ID. I was convinced that you were in cahoots with each other and were cunningly about to use my week away to your full advantage.

I bet you both planned your choice of flight together and even debated over what the best time options were so that you could spend as much time here as possible. My mind was working overtime with all the questions I didn't have answers to but so desperately craved.

The last time he planned to meet you, he did the right thing and changed his mind. But this time in my absence, I can't be sure he'll be smart enough to do the same. That's why I absolutely refuse to sit back and do nothing while the two of you creep around behind my back. I have to do everything I can to look after my best interests now. The two of you might think you're excitedly plotting against me but believe me it will be very short-lived, and I will catch you. I'll catch you both; snare your deceitful souls in my little game of mouse trap, because this is my home, and he is my husband – not yours. Some things aren't supposed to be shared, and it's about time that you realised that.

I curse your parents for raising a girl like you. You seem to know nothing about morals or the simplicities of what is right and what is wrong. Say you were happily married, entirely devoted to your husband, a bright future of a family together on the horizon. Would you welcome an intruder? Would you sit back and let someone else steal what is yours? I don't believe that you would, because if you're ballsy enough to come after what is mine, I can't imagine you allowing someone else to take yours.

I imagine you to be the spoiled child at the birthday party, the one who isn't satisfied that another kid has successfully unwrapped the prize in a game of pass the parcel. I wonder if you screamed and caused a fuss and so your parents gave in to your relentless tantrums that really, they only had themselves to blame for, or if you were cunning. Did you wait until the winning kid put down their precious gift and was out of sight before you snared it into your grasp? The irony of you doing the same thing to me hasn't gone unnoticed.

With what little time I had left, I trolled the Internet searching for something that could help me keep a watchful eye on you. I had something in mind, but I didn't know if it even existed, it's not like I've ever had a need for anything like it before. By sheer luck, though, I managed to source three-minute cameras that were barely the size of a garden pea from a small gadget shop down the bottom of my local high street. I rushed straight out to get them, fearful that someone else might nab them before me, and when I got those precious gems home,

I immediately downloaded the required app to my phone that allowed me 24-hour surveillance from wherever I may be. I imagine people use these for keeping tabs on their pets or just for security purposes. I suppose this is for security purposes though; the security of my sanity, my power, my upper hand.

I hold the three of them in the palm of my hand as I examine them. They don't look like much, but they were fucking expensive. That didn't bother me though, they're a necessity, and anyway I used Jacob's credit card – not mine. It's the least he could do, right?

As I look around our kitchen, I ponder my first move. Hmmm, if I were a hidden camera, where would I like to be? My eyes land on my first target and so I balance the first little black eye discreetly in the centre of an artificial flower with a muddy centre that rests in a stunning silver vase on top of our dining table. This one will allow me to see anyone and everyone who enters my house through the back door, while still giving me a full and clear view of the kitchen and beginning of the dining area.

Now for my next victim, I think as I tap my bottom lip with my finger. I don't think Jacob would be stupid enough to walk you directly through our front door; not for all our nosey neighbours to see, but still, I need to cover all areas just in case. I tuck the second inside the back of the heel of the black Louboutin's that Jacob bought me last Christmas. I think he had been at the pub on Christmas Eve much longer than he realised and panicked; resulting in an extremely expensive purchase for him, but a delightful luxury for me. It's not normal for me to leave them lying around but I don't see him bothering to tidy while I'm away, so I'm confident that they'll stay where I leave them – stacked neatly beside the front door, pointing into the hallway. This will successfully cover the entrance into our home, the entrance into our living room, and unfortunately also providing me with a sickening view of anyone that heads up stairs. I feel satisfied so far with my decisions. There is no way anyone could enter or leave my house without being seen.

The third camera is the most difficult to place by far, but for an entirely different reason. I know where it has to go, but I'm not totally convinced that I could stomach the sight of anything taking place in our bedroom. The thought of the two of you rolling around on my bed caused my stomach to heave, and I lurched forward, grabbing on to the banister. It has to be done though, no doubt about it, and so I lift my head up slowly to avoid a bout of dizziness and I rest my hands on my thighs, bracing myself for the climb. I have to pull myself together, it's much too late to wimp out now.

As I head up the stairs, I tell myself over and over again that I need to do this; I need to make sure that I have solid evidence to confront him when I return home. I picture it playing out in my mind's eye. I'll fire the first shot. An introductory accusation of his betrayal. It will come from nowhere, and I won't tell him how I know to start with, because what fun would that be? I'll let him deny it – because he will – and I'll listen to his weak and pathetic attempts of convincing me that I'm wrong, that he would never do that to me, and then I'll wait for him to become defensive as he tries his best to convince me that I'm crazy, because that's the ugly narcissist in him. Then when I'm completely satisfied that he's buried himself too deeply in the dirt to climb out, instead of offering him my help, I'll launch my second attack with the sordid camera footage. I'll watch his face crumble as realisation finally sinks in. There is no way out for him, not now.

Just the thought of seeing him suffer gives me the boost I need to carry on as I dart into our bedroom. Once again, I examine the room as if it were a crime scene and take my time to pick the best possible place for the evidence to be planted. It doesn't take me very long to decide. I whip open a drawer in my dresser that holds all my bits and bobs and snatch up a tube of eyelash glue. I apply it to the back of the third little diamond in the mud and collect my favourite black earrings from my jewellery dish. I push the little black dot firmly into the earring's centre, disguising it among the rhinestones until my thumb turns red from the excessive pressure.

I plod over to my bedside table at the right-hand side of the bed – the furthest away table, because if I manage to lay them down in just the right position, they'll capture the entire room – whether I liked it or not.

Finished with planting my poisonous seeds, I take a seat on our bed and stare blankly out the window. I can't quite believe that this is real. That he would even be so stupid to entertain you if it meant breaking my heart. The heart he promised to protect. I run my hands over my duvet as overwhelming sadness overcomes me. This room used to be a happy place, somewhere we'd enjoy the best parts of each other as we grew closer as husband and wife. There is no more happiness in this room. The life has drained from it, all its colour melting away like hot crayons under a London summer sun, and even with the curtains wide open, it looks nothing but dark and tainted. For the first time in my life, I'm grateful that I only need to spend one final night here before I'm able to escape tomorrow.

CHAPTER TWENTY-TWO

'**D**o you have everything?' he asks as I'm fiddling about with my hair one last time before leaving for the airport. I answer him privately in my head – *Sure, I have everything I need for my holiday, but I don't have what I need from you, Jacob* – before actually replying.

'I think so. I'm sure one of the girls will have whatever I need if I've forgotten anything, anyway.'

He's talking away at me, but I'm not really listening to what he's saying, at least not until I catch a hint of humour in his voice, a light-hearted tone indicating that he's making a joke. Something about staying at home with him instead of going away.

I slowly draw the lipstick away from my bottom lip and place it down on the dresser in front of me.

'Do you not want me to go?' I ask him curiously.

For a brief moment I wonder if he would really be suggesting that I stay at home if he had made plans with another woman. There would be no sense in that. I wonder what would happen if I did change my mind and decided against going. Would I be spoiling his plans, or have

I just got all this horribly wrong? A fleeting thought that I might have escalated this little demon in my mind beyond the realms of reality strikes me sharply. What if this is all in my mind and I'm making something out of nothing, something that isn't actually there?

The idea begins to taunt me as I play over the solid facts in my mind. I haven't actually found anything that would suggest they are planning a hook up; I just ran on gut instinct, which is silly really, but it's something that's never failed me before. He interrupts my naïve train of doubt, forcing it to an abrupt halt, when he tells me he is of course, only joking about me staying at home. I sneer in response. Of course, he's joking, I bet he can't bloody wait until I'm gone. I curse myself under my breath for even giving him the benefit of the doubt.

I smooth down my clothes, wondering if he's noticed my choice of travelling attire. Does it look similar to something he's seen before, but on you? I took inspiration from you. I decided to dress just like you to entice a reaction. I bet you're wondering how I did that though, eh? It was quite simple really; I flicked through your Instagram account that was foolishly linked to your Facebook. Your need for attention and desperation to be seen was your downfall here.

I knew that your page would be public and not private. The vanity of it didn't shock me at all. I took my time to browse through your feed, starting at the beginning of its creation and then following your journey to where we are now. I could have worked in forensics or something really, because I examined every single photo with a fine-tooth comb before I selected a handful of pictures that I felt able to imitate and took screenshots as an aid to help me pick out the exact same if not very similar garments. So now, I stand here in a little black playsuit of my own, one just like yours.

He comes up behind me and pulls me in close to him, wrapping his muscular arms around my waist and resting his chin on my shoulder. It feels like a hot dagger plunging into my flesh and I want so badly to push him off me, tell him not to come anywhere near me, but I don't – it's not time for that yet. Instead, I smile as best as I can and play my part of his leading lady perfectly, knowing that in no time at all I'll have my answer, one way or another.

GEORGIA PICKED ME up in a black cab about an hour later, stopping only a few streets away to collect the rest of the girls who had met up for coffee first in Costa. Georgia and I very rarely separate from one another, doing everything together at all times. We've been best friends since we were kids, our families were constantly intertwined with each other and we were encouraged to look at each other's parents as family rather than just our mum and dad's friends. I'm so glad I have her here. I don't think I would manage to get through the next week without her. Even though she didn't know anything, her calming presence was enough to make me feel safe.

My four friends hopped in the cab and each had an iced brew to go. Great, that's all they need, more fucking caffeine! They were giddy with excitement, which lasted the entire cab journey to the airport and then more relentlessly throughout the flight when they got their hands on the miniature bottles of wine and vodka. Their chitter chatter irritated the hell out of me. It buzzed furiously in my ears and I just wanted everything and everyone around me to shut up. I was very irritable about what was about to happen, what I'd just allowed to happen, but also a little jealous that they were having so much fun, completely oblivious to the heaviness that was weighing my soul down.

CARS WITH THE remnants of sand stuck to their bumpers zoom by us as we stand on the pavement outside of our hotel. We wait patiently for the lift doors to open because there was absolutely no way that any of us were about to climb the steep set of stairs directly in front of us. The afternoon air is uncomfortably sticky and muggy, and I feel a trickle of sweat run down my chest. I dance on the spot impatiently. I can't think of anything better than being able to take an ice-cold shower and change into something fresh and more comfortable. The playsuit is nice, but it's also incredibly clingy and is wrapped tightly around my body. What I'd give to be in a pair of sweats right now.

The girls, who had bulldozed their way through the drinks menu on the flight were laughing loudly among each other and causing a scene. Locals who approached our direction started to cross the road before reaching us so that they could avoid any unnecessary drama of drunken holiday makers. Even Georgia was taking part, and I watched her cackle among the other witches around an invisible cauldron. I'm actually quite annoyed with her for not noticing that something is wrong with me. Surely, she must be able to tell that something is a bit off and that's why I'm not joining in on the fun?

As soon as we had landed, I switched my phone back to its normal state from aeroplane mode and urgently clicked open the surveillance app. It was strange looking at my home through a screen and it felt abnormal as hell; a bit like watching the film *Paranormal Activity*, waiting for the worst to happen, and although you don't really want to see it, you just can't help yourself. From what I could see from the live stream, nothing looked out of place and I felt a wave of relief wash over me. My single moment of comfort didn't last long though, vanishing just as quickly as it had appeared when the devil on my shoulder reminded me that they could still be together – just not in my house, or just not yet.

The doors finally open, and we all pile into the cramped, sweaty space. It takes forever for it to get going, but when it does, I can hear the faint clicking of rusty metal cogs. I start to panic, and my heart begins to flutter. What if we got stuck in here? How would I be able to check the app? I looked at my phone and seen that the signal had dissipated during the confinement. I'm being silly; catastrophising when I've got enough to worry about and give myself a quick shake.

The lift smells bitter and yet also a little sweet; a variety of different perfumes blended with fumes of alcohol and body odour from all the different people who had graced it with its presence. It continued its ascent slowly but surely, and the doors finally open. We are brought out at poolside and the girls stumble out one by one, giggling like children as they haul their over-packed and bulging cases behind them. I shouldn't be so harsh on them, I know this. They're just excited to start their holiday, I would have been too under normal circumstances.

I need to try a little harder to join in on the fun and brace myself, ready to at least attempt to pull myself together and plaster a smile on my face, for their sake, but as I pull on the handle of my suitcase, it resists my jerk. I notice that one of the wheels has twisted the wrong way around and found itself stuck. I give it a heavy tug and kick the wheel with the side of my foot, forcing it back into its rightful position. I groan in irritation as I take my first step out of the doors. I push my black sunglasses off my face and on to the top of my head, but I'm caught completely off-guard by a pretty brunette impatiently waiting to enter.

My heart falls through my chest and into my stomach, my eyes widening in horror at the recognition of your face. Although I've only ever seen you in pictures, I recognise you immediately.

What. The. Fuck? How did you ... where did you ... WHY are you here? I struggle to comprehend the situation I've just stumbled upon. You for some reason look just as startled and dismayed as me; a vulnerable rabbit caught in headlights of a car as it naively travelled down a dark country road. I can't believe what I'm seeing. I played out every scenario that I thought possible in my head, and not one of them resulted in you standing before me today.

The time and effort I spent arranging those stupid, fidgety cameras around my house and here you are blowing it all out of the water. You have surprisingly not gone to see my husband after all, instead you're here for me. But how did you know where I would be staying, you crazy cow? Oh, shit! I could slap myself in the face right about now. Of course, the pictures I uploaded to my Facebook, the ones of our hotel that were intended to offer you confirmation that I would definitely be out of town, that's where. My own foolish actions have come back to bite me in the ass, and I can definitely feel the sting.

The girls have started to disappear from my sight, and I'm faced with two options here. As much as I would love nothing more than to plunge straight towards you and attack, I can't. Yes, you think you've been very clever, and no I don't quite know what your next move will be just yet, but what I do know is that in your warped mind, I could never recognise you. To me, you're merely a stranger. Taking a deep breath, I begin my stride away from her without a second glance in her direction.

CHAPTER TWENTY-THREE

A cool breeze blowing gently through the open balcony door rouses me from a distressed night's sleep. I tossed and turned and got up and lay back down more times than I can even remember. I was torn with what the best thing to do next was and to be honest, was still completely mortified that you were even here, that this was actually happening.

After seeing you, the rest of last night turned into one big blur. We checked in at the reception and as the girls handed over our passports and placed deposits for the air conditioning and use of the safes; I stayed at the back, silently shitting myself for what was about to come next. I knew that there was absolutely no way that I could carry on with this holiday as normal; a sordid pretence looming over my head like a dark, violent cloud, whispering to me that everything was fine when in reality, it was far from it. I knew I couldn't keep this to myself for an entire week, and that's why I decided the only option left was to come clean to the girls.

I gathered them round a small wooden table in the living area of one of our apartments. Nobody took a seat which made everything seem all the more nerve-racking, and as we all remained standing awkwardly, I told them everything. I barely took a breath, purposely spitting the story out like wildfire before anyone could interrupt or ask me questions until they knew the full story. I told them about the first time I'd ever heard of you and why I believed that you weren't that big of a deal. I told them that last year I'd seen his phone, and how I thought that he was about to take a dangerous step towards infidelity, and so soon into our marriage. I told them that he had seen sense though, that he had changed his mind about going through with anything stupid and how he returned home to me, where he belonged and so I saw no reason to do anything drastic. And finally, I told them about the mysterious like that I received on one of my Facebook pictures and how it led me to the conclusion that I believed that you would be visiting Jacob while I was here.

They stared at me as if I'd told them everything in a foreign language, their mouths slack and their eyes wide and bewildered. I held my breath and waited for one of them to say something, especially Georgia, but I think they were, as cliché as it sounds, lost for words.

There was only one final thing left to tell them and really the only reason I decided to tell them about you at all. I exhaled slowly and lowered my head as I focused on a hairline crack on one of the white tiles on the floor and then I dropped the final bombshell; that you hadn't gone to see Jacob after all – you were here, in this country, in this town, and in our hotel.

There was a deafening silence for a couple of seconds, but it felt like hours, and then the room erupted. Voices, so many loud voices,

179

shouting and screaming and demanding more information. I held my hands to my ears and shook my head vigorously. The room was spinning out of control and I felt dizzy and dehydrated. I slowly lowered myself onto the blue and yellow striped sofa and braced to lift my head to face them. Although completely baffled by the whole fucked up situation, they reacted like true friends would and demanded that they be granted permission to go and find you, corner you and interrogate you on my behalf. I couldn't let them do that though, this wasn't their battle, it was ours – mine and yours.

Admittedly, I did leave out the tiny, but irrelevant detail of setting up those stupid spy cameras around the house. I didn't want them to think I was crazy. I didn't think they would understand why I wanted to catch you both in the act, why I wanted to see it for myself, watch you both with my own eyes as my irises burnt raw. I needed that proof to solidify everything in my mind, to watch any time I felt my resolve weakening as a result of my overpowering love and adoration for Jacob.

Georgia reacted the worst out of them all, which I expected, of course. Your best friend is always someone who takes on your pain as their own, who gets angrier about your hurt than you do, who will stop at nothing to protect you. Rage fizzled from her dark emerald eyes as she rocked back-and-forth on her heels. She was so visibly upset for me, just as I would have been for her if roles had been reversed, but I also think she was a bit hurt. It must have felt like a betrayal for her in some way. She hadn't known about any of this, about you, and part of me felt like I'd stabbed her in the back by keeping you from her. I wanted to tell her, of course I did, but she wouldn't have understood why I chose to stay with him. She would have made things awkward and difficult and might even have stopped coming round the house altogether. I didn't want the dynamics of our friendship to change because Jacob fucked things up. Why should we suffer for his stupidity?

I struggled to meet her eyes. I felt ashamed, and I had no idea what I was going to do next. My head was filled with a suffocating, thick fog that prevented me from thinking clearly; from making a rational decision. I knew one thing though, that I couldn't allow the girls to approach you. Whatever happened next was down to me. I had to be the one who took a step into whatever game you were playing, and I knew I had to be a better player.

I GENTLY PROD my face; it feels puffy, a mixture of lack of sleep and the sweltering heat. I feel extremely groggy and my mouth is dry; my tongue sticks to the roof of my mouth. Georgia is no longer lying beside me in the adjacent bed, but I can hear the faint whisper of voices flowing from the balcony. I peel a strand of my damp brown hair off my forehead and swing my legs out of bed forcing myself to get up before I changed my mind and curled back into the foetal position and pulled the lightweight sheet over my head.

I make my way out of the glass doors to greet the girls who have gathered around the plastic table. It's only Georgia and I who are staying in this room and yet they're all here this morning, presumably discussing me. Their heads swivel in unison as I emerge into the light.

I don't even need a mirror to tell me that I don't look my best right now I can tell from their ghastly expressions.

'Oh, morning, babe – we didn't want to wake you,' Lilly says, smiling at me with pity. 'We're going to go put our towels down at the pool before it gets too busy and then go for breakfast and sort all this shit out. You coming?'

I hesitate before I reply, unsure if I'm hungry or not. My stomach gurgles gently at the thought of something to eat, but I decide that I want to be left alone for now. I don't want to hash over the same details I fed them all last night. I need a clear head to think things through.

'It's OK, babe. I think I'm just gonna go for a shower and hang here for a bit. Would you mind grabbing me a pastry from the shop on your way back?'

'Of course.' She beams. She's always so sweet and innocent which is why it was such a shock to see her so angry last night.

They re-enter the apartment and then shuffle out of the door one by one, the sound of their flip-flops snapping against the tiles. I close the door behind them and wince at the state of our living room. Glasses with toenails of wine are still abandoned on the small wooden table, and more than a few empty bottles are lined up on the floor. It was best for all of us to stay in last night, even though it was our first night here. To be honest, I was scared of bumping into you again, but not for the reasons you might think. It wasn't that I didn't want to see you. Oh, I definitely wanted to see you, but the girls – their anger was so raw and unpredictable. If you mixed their emotions with alcohol and threw in a slice of you, there would have been nothing left of you for me to play with.

I think back to their expressions, the horror, the disgust – some of it maybe even directed at me. As the night unfolded, they let rip with their opinions. They were dumbfounded I'd kept such a huge secret to myself, and for so long. They also couldn't believe that I chose to stay with Jacob. I think they even took the whole drama a bit personally, as though I didn't trust them with such a secret, but it wasn't that at all. Naturally, I wanted the comfort of my friends. I wanted it as soon as I found your messages. I yearned for them to hug me tight and tell me everything would be OK. I wanted all of their shoulders to cry on, especially Georgia's, but I didn't want their judgement. I didn't want to hear their advice. I didn't want them to tell me to leave Jacob.

Silent tears begin to escape my eyes, dripping gently down my cheeks, and for the first time since seeing you yesterday I allow myself to cry. I didn't show any weakness last night; I kept the truth matter of fact and almost military like. I wasn't ready to fall apart, not in front of everyone. Today though, my tears flow like waterfalls, fresh and pure. I feel so many emotions right now; anguished by the reality, betrayed by my husband, relieved that I could finally share my pain, but most of all I felt achingly vengeful.

CHAPTER TWENTY-FOUR

After I'm satisfied I have no more fluid left in me to produce any more bloody tears, I take a nice long, cool shower. It makes me feel a little better and washes away the lethargic heaviness in my head. I wrap a large towel around my body as I head out to the balcony, grabbing a large bottle of icy water from the fridge as I pass. My feet are still damp on the hot tiles and leave dainty size three footprints.

Our room is on the seventh floor and has a bird's-eye view of everyone and anyone, something I'm now extremely grateful for. Peering down, I notice that the girls have put down their beach towels and belongings at a little sun trap on the far side of the pool. Their beds are empty, so I suspect they're still out for breakfast. Enjoying themselves and gossiping about me no doubt. I hope Georgia isn't too harsh on me, she usually has my back in any situation but this time, I'm not too confident.

I run my fingers through my wet hair, attempting to de-tangle some knots without a comb and take a few minutes to admire the beautiful view that has gone unnoticed since arriving here. In the distance you can see gentle waves ripple throughout the warm, salty sea. It's too far away to see other people, but you can just about make out the shape of a few sailing boats and even a parasail that has been propelled high into the sky but is safely secured to the end of a speedboat. It really is a stunning view, one that you could only really admire from such a height like our hotel room. I inhale the earthy scent of the air. It's not really something you can describe though, it's just a different smell to back home; one you can only experience in hot, foreign countries. The large, warm sun perches above a single puffy cloud in the bright blue sky as it prepares to shoot blinding rays of light over scantily clad bodies.

When my gaze reverts back to down below me, I notice that one bed appears to be sitting on its own. It's peculiarly positioned too far away from any of the beds at either side of it for it to be part of a group. And a pink and white towel lying gently on top makes me wonder if it could be yours. It might be too big an assumption to make though. I don't know if you have anyone else here with you. Just because I only stumbled across you yesterday doesn't mean that you're alone. You might have brought a friend for support or someone that will be useful to you for whatever it is you came here to do. I guess I'll just need to wait and see.

MY STOMACH HAD started to growl furiously as I waited patiently for the girls to return, but when they did, only Georgia came back up to see me. She brought me a fresh litre bottle of water and a chocolate chip croissant without saying much and then pottered off to join the rest of the girls down at the pool. I didn't try to talk to her much either though; I was a bit miffed at her being so stand-offish with me. I never expected her not to go for breakfast with the others, after all, a girl's got to eat, but surely my best friend would at least have offered to spend the day with me up here – you know, to make sure I was all right. But she didn't. Instead, she left me by myself and I can't help but wonder if she's still annoyed at me for not telling her about Jacob. It might just be that I've thrown a big ugly curve ball into what was supposed to be our fun annual holiday, but that would be a little selfish of her. It's not like I asked for any of this.

No, it's probably the first option. Knowing her, she'll be thrashing around solutions in her head, cursing me for not handling this whole thing differently. She usually, and always has had a strong and forceful opinion, one that she always believes to be the correct one, and I have no doubt she would have an unsavoury one about this.

Even though I'm seated, I've positioned my chair so that I can still see the pool area below through a gap in the railing. What should have been my bed is lying at the end of the row, vacant and lonely. I have no intentions of taking my place on it today, but I want to keep you on your toes; leave you wondering when I'll show up. Even if that empty recliner wasn't yours, I imagine you will still be on the lookout for me today.

The croissant melts between my fingers as I tear off little pieces and pick at the chocolate chips. I lick the mess away to avoid lingering sticky fingers. I feel you arrive even before I see you. The hairs on the back of my neck stood up despite the summer heat, alerting me to your presence through female intuition. I watch as you take your place on the bed that I suspected correctly was yours. You are alone, nobody comes to join you, and I wonder if you've really been crazy enough to come here by yourself. Quite a bold move.

You do little to hide that you're blatantly staring over at my group of friends. You must have recognised them from yesterday. My lips curl upwards into a satisfied smile as I watch you in amusement. You're thirsty for attention, but the thing is, my girls don't know what you look like, and so they don't notice you one little bit. Instead, they apply sun cream to each other's backs and adjust themselves into perfect sunbathing positions. They are all completely oblivious to you. Did you expect a reaction from them? Is that why you can't tear your gaze away from them? But they don't know you, or know of you, remember? You're here on the basis that I don't even know who you are.

I adjust my chair slightly so that I have a clearer view of you and honestly; I enjoy just sitting here watching you. It's a bit exhilarating being able to examine you in person from my secret hideaway. You have chosen to wear a yellow bikini with white spots or flowers – it's hard to tell from a distance, and your dark hair is tied up in a more of a dishevelled bun than a styled messy one. That strikes me as a little odd. You don't look as neat and tidy as I would have imagined you to be. Jacob likes his girls to be pristine and beautifully presented. I expected that you would be flaunting your seductive curves in lively eye-catching colours, fully accessorised with statement jewellery and with not a single hair out of place. Interesting, I tell myself. Very interesting.

At the moment you're not doing anything remotely interesting, and quite frankly you're beginning to bore me, so I pull over one of the other chairs and prop my feet on top. I push my dark sunglasses on and let my head lull back, allowing the warm sun to beat down over me.

Of course, I check on you from time to time, but still there has been nothing to write home about. Considering how brazen you've been by coming here, I half expected you to go over to the girls at some point or another and introduce yourself, but you haven't budged. Hmmm, what exactly did you come here to do? What is your great master plan? If it's simply to lie around like a corpse all day then crack on, sweetheart. It's your time you're wasting, not mine.

I push my chair away from me with my feet and begin to stand up to stretch my now stiff legs. My foot barely lands on the scorching tiles when I hear it; a muffled whimper emanating from down below. What is that? I tiptoe so that I can peer over the balcony fully to find the source of the noise, but I can't see anyth ... Wait. It's you. But you can't be. Are you fucking with me right now? Are you ...? Are you crying? You struggle to catch your breath and the elderly couple sat next to you – much to my amusement – do sweet fuck all but glare at you in bewilderment. I look over at the girls, who don't seem to have even noticed the drama at the opposite side of the pool, and for the first time in my life I've never been happier that I have such self-absorbed friends.

George is the exception though. She slightly lifts her head from her book for just a moment or two, apparently intrigued by your random outburst, but decides to ignore you like everyone else and goes back to reading her book. She isn't stupid though; she's probably the smartest out of all of us, and so I wonder if she suspects that the blubbering mess is you. You see, my reasoning behind this assumption is that I can't imagine Georgia not wanting to help in some way if she sees someone so distressed, even if it's a stranger. Ever since we were kids, she was always the one who took on other people's problems as her own; protecting them and taking care of them. She has a big heart, one of the many reasons why I love her, and so it's odd for her to seem so nonchalant about the exhibition, which makes me think she has clocked on to who you are by herself.

If I'm right, and she has figured out who you are, she doesn't let on, just as I'd begged her not to, and I'm grateful for her loyalty. Given that Georgia is now unlikely to react, I feel safe to allow my eyes to dart back to you, and I notice that your pathetic sniffles have now stopped, as if by magic. Well, that was fast. Whatever upset you can't have been that bad. I barely finish my thought process when another light bulb moment jolts me. Oh, come on, really? Surely, you weren't faking it. I watch you even more carefully now, studying what I can from the varied expressions splashed across your face. There are no more tears, no further signs of discomfort, and your breathing is back to a normal, steady pace.

Even if I'd been gullible enough to believe you, for even just a minute, you're oblivious to the fact that you would have just ruined your unknown victory. Even with your eyes masked by your dark glasses, your slip-up here is the positioning of your head. It's rigid and focussed in the direction of my girls, waiting patiently for a reaction of some kind. I wonder if you believed that one of them would have made their way over to you. Is that what you wanted, for one of them to befriend you? I cover my mouth with my hand, masking the laughter that has escaped my throat, even though there's no way you would be able to hear me from all the way up here.

Your bed is pushed back with a loud screech and you storm off like a little brat in the direction of the hotel bar, returning a few minutes later with a half-empty plastic cup of something you clearly have made fast work of. I continue to watch gleefully as you throw yourself down onto the bed in an undeniable strop and rest your head on your arms above your head. I chuckle once again. What a nutcase you are. Maybe this day will turn out to be eventful after all.

CHAPTER TWENTY-FIVE

After your little melodramatic melt down earlier, I hoped that you would delight me with some more humorous entertainment, but annoyingly you've decided to do nothing but sleep. It's been more than a few hours now and I'm growing agitated at your lack of effort. I need to get up for a bit and move about. I jump to my feet and a sharp rush of pain similar to a plaster being ripped off a hairy arm causes me to wince. The backs of my thighs had melted into the white plastic of the chair and evidently weren't ready to budge.

I check the time on my phone and see that it's now quarter to four in the afternoon. The heat has been blazing today; one of the warmest temperatures I think I've ever experienced, and plenty of people down below have erected their umbrellas to shelter themselves from the sun. You haven't though; you weren't thinking properly and so as you slept the day away, the yellow ball of fire in the sun has taught you a lesson by branding your skin with its furious wrath. Your back looks raw and painful, something you will no doubt feel as soon as you decide to wake up. This makes me happy. You deserve to feel pain.

The girls are still lying across from you; their skin a stark contrast to yours as they glisten under the sun while slowly but surely turning a beautiful shade of bronze. I think I'll go down to see them for a bit after all, I'm starting to feel the effects of cabin fever being cooped up here all on my own.

I pull a pair of denim shorts and a cheap tank top from my suitcase in the corner of the room that's still waiting to be unpacked and quickly dress myself, removing the headband from my hair allowing it to fall freely around my shoulders. I give it a quick ruffle, creating some extra volume now that it has dried naturally in the sun. I leave the apartment and make my way down the many flights of stairs instead of taking the lift. It's much easier to go down seven flights of stairs than it is to climb up I imagine, and I'm enjoying being able to relieve some of the stiffness in my legs seeing as they've barely moved all day.

Eventually I emerge at the rear of the pool – behind you – and I pause so that I can use these precious moments to really savour the opportunity to study you from a much more intimate angle than I've been able to before. I see all of you now; the painful blistering of your fried skin, the faint white line protruding from where your bikini has lay across your back and managed to escape the blanket of heat, the richness of your dark hair – a richness just like mine – scooped up on to the top of your pretty little head, your tiny waist that only heightens the curve of your ass which is undoubtedly supported by your shapely thighs. I swallow those details down with a large gulp, keeping them tucked away inside me.

A little blonde-haired boy starts to run in the opposite direction of his parents and jumps into the pool, not only causing a large splash that propels drops in your direction, but also a stern whistle from the teenage lifeguard. The tanned boy in the red shorts drops the whistle from his mouth and wiggles his finger at the little boy. Some cold water has landed on your back, disturbing your slumber, and I watch as you use the palms of your hands to push yourself up slowly and onto your knees.

What's interesting here is that you don't even look for the source of the splash. Instead, you stare straight ahead as you had done earlier today, directing your attention towards my friends who are now all sitting upright and chatting among themselves, completely unaware that they have a spectator.

I don't want you to see me; I thought that I would be able to creep down while you slept and be gone by the time you eventually woke up. I should retreat, turn back and head up to my room, but I just can't seem to tear my feet from the spot. I'm quite transfixed on you, and what makes it even more exciting is that you don't even know I'm here. You seem to have bounced back to life quickly and I watch as you pick up your phone. Your fingers move rapidly over the screen, presumably replying to a text. A horrible acidic taste forms in the back of my throat as I wonder if you could be texting Jacob. Surely you haven't told him you're here, have you? What good would that do? Then again, I'm still not sure what your plan even is and so anything is possible I suppose. Maybe you're not here to speak to me, but simply to put the frighteners on Jacob by showing just how far you're willing to go to be with him. You could be taunting him, teasing him, relishing in his fear. I enjoy the idea of him suffering, but as I glance down at my hands; I notice that they've started that now familiar tremble that only appears when I think of the two of you together. And then I hear it. The same noise from earlier. My head juts back up to find you sobbing once again into your hands, only this time the snivelling is much, much louder than before.

I lean against a large white pillar and cross my arms and allow you to do your thing. Who am I to stop you? I mean you're really going for it; an Oscar winning performance that I can't fault, but what's really brilliant about the whole damn thing is that nobody gives a flying fuck. Nobody cares about you. You have failed again; I almost want to applaud you for your efforts, but one of those disingenuous slow claps that make things really awkward.

Realising that you aren't getting the response you want; you start to fumble around; collecting your belongings and throwing them into your bag. I realise that you're packing up to leave, but something inside me tells me to stop you. I can't let you leave. I need to take control of the situation. Impulse shakes me into action and before I know it, I'm standing right beside you with my hand placed gently on your clammy shoulder. You glare at me: stunned, baffled, confused – perhaps even scared.

I take a seat on an empty bed and scoot in close to you, pulling your dainty hand into mine. I move in even closer; our knees are just about touching; a complete intrusion into your personal space. I clear my throat and the words begin to float from my mouth like a well-rehearsed song.

'Sorry, I don't mean to be nosey.' My voice is remarkably calm and soothing. 'I've been in and out of my balcony today, trying to catch some sun as I've not been feeling too good and I couldn't help but notice you.'

You exhale loudly at the sound of my voice, almost as if you didn't expect it to be real. I continue to ride the dangerous wave that I've started to surf.

'I couldn't bear watching you any longer, and you don't need to tell me what's wrong, but are you OK?'

Come on now, babe, take the bait. It was a catch you were after when you were fishing, was it not? I watch as your forehead creases, a sign that you're wandering around my face, examining every bit of me intricately. Before you speak, you remove your hand from my tight grip and push those large, tacky sunglasses up on to the top of your head. Your eyes, they look puffy and strained, which is strange considering your discomfort hasn't been genuine. Your mascara is ugly, smudged across your cheeks like war paint, and you appear timid and weak under my powerful glare.

'I'm so sorry, I didn't mean to disturb you.'

Your Scottish accent slaps me across the face. Your Glaswegian twang is unfamiliar to my ears, although not as difficult to interpret as I expected. Now that you've found the balls to finally speak, you don't want to stop.

'It's my boyfriend. He told me he didn't want to be with me any more – a day before our holiday.'

You puff your chest out and force another couple of sobs for good measure. It takes every bit of strength I have to stop myself from slapping you across your jaw. It seems that you've thought this through. You have a lie freshly baked and ready to serve me, so I let you continue.

'I didn't know what to do, so I came on this stupid holiday by myself and now everything is just a mess.'

I consider the tangled web you've expertly spun me for a few seconds. Had I not known who you are, I might actually have been gullible enough to take pity on you with such a sob story, but fortunately – or unfortunately for you – I do know who you are, don't I?

I keep my attention firmly on you, my head painfully rigid and in position with my jaw clenched. My back faces the other side of the pool – the side where the girls are – and although I can't see them, I can definitely feel their sharp eyes bore into the back of my skull. By now they'll all have realised who you are and be wondering what the hell I'm doing, and what I'm going to do next. Maybe they're bracing themselves for a cat fight, claws out, sharp and ready for a showdown, but that's not going to happen. What I do next will shock them, I know this. It's probably going to shock you too.

I stay as calm as I can be and tell you that I'll look after you – be your guardian angel of some sorts. It was a friend you were after, wasn't it? Isn't that why you've been trying your best but failing miserably to grab the attention of one of my girls? Let's cut out the middleman, shall we? We both know that it's me you're really interested in, and so I invite you out to dinner with me this evening. It would have been rude of you to refuse, and also quite strange considering you're here alone, so you don't.

I bet you never thought that I would be the one to approach you, especially since I've been out of sight today, but you see, that's the power of having the upper hand; something you believed you had by coming here. I tell you to meet me later tonight, around 7 p.m., and then leave you alone with your thoughts – I imagine you will have many now. I rise slowly from the plastic bed and begin to head back to my room, purposely not looking back because over my shoulder are the girls and I don't want them to make a scene. It won't take long for them now to pack up their things and scurry upstairs to demand answers from me.

The four of them stand in front of me in my apartment; lined up like obedient soldiers waiting for command. The room is silent for a long time before anyone dares to speak first, and so it's left to me to be the one who does. I speak first, explaining the ins and outs of our conversation and confirming that yes, it was you, you're the crazy bitch who has followed us to Tenerife. I tell them my plan for you, not just for tonight, but for the week.

'You can't be fucking serious, Lauren,' Lilly says. I flinch slightly, it's always so strange when she curses.

They all wait for me to reply, to tell them that I'm only joking, but of course, I'm not. I shake my head, unable to give them the response they want and deciding not to waste another breath on trying to justify my actions.

Danni is the second to shoot her shot.

'So, let me get this straight. You are ditching us, your actual friends, to spend the entire week with her, your sleazy husband's bit on the side?'

Her finger jabs the air furiously, something she does when she's extremely angry and desperate to start an argument. I try to stay as calm as possible and not let her rile me, even though the way she just spoke about my husband was a little out of line. Yes, he has done wrong, but it's not her place to throw names around.

'It's not quite as straightforward as that,' I reply.

I look at Georgia, desperate for her help, but her face is blank, as if it has been turned into stone.

'Look, it's like this. I have to spend time with her to find out what she's like, you know, see what's so special about her – if anything! I can really get to know her by pretending to be her friend, and then maybe she'll come clean.'

'And then what will you do?' Georgia interrupts.

'I don't know, George!' I snap, angry that she has finally chosen to say something but only to attack me. 'Maybe I'll record a confession or something on my phone so that I can play it back to Jacob when we're home.'

They all look at each other, silently mocking me, not quite understanding or even trying to comprehend what I'm trying to say or why I need to do it, and I'm growing more irritated by the minute.

I hadn't actually made my mind up yet on whether I would include the girls at some point, but their reactions do that for me. They cannot be trusted to support me, and I now don't want any of them to get involved – even George, which stings a little. I'll do this, all of this, by myself, and I order none of them to approach or confront you. If you pass them, they should look the other way, if you talk to them, they should be polite but disengaging.

Their faces are a mixture of emotions; two of which definitely being disbelief and confusion with a third quite possibly being anger. The final person to say anything is my best friend, who approaches me in one quick stride and positions herself extremely close to my face, so close our noses are almost touching. She looks me dead in the eye and spits her words like venom.

'I hope you know what you're doing.'

She turns on her heels and swings open the apartment door. The rest of them all follow and leave the room behind her. The room falls eerily quiet and I bite down on my bottom lip hard, hoping that it will stop the tears that have begun to form in my eyes. So that's that then. It's just me and you now, all alone.

CHAPTER TWENTY-SIX

The right outfit for tonight didn't come to me instantaneously, but after a quick scroll through your Instagram using my fake account, I managed to find exactly what I was looking for. The blood red jumpsuit that I bought before coming here is perfect. The shade is really out there and in your face. A simplistic item of clothing and yet still very much a statement in its own right. It's the kind of outfit that you wear when you want to say something, whether it be to yourself or someone else. I hope you feel intimidated by its boldness, and I'm sure that you will, but just to tweak it slightly, I add a little more emphasis to my small waist by pulling out a thin black belt from my case and securing it tightly around me. I admire myself in the mirror. I suppose I have what you call an hourglass figure. I'm petite, but my curves are always something I'm proud of. They make me feel seductive and powerful, and you know what they say – if you got it, flaunt it. I guess the strangest thing is that I didn't ever imagine I would be flaunting myself to you.

It's still a bit of a shocker to be honest; you being here, I mean. When I packed my case, I did it meticulously with photo opportunities in mind. I only ever expected Jacob to notice the similarities between us – play with his mind a little. But hey, you're here now so I guess that means I'm lucky enough to be able to toy with the both of you.

At quarter to seven I'm ready to go, but I decide to bask in the sunset of my balcony. The world below seems peaceful. The last of today's sunbathers have started to pack up their things from the poolside, and there's a stillness to the chlorinated water that you don't see or appreciate until this time of night. I always remember thinking that the water itself was that dreamy blue colour. I couldn't believe it when my mum told me that it was in fact the tiles on the ground that made the water appear that colour. Such a simple and small snippet of information that changes your outlook on the surface of things. It's a bit like life, really my life. It appears perfect to the naked eye; some might even say I have the ideal marriage. To my friends and family, everything between us is rosy and beautiful and bright and I used to agree with them, I truly believed it too. But just like when my mum told me that one tiny truth about those pool tiles, I now see things for what they really are. Our life isn't rosy and bright at all, it's grainy and dull.

I take a deep breath and inhale the warm air. Is this what it feels like – the calm before the storm? Although I told you to be there for seven, it has always been my intention to be late tonight. I want to keep you waiting for a while, just for fun – mine of course. I imagine that you will be really racking your brains now, conjuring up a wicked plan of your own, something entirely new and different from what you had originally thought of. Maybe you've been smart enough to think of something else already, but by personally choosing to befriend you I'll have almost definitely thrown a cat among the pigeons. There is no doubt in the fact that you will have been forced to reassess the situation.

I wonder if your conscience could have got the better of you. You might not be thinking of a way forward at all, but a way out of all this instead. Let's be honest, things have gone a bit too far now, haven't they? Perhaps things just seem that bit too real now that you've met me, and you've decided to call the whole thing quits and set off home. That's really what you should be doing, and yet I just don't believe that you're capable of being so rational with your actions. There's nothing more dangerous than being left alone with your own thoughts, and you are one dangerous girl.

After allowing a further ten minutes to pass, I start to make my way down to the bar to meet you. I feel confident as I walk towards you. Do you know that red is Jacob's favourite colour? I wonder what other intimate details you know about him. Do you know that even though he is half Italian, he can barely string a sentence together? Do you know that he has two brothers that look absolutely nothing like him? Do you know that he wears socks with his sliders even when he's in the house? You can't know him like I do.

My perfectly curled hair bounces delicately with each click of my solid wedged heels, and the narcissist in me can't help but wonder what you think of me as I approach you. For the second time today, I'm confused by your choice of clothing. I'm not being mean, it's not that you're dressed badly just not how I expected you to be – not after seeing your pictures on Instagram, anyway. You're always so extra and thirsty for the attention and the likes. I examine you subtly, taking in your petite legs that have been squeezed into pale blue skinny jeans and are dangling loosely from the high stool that you're perched on. You don't have on heels either. Instead, you've opted for a flat pair of flat sandals that I suppose match your equally bland white top. I don't have anything against a pair of skinnies and some flats, but again, it's just not what I expected from you.

I make my apologies for being late of course, and now up close to you I can see that you've chosen to leave your make-up behind tonight. Could it be that you've misplaced your foundation in the same place that you appear to have lost your fashion sense? Oh, meow Lauren. I guess that was a little catty of me, but you look demurely pretty and painfully innocent sitting in front of me, with hair that's been straightened within an inch of its life.

I can't understand why you don't look the way you should. None of your pictures show you in this light, not one. Is your Instagram merely a facade? So many people post the best versions of themselves online in a pathetic attempt to dupe people into thinking that their lives are flawless and complete. It's become the social norm to filter the life out of your pictures, crop your waist a little and smooth out any stretch marks. Who do we do it for? Is it for ourselves? Is it to look better than someone you're secretly in competition with? Or is it for men's approval? In your case, I'm going to shoot my shot here and run with the latter, except the man you want to impress isn't yours, is he? He's mine.

Slowly I start to realise that you're far more cunning than I first had you pegged. Of course, I've seen what an impressive actress you can be and I'm very aware that you're slightly unhinged, but this – all of this – all of you right now, it's an act isn't it? You've intentionally dressed like a lost lamb; weak, fragile, and looking for guidance. I shake my head in amusement. You crazy, crazy, bitch. You definitely have some balls on you, I'll give you that.

OK then, I decide, if you're here to stay and ready to play then tonight, I'll be your trusty shepherd.

JACOB

What's going on, babe? Haven't heard much from U x

I'm surprised you've even noticed! X

Of course, I notice, I always notice when you ain't doing my nut in x

Is that what I do yea? Do you not like nutters? X

Only when they're as fit as you x

I'll remember you said that x

I'm sure u will, dick-head! X

Charming. You're always so nice to me ... are you as nice to all your other girls? X

Just you, babe, always you x

CHAPTER TWENTY-SEVEN

LAUREN

To this day, whenever I go to my old man for advice, he tells me the exact same as he has always done since I was a little girl – Baby girl, failing to prepare is preparing to fail. His ability to research and organise things down to the very last detail is only one of many things I admire about him, which is why I searched for a restaurant earlier today instead of leaving it up to chance. I browsed the Internet for top rated restaurants nearby and scrolled through several reviews that boasted about the quality of food or exceptional customer service – sometimes even both. Even though there were many to choose from that would have been suitable, I settled on a beautiful Moroccan themed restaurant that looked cosy and intimate. I didn't want lots of eyes on us. I didn't want big, flamboyant cooking exhibitions. I simply wanted me, you, and our meal. I'm pleased with my choice now that we are here. The pictures didn't do it justice; it's much more beautiful in person.

I watch you discretely over the top of my menu as you debate your choice of meal. Would you be a plain eater; fussy and uninteresting, or would you opt for something a bit more flavoursome; something spicy and wild? Much to my amusement you choose quite a simple chicken dish and part of me suspects that you might not be quite the dare devil you portray yourself to be. However, in order for me to form a strong alliance with you, I have to make myself likeable, someone you would naturally gravitate towards in a normal setting, and so I quickly decide to match your taste and order the exact same dish. You smile at me fondly and it's all the reassurance I need that I've successfully created common ground between us.

You are extremely chatty and upbeat tonight, not the damsel in distress I'd met earlier today. The heavy sobs have disappeared, and your frown is now replaced with a smile. I try my best to act normal. Well, at least as normal as I can be in this situation. But I admit, it's difficult. I feel like I'm on a really awkward first date or at an interview for a job that I don't really even want. I almost wish you had gone to see Jacob after all and allowed me the time with my own friends.

Despite this, I answer all your questions, watching carefully for any signs of approval or disdain that you're willing to give. You are relentless though, firing them wildly at me; your mouth a loaded gun, and I'm honest about most things. I imagine that Jacob will have already told you quite a lot, so I see no point in wasting energy trying to lie to you.

I hope you never try your hand at poker, your face is unforgivably honest. A wave of jealousy crashes over you as I discuss life at home

– especially at the mention of my own salon. Your pretty face twists into something sour and even though you try to hide it, you look just like a spoiled child who has pinched a fizzy sweet from someone else's bag and then was caught off-guard by its bitterness, giving the game away.

Through all this chitter chatter, there has been no mention of your connection to Jacob, and I wonder when you're going to drop the act and come clean by telling me who you really are. I wait for you to tell me that you know who I am and that you've some sort of relationship with my husband. You could even swing it that you're here following the girl code and wanted to tell me woman to woman what type of man I was married to, and yet nothing even remotely like that escapes your mouth. I'm a patient girl, but eventually my patience will run out, especially when I know for certain that I'm being lied to. I mean, you've even lied to me about your real fucking name, introducing yourself as Zara instead of Karly. The more lies you tell, the quicker I realise why you've done this, though. By giving me a false name, you've successfully covered your back if I was ever to speak about you with Jacob. If I was to mention that I'd bumped into a Scottish girl named Karly, I'm pretty sure that he would have been thoroughly alarmed. It's clear you don't want to risk any interference from him while we are here, and for that I am grateful, because neither do I.

I decide to try to force your hand, turn the heat up a notch and put your acting skills to the test. It's my turn to ask the questions now, and I'm sure that they'll be much tougher to answer seeing as all the answers will be blatant lies. You will have to think quickly on your feet here, and I'll quiz you thoroughly on this so-called boyfriend of yours – you remember, right? The one who has just dumped you so callously. Maybe you will trip yourself up and realise that you've turned the wrong corner by coming here and meeting a dead end. It might even speed up whatever it is that you've actually come here to do. I know that you intended to chat to my friends, but I'm not sure what for. I know that you still think that lying about who you are and why you're here is something you're sticking with firmly for the time being. What I don't know though, is when this will all come to a head. When will you tell me who you are?

As you tell me your story, I listen carefully for any hint of a contradiction, but impressively there is none. You have clearly rehearsed this well and know exactly what to say to make yourself sound believable. Perhaps this is the story you would have told my girls.

It's boring, you're fucking boring, and as much as it pains me, I have to keep up the pretence that I sympathise with you, but I just can't bear to listen to your voice any longer and that's why I jump on the opportunity to offer you comfort as I push out of my wicker chair and pull you into a tight hug. Your dark hair – smelling of banana with a hint of coconut – tickles my cheek as I hold you firmly. I want to rip every inch of sweetness from your skull.

After dinner we walk casually through the strip of restaurants and bars and I grow more and more curious about what you could be up to. You have come across so lovely tonight. And yet you've gone to such an extreme effort, to not only stalk me, but then follow me all the way to the fucking Canary Islands. Also, I can't for the life of me work out why you haven't pounced on the opportunity to divulge what my husband has been up to. Surely sitting down to dinner in a public area where you're unlikely to cause any sort of scene or embarrassment would have been the perfect place to come clean, and yet you don't.

You suggest that we go for a drink before we call it a night and I indulge you, allowing you to take the lead and pick a busy rooftop cocktail bar. I pop to the toilet to freshen up and make sure the humidity hasn't done too much damage to my hair. I just need a few minutes to myself more than anything, away from you and all your lies. As I grip the edge of the cool magnolia sink, I stare at myself in the mirror and take deep breaths, in and out, in and out. I ready myself for what might come next and pray that I can keep my cool. I've never had to exercise self-discipline like this before. My temper is usually short and snappy, and I offer no apologies for it.

I give my hair a quick ruffle and exit the cubicle, bumping into a pretty red-headed girl who is standing waiting with her arms folded tightly. She looks pissed that I've taken so long, eyeing me up and down from head to toe, but I honestly couldn't care less because she really doesn't want to mess with me right now. Glaring into her wide eyes, I mouth the words *f u c k y o u* and glide away from her slowly. Although I don't bother to look back, I can tell there is a delay in her entrance to the cubicle as the door doesn't close for another few seconds. Silly cow. I hope she gets stuck in there.

As I approach you sitting at a table of your choice, I can see that you've already bought us drinks, which I recognise as long island ice teas; one of the strongest on the menu. Next to my cocktail is also a shot glass of a transparent liquid, which I imagine is equally powerful.

I smile at you and take my seat. You must think I'm really thick, babe. I bet your plan is to ply me with copious amounts of alcohol, right up until the point where my reactions are slower and am less likely to lash out at you with any success when you tell me who you are.

I throw back my shot of what I now taste is tequila, and it burns the back of my throat. It's disgusting, but I needed that rush of fire to keep me going. I don't drink my cocktail with the same urgency though. Instead, I take slow and steady sips, careful to only allow a small drop of the dark potion to enter my mouth at any one time. I block the rest of it by pressing the tip of my tongue against the opening of the straw.

To everyone around us, our conversation probably looks like a normal one between two friends. You laugh at all my jokes, even though they aren't very funny, and when you do, your smile reaches the corners of your eyes, which makes me think that you might actually be having a good time. I bet you never saw that coming. Our conversations include nothing of importance; no more talk of boyfriends or husbands. Instead, we gossip about reality TV programs and what our go-to brands of make-up are. You seem to know a lot about make-up for a girl who doesn't wear much.

Eventually you excuse yourself politely to use the loo, and I watch your shapely hips sway as you walk around the corner and out of my sight. Confident that you will be gone for a few minutes, I pick up my tall glass that's still more than half full and take a quick look around me, glancing over each shoulder, making sure that nobody is watching. With a sharp flick of my wrist, the glass swings over my shoulder; successfully pouring the majority of the liquid over the roof.

I grab my bag from the ground and rummage inside for something that will assist me in looking tiddly, but I'm not sure what will. It's just lipstick and chewing gum and they won't help. As my hands fumble furiously over each item, they discover a small bottle of perfume tucked away at the bottom and I twirl it around my fingers, debating with myself of its necessity. I give myself a wiggle, shaking any doubt off my tense shoulders. I don't have the luxury of time to think things through in great detail, and so I hold the bottle a couple of inches from my face and widen my eyes. I spritz only twice, but it's more than enough as it stings my eyes violently. I rub them hard, trying desperately to ease the burn, but the more I rub, the worse the pain gets. I scoop a handful of ice from my drink and press them into my closed eyelids, hoping that it will provide even just a bit of relief.

My vision is still a bit hazy when you return to the table, but I notice you glance down at my now almost empty glass. You then divert your attention to me, pinning my eyes with yours in suspicion, and so I shrug and giggle childishly. I guess I'm just a fast drinker after all.

'Com … come on then,' I slur, as I nod my head at your drink, encouraging you to catch-up with me.

You seem amused and are more than happy to let me lead the conversation any which way I like. I bet you're giddy with excitement, waiting patiently for the alcohol to seep further into my veins which will unleash some juicy secrets that might interest you. That isn't going to happen though, because once again you think you have the upper hand and once again you are wrong. I talk a pile of nonsense, blabbering on about everything and yet nothing. For good measure, I pause a couple of times as if to forget what I was saying.

On a good night out, when I'm really inebriated, I like to tell all my friends just how much they mean to me. I'm a bit of a closed book sober, and so it's a rarity when I'm overly affectionate. I decide that I'll mimic my drunken self and tell you just how much you mean to me, and so soon as well. I go on and on about how happy I am to have met you, and that it must have been fate that I'd even seen you earlier this afternoon. What are the chances that I would have noticed you from all the way up in my apartment? You lap it up; a feral cat presented with fresh cream, relentlessly consuming every drop.

As the night drags on, many precious drinks are wasted from tossing them over my shoulder at any opportunity. It's exhausting pretending to be so fucking wasted, and so I'm thrilled when you decide to call it a night. As we walk back to our hotel, I use the journey to have some more fun with you. Seeming to have lost the ability to walk in a straight and stable line, I grab on to you tightly and almost pull you down with me. I focus on the cracks of the slabs as I take each step, being ever so careful not to step on them – a game I used to play when I was a child. I've always had a vivid imagination, and it seems to have come in handy tonight.

The sound of your laughter catches me off-guard and my head whips round to face you. Are you laughing at me? You must really believe that I'm too far gone to realise, but I do and to be quite honest, I'm furious. What gives someone like you the right to laugh at me? You're the joke in all this, not me.

I scream silently. I can't confront you right now, and I'm stuck with all this fury trapped inside me. It kills me, but I do the only thing that I can do right now, and so I join in on your arrogant laughter, playing your joker. I still don't know what your fucking plan is, but I know that you firmly believe that you have the upper hand and that's why my own laughter starts to become less false and instead more genuine at just how naïve you really are.

CHAPTER TWENTY-EIGHT

We spend the next few days of our trip attached to each other; joined at the hip like Siamese twins. Sadly, I barely saw the girls. They decided to spend their days at the beach instead of poolside, and at night they kept to themselves and went their own way for dinner and clubbing. I know I asked none of them to approach you, but that didn't mean they had to cut me out completely. I'm still here, in this hotel, and they're supposed to be my friends. The least they could do is check in on me from time to time, but they seem to have forgotten all about me.

To make matters worse, Georgia has moved all her belongings into the other girls' room instead of staying with me in ours. I don't like to think she was being malicious – at least I hope she wasn't. She's just giving me what I asked for I guess; space to spend time with you without any distractions. I do hope she isn't mad at me though and that it was easier for them all to be together in the one apartment, but it still stung a little.

Once again, we've found ourselves in a busy bar, full of rowdy men who leer at the shot girls doing their rounds of the tables. I've noticed that some girls do better than others; some approach mixed tables of male and females, politely selling their services and bowing out when they're rebuffed. The others wear tighter tops and shorter skirts and focus solely on the male only tables. They flirt furiously and shamelessly in a desperate bid for the drunks to buy the full tray rather than waste their time trying to sell one at a time – they're usually the most successful ones.

I watch you from the comfort of my stool as you dance on top of the bar, confident and carefree. It's been four days now, and you haven't slipped up once about your true identity, or even shown any signs that you're about to come clean.

'Come up here! Dance with me!' you holler at me over the music.

I fake laughter and shake my head. I'm losing patience with you, but I won't crack first. You hop down and shimmy your way over to me, slithering in and out of people's way like the snake that you are. A bunch of bloke's wolf whistle in your direction and you smile back at them over your shoulder, revelling in the attention. I swear if I could roll my eyes any further back, they might fall out of my fucking skull. What a difference a couple of days can make. You might not have told me the truth yet, but there's no doubt you've started showing more of the real you, the you I see online. You're more confident now, more eager for action. That was definitely some heart-wrenching break-up you went through eh, babe?

You whine at me; that annoying, needy way you've grown so accustomed to when trying to convince me to do something. You want me to get up and dance with you, and it seems that it doesn't matter how many times I tell you no, you just aren't having any of it.

'Lauren, listen to me, there is no point sitting here on your todd with a sour face when you could be having the time of your life dancing on a bar, Coyote Ugly style with me – now get up,' you demand.

Who the hell do you think you are, talking to me like that? I wonder if this is why you're here alone. Maybe you don't have any friends. I've been wondering why you don't have anyone with you for a while now as this was quite a big task to take on by yourself, but now it wouldn't really surprise me if there was nobody you could bring with you given that's how you speak to people.

You take my drink from my hand and pull me to my feet with a force I didn't know you were even capable of. Your tiny fingers burrow into my arm as your grip tightens. I decide that I'm not going to make this easy on you and allow my body to fall limply into your grasp as I trip over my own feet. You push me in front of you and take hold of my waist to support my fake, drunken wobbles that I've grown to perfect now, and lead us to the front of the bar, via the wolf whistlers of course. It really is such a waste; the amount of money that has been spent on alcohol that I've had to chuck under the table or in the nearest plant pot. I'm quite impressed by my acting skills actually, and I bite the inside of my cheek to stop myself from smiling. Tonight, is another night where I've had to pretend that I'm completely out of my face because you seem hell bent on getting me drunk for the entirety of our holiday.

You haven't got the faintest idea that I've been faking it, which brings me to the assumption that you're gullible enough to fall for just about anything if you think it's serving your purpose. You're just so fucking self-absorbed, caught up in your own little head. A pretty head yes, but one filled with disillusion, lies, and deceit.

You order us three shots of tequila each, I've noticed that tequila is always your preferred choice of shot. If I've tried to suggest anything else, you instantly dismiss it. Maybe tequila is the only shot that you know agrees with you, the one that allows you to feel that intoxicated high but still remain completely aware of your surroundings. I must remember that.

You catch me staring at you, but I think you believe I'm looking to you for reassurance.

'Go on then,' you taunt, encouraging the glass towards my mouth by pushing the bottom upwards.

The first one is difficult to swallow. I have no choice but to drink them now that you're watching me so intensely. You want me to drink all of them, one straight after the other. I know what you're doing, but the thing is, tequila is always my shot of choice too. A rush of pure adrenaline hits me at the same time the empty third glass hits the surface of the bar.

You shoot yours without any difficulty of course, and I watch your throat as it greedily gulps the liquid down. I imagine what it would feel like to have my perfectly manicured hands wrapped tightly around your pale neck, pushing my thumbs deeply into your windpipe and watching you struggle for air as you cling to the last drop of your pathetic little life. I bet you thought I would be no match for you. You must have if you thought you would be able to come here and manipulate me into doing what you want. I wonder what made you think that way, was it something on my Facebook that I posted, or even just snap judgement of my photos. Either way, you've judged this book very wrongly by its cover, haven't you? Let this be a lesson to you – not everyone is how they appear online.

You push the empty glasses aside, turning your back to me, and use your arms to hoist yourself back up and onto the bar. Although petite, you stand tall, looking down on me with the aura of a goddess, and I don't like imbalance between us. Yes, you're beautiful to look at, but you're ugly as sin on the inside. You stretch your hand out to me, encouraging me to join you, and I know that you aren't going to give up until you get your own way. I mull it over in my head for a few seconds. It's not that I think I'm too good to be dancing on a bar and letting my hair loose or anything like that – far from it, it's just not something I want to be doing with you. I don't want to enjoy anything about you, or my time spent with you. Moments like these should be enjoyed with real friends, not enemies.

I allow you to pull me up, a little part of me hoping that I might pull on your arm too hard, causing you to fall flat on your face, but you don't. There's something different about you tonight. You genuinely look like you're enjoying yourself and it just doesn't make sense to me. How can any of this be enjoyable for you? You dance erratically beside me, grinding your shapely hips, and swinging your long dark hair around like an eccentric stripper. I don't want to be here.

I try to keep my body rigid and I'm reluctant to allow myself even a moment to relax and have some fun but before I know it, you've made another decision for me; grabbing hold of my hands and pushing them into the air, forcing me to dance with you.

You pull me closer to you, so close I can smell your musky floral perfume. You appear to be trying to dance seductively, and I'm absolutely mortified. What's going on here? It's only when I follow your line of vision that I see the blokes in the corner of the room once again. They are enjoying the show, enjoying the performance you're forcing me to take part in. They wolf whistle return, and I can't help myself as I let out an almighty laugh at just how pathetic you really are; just how much you crave attention and the buzz it gives you.

I'm relieved when a couple of other girls decide to join us on top of the bar. I use this golden opportunity to dance away from you, as far away as I can get, taking one of the other girls with me. Only when I'm away from you do I really start to have any fun; something I've not had much of during this trip.

I'm still completely aware of my surroundings despite what you might think, and that's how I notice that you've now shimmied towards the blokes in the corner. You jump down, just a couple of feet from them, and I can't quite believe what I'm seeing as I watch you walk confidently towards them. You can't be that invested in my husband if you're still interested in other guys.

You chat casually to a few of them, introducing yourself I assume, before singling one of them out. Your hand is placed gently on his chest and you begin to whisper something into his ear, your body now pressed firmly up against him. I see it now; I can't believe it's taken me so long to realise. I know exactly why she's showing interest in this guy, it's because he looks a bit like Jacob. He has the same wide, cheeky grin with pearly white teeth that have the ability to persuade you to do anything and everything. Just when I think that there is nothing else left for you to do that would shock me, you do this. Are you not satisfied enough with your attempts to worm your way into my marriage? Clearly not, I guess. The homewrecker now wants a slice of his doppelgänger, and it makes me sick.

The two of you step away from the rest of the group and a few of the lads thump him on the back in admiration. My heart starts to beat faster, and I can feel the blood rush to my ears as you lead him over to me. I feel hot, very hot. I do my best to act oblivious, keeping up the pretence that I wasn't watching you, but now you're pulling at me, yanking at my ankle to get my attention. I crouch down to hear what you have to say, but you start to wipe at my face. I flinch but try my best to stay steady even though your touch feels like it's burning my flesh. You smooth down my hair before finally telling me what you want.

'Come on, babe, we're going for a walk,' she shouts over the sound of the music.

I can't speak, my mouth feels dry and desperate for water. I have no idea what you're up to here, and why you need me to join you in entertaining your Jacob lookalike. I jump down swiftly and obediently, but as soon as my feet hit the sticky floor, I scald myself for slipping out of character. There was no struggle, no wobble, no clumsiness. Nothing even remotely close to the drunk that I'm supposed to be.

Thankfully, I think you're too wrapped up in your male friend to notice.

CHAPTER TWENTY-NINE

We walk for a little while; not too long, just enough that we are now away from the hustle and bustle of the busy bars and clubs. We seem to have found ourselves at the beach. It's quiet, maybe even a little eerie without mass gatherings and loud voices. The light from the street has faded into the distance and we all would be in complete darkness if it wasn't for the crisp moonlight.

Jack seems like a nice lad. He's attractive and extremely funny and if I was single then sure, I would think about going there, but unfortunately for both of you, I'm not single and I definitely haven't forgotten about the rock on my finger.

We sit on the damp sand, just the two of us; away from you and your poison. The cool salty air washes over us gently and I'm enjoying spending some time with someone new – someone who isn't you. Jack is a nobody to me, I can be completely myself with him, but still, I'm aware of your presence and the fact you can't take your eyes off us. You sit by yourself only a few feet away and I can't remember if we chose to walk on in front or if you stopped behind deliberately but right now, I don't really care as long as you're not suffocating me.

What I do care about though is what you plan on doing next. I know now why you wanted me to tag along. It wasn't so that I could play gooseberry, it was so that you could. I was very much aware that this bloke had been giving me the eye in the bar earlier, but you didn't think of that did you? You thought I was too pissed to notice and instead you spotted a wild opportunity; jumping at the chance to cause some trouble.

In your warped and twisted mind, you believe that if you dangle this handsome guy in front of me; one who has striking similarities to Jacob, that I'll stray from fidelity. The alcohol you think that I've consumed throughout the night is what you will be counting on, and like a little rat you will scurry back home and tell my husband that his wife is a filthy cheat. It seems that alcohol has always been your weapon of choice and something you counted on being the instrumental factor in my demise. I wonder though, how did you plan on presenting this information to him without giving away the game that you were here too?

I've already made it crystal clear to Jack that nothing will be happening between us. I'm flattered by the attention, of course I am, but I've never been the type to lead a poor bloke on. He's completely wasted but I think he understands because after I politely rebuffed him, he's spent the majority of our time together chatting shit about his ex-girlfriend back in Liverpool and how he thinks he'll give things another go between them. You don't know any of this though. You don't have any idea what we're talking about, and so I'm milking every drop by laughing loudly at his jokes and gently touching his arm.

I might not be happy about leading Jack on, but leading you a merry dance, I'm more than happy to.

You've decided to interrupt us. Perhaps you've grown impatient with me because there's been no snogging or heavy petting. 'OK, you two lovebirds, let's take this party back to the hotel, shall we?'

It takes everything I have not to put you in your place right here. Every inch of my shivers as I try to practise the utmost self-control. I bite down hard on my bottom lip, piercing the skin. The coppery taste of blood streams onto my tongue and I swallow it down.

Jack, although still clearly pining after his ex-girlfriend, seems to think he might have caught chance of a second wind with the suggestive invitation back to our hotel and springs into the air, ready to go. I'm not so quick to get to my feet, after all, I'm very drunk ain't I?

I stumble my way back to our hotel, grabbing onto your arm tightly, making it difficult for you to manoeuvre me. I make a point of causing a scene when the lift brings us all up to the poolside. Nothing major, just faffing around and shouting obscenities. The security guard shushes me, but I just laugh at him. You look absolutely mortified and I realise that this is probably the most fun I've had yet. I make a mental note that I should try to embarrass you more often.

When we finally get upstairs to your apartment, you pull me away from Jack and into your bedroom and we both fall back on to the bed, laughing in unison. You turn on your side to face me, our noses almost touching, and I feel really, really uncomfortable so I flutter my eyelids a couple of times as though I'm falling into an intoxicated sleep.

Maybe if I fall asleep, you will go away and leave me alone. I can smell the sweet tang of tequila on your breath and your hair is gently tickling my cheek. I'm repulsed by you.

I wrack my brain nervously trying to piece together what your crazy ass is about to do next. As if I ever had any doubts before, it's abundantly clear that you invited Jack back here for no other reason than to wingman him into a quick shag. To be quite honest, I'm a bit stunned that you're willing to go this far. Surely with the amount of alcohol you've attempted to ply me with, you know that this isn't right? Had I been as drunk as you think I am, there's no way I would be in any position to have sex, and yet you've continued to orchestrate this whole thing. There might have been a time where I held some respect for your ballsy-ness; coming all the way here by yourself with a grand master plan – but not now. You've forfeited the right to any respect at the same time you forfeited my right to safely consent to going to bed with a fucking stranger. You're vile, and I hope to God you struggle to sleep peacefully at night.

While I feign sleepy unconsciousness, there is a brief moment where there is nothing but silence; no movement, no speaking, no laughing. Suddenly a sharp pull underneath my arms causes me to flinch as I'm hoisted upwards. I feel your warm body pressed against my back and I allow my head to lull to one side. You tug my dress up and over my body and then release my dead weight, allowing me to fall back down flat on the bed in just my underwear. I can hear the blood whirling furiously in my ears and I do nothing but remain completely still, anticipating your next move. The only thing comforting me in this freak situation is that I have sobriety on my side; I'm able to defend myself if I really need to. But I still can't believe this is even happening. I wish we were in my apartment, not yours. Georgia would come home and see what you were up to and would put a stop to this madness and then she would, she would … she wouldn't do anything – because she's not staying with me anymore. My best friend left me when I needed her the most.

A crash erupts from the kitchen where we left Jack.

'Jack … Jack,' she whispers, and I hear him bound into the room like an obedient puppy dog.

My eyes remain firmly shut, mostly because I don't want to open them and for all of this to be real.

You encourage him to lie down next to me. 'Here, lie down next to Lauren. She asked me to get you.'

Oh my god, my heart begins to pound against my chest. You're really going to do it; you're really going to let a stranger take advantage of an unconscious and un-consenting girl, aren't you? This is a joke, right? It has to be a joke. Maybe you do know that I know who you are and are testing me, tempting me to make another move on your wicked chessboard. Surely you can't be serious, I just can't believe that you could be. This isn't right. Neither of us know this lad, he could be anyone. We don't know his past; we don't know what he's capable of. Sure, he seemed lovely to chat to, but he's drunk too, and he has been invited back to our room. He might think this is OK. He might not see this for what it is. This is rape.

There's a struggle between the two of you. I think you might be helping him undress, but I can't be sure. All I know is I heard the crack of a belt hit the floor. The bed dips as he falls beside me, the strong woody smell of his aftershave filling my nose as he throws an arm over me and pushes his face against my neck. My body stiffens at his touch; a touch so foreign and unfamiliar to my husband's, and I realise that I'm torn between two very strong emotions – fear and rage. I feel paralysed, too scared to move a muscle, and yet there's still something much darker and much more intense lurking in my body that wants me to lunge from this bed and tear you apart, limb from limb.

I wait for another movement from Jack, ready to swipe away the creep of a hand or a hot mouth pressed against my lips, but nothing comes. I try as best as I can to push past the pounding in my ears so that I'm prepared for anything, and when I do, I realise that the rhythm of his breath has changed. He's asleep, oh thank God he's fallen asleep.

The bedroom door creaks as it's pulled over, and a sharp sigh of relief escapes me. My eyes dart open wildly, and I lift up Jack's limp arm and slide away from him, slowly rolling my way off the bed. I creep over to the door that hasn't been shut properly and peer through the crack and there you are, sitting on the couch, your feet up comfortably without a care in the world. Your stupid face a picture of glee as you flick through your phone. You seem satisfied with yourself, but I don't understand why because nothing happened. He fell asleep. We didn't sleep together, nothing happened for you to be happy about. You don't have anything to use against me, and yet you look thrilled.

I continue to watch you through the gap as your finger swipes right and then left, and then right again as if you're looking at something more than once. It's almost as if you're scrolling through some happy memories in your photo album. Tears begin to form in the corner of my eyes, and I clasp my hand to my mouth in realisation. My eyes bulge, forgetting how to blink, and I force myself to take slow and steady breaths. You do have something, don't you? In fact, you have all that you need, regardless of how this night has panned out. You don't need a serial killer to perform in front of you when you're staring down at their crime scene because you have all the evidence you need in one clear snapshot to convict. You have fresh ammunition to take me to trial. You have pictures.

CHAPTER THIRTY

I barely slept last; a turbulent combination of lying half naked in an unfamiliar bed while being left for roadkill. I was so angry at myself for being so fucking stupid. Of course, you were going to take pictures; you aren't stupid. You are many things: cunning, sly, wickedly manipulative, and I knew all this about you from our first few days together, and still it never crossed my mind to think you were capable of such evil.

I know that nothing happened between us, but I'm not so naïve in believing that any Jury examining those pictures wouldn't find me guilty of adultery – if that's what I was to be accused of. What evidence would I have to support my case? It would be my word against yours, just the two of us battling against each other. I wouldn't have Jack to confirm my story of events because I didn't plan on seeing him ever again.

I scratch furiously at my head in frustration. I desperately need to get out of this hot and sticky room; the balcony doors have been shut all night, and the room is stifling. I can smell last night's alcohol circulating among us. I need to get to the shower fast and scrub away the fear and disgust that accompanied last night. I still can't wrap my head around the fact that if I'd drank too much, and I wasn't as aware as I was last night, what could have happened. The way you behaved last night, that's a whole different level of crazy, a much greater scale than the one I had you pegged.

I won't be able to get to the bathroom without you knowing because I'll need to pass by you in the living room. I'm not ready to spar with you yet, but I have no other choice than to confront this head on and allow you to play puppet master and so I call your name. Silence, you don't answer.

'Zee, are you awake?' I call again, but you still don't respond, and instead Jack starts to stir beside me.

For fuck's sake, where are you? My hands start to shake with rage or nerves, I'm not too sure which one, and I slide them under my thighs to stop their trembling. You're only in the room next door, so I know that you can hear me but for some reason are choosing to ignore me.

I shout on you again, louder this time, and the fresh anger spikes tears in my eyes. The patter of heavy footsteps thudding against the tiles tells me that finally, you're moving closer. The door flies open and clatters against the wall, causing the paint to crack, fall, and sprinkle lightly onto the floor. You stand completely still, gawking at me with those big stupid eyes, issuing me a disapproving glare that a parent would give their kid when they've behaved out of turn.

What the hell have you got to be so righteous about? You know nothing happened between the two of us, as much as you clearly wanted it to, and yet here you are standing in front of me with your hand placed on your hip and the audacity to look at me with such revulsion. You silently dare me to make the first move in today's game, and reluctantly I play my hand.

'What happened last night, Zee?'

My voice is hoarse and panicked, but not by the fear that you expect me to feel this morning. It's a different kind of fear, a fear where I don't know if I'll be able to control myself enough to carry on with this farce.

'Come off it, Lauren.' You belittle me. 'You mean you don't remember?'

I can't speak, I keep my tongue firmly pressed to the roof of my mouth to prevent me from responding irrationally. I'm too angry, too close to the edge, too close to exploding, and blowing up your entire world to even try to speak to you. Instead, I shake my head. It's all I can stomach as I pull the thin white bed sheet tighter around my partially exposed body and sit there silently as you relish the opportunity to tell me everything you want me to believe. Delighting in telling me just how drunk I was, you dive in without hesitation, adding that you understand that it was a mistake, and it wasn't my fault.

'Blame it on the alcohol, babe, we've all been there.'

I taste the venom on my tongue, and I force my lips apart, doing everything I can to speak to you without spitting obscenities.

'What wasn't my fault? Where are my clothes?' I demand; an icy stare fixed on your face.

You nod your head in the direction of the corner of the room, where my white sundress lies in a heap, accompanied by Jack's red T-shirt.

'You slept with Jack, Lauren. Don't worry though, obviously I won't tell a soul.'

The way you speak, so nonchalant about the whole thing raises bile to the back of my throat. Swallowing it down, I pounce from the bed and grab my dress, throwing it quickly over my head and barge past you with a thunderous force. I can hear you shout on me, telling me to come back, but I'm too fast for you to try to stop me. I quickly unlock the apartment door and make my escape. Stuff the shower, that can wait, I just need out of this fucking apartment.

I hurl myself around the corner that takes me to the stairs and start to power my way down. I realise that I'm not wearing any shoes and the tiles are cool on the soles of my feet. What can I do? Where can I go? I pause, thinking that maybe I should head back up the stairs with my tail between my legs. I could chap on the door; I could tell them what happened last night and how dangerous it was. I'm sure they would understand, they would let me in, they wouldn't hold anything against me. My hand grips the railing as I decide if I'm going up or down. I decide to go down. I can't tell the girls about last night, of course I can't, that will only open a whole new can of worms. I can see their faces now, glaring at me with that I-told-you-so attitude. I started this by myself, I have to go the distance by myself, no matter what happens. I take another step down and slowly continue my descent. I'll sit by the pool, maybe dangle my legs in a little while I wait for you and Jack to leave my apartment. I just need to give myself a shake, gather myself again after the wreckage of last night. I'll be OK; I can do this.

The last couple of days were the most stifling of them all. To carry on acting like I'd done something wrong, gifting you the satisfaction of having something over me was a nightmare. It made my skin itch to even be around you. In hindsight, I should have just told you that I knew who you were after that night. Ended the whole thing while I still had you face to face. I should have done, but I didn't, because that would have been too easy on you. You might even have enjoyed the confrontation in some sick way, who knows what goes on in that twisted head of yours, and I didn't want you to enjoy anything about this. You didn't deserve to. I needed you to suffer for what you had put me through – hell, are still putting me through – and outing you then was not going to satiate me.

THE PLANE JOURNEY home was frosty, and I'd expected it to be. I'd missed out on a fun week with my friends – my real friends, and I couldn't join in on any of their gossip or private jokes. I'd spent all my time with you and ruined what should have been such an amazing trip.

I was sitting next to Georgia and had tried to make small talk, but she wasn't having any of it. She was still mad at me. When I thought about giving up and just putting my headphones in and sitting in silence, she eventually spoke to me, bringing up the subject of you of course, what else? And I reluctantly filled her in on everything that had happened during the week. She followed my lead and fed me snippets of her holiday. There was such a stark contrast between our two trips; she'd spent her week tanning her perfect body and drinking sangria while I spent my time befriending my husband's bit on the side.

I wasn't going to, but I ended up telling her about Jack from the bar, and how you were a crazy bitch, stripping my body of clothing and encouraging a stranger to take advantage of me. She was horrified, but listened intently, scraping her thick blonde hair into a high pony as if somehow that would help her soak all the information in.

After a while, Georgia stopped speaking again. Her green eyes pierced the back of the chair in front of her as she sat in icy silence. It sent shivers down my spine, I just wanted her to comfort me both physically and emotionally, to tell me that I'd done the right thing by not outing you. I craved her guidance on what I should do next, but she refused to give me anything more. I decided to leave her to digest everything I'd told her. She was understandably stunned by the whole thing, and I knew better than to push her. If you think my temper is bad, you should see hers.

CHAPTER THIRTY-ONE

Now that I'm back home, I'm really struggling to be around Jacob. Knowing that he could even betray me with anyone, never mind someone so hateful and devious made me question who the hell I'd married. How could he find those traits attractive in any way, and if he did, why did he marry me? I'm nothing like you.

Sometimes I've caught myself watching him as he goes about his day; washing up or lounging around on the sofa watching the TV. His face, that beautiful, strong, smouldering face that so often made me melt was now making me want to heave. I recoil every time he tries to touch me because it feels wrong; it feels like a lie. Things can't just snap back to normal, it will take some time for me to get over this, for us to be able to go back to the way we were. I still don't really know what I'm going to do going forward, but my week with you is still too raw, too fresh in my mind to push aside. We will get through it though; I haven't gone through all this shit just to hand him over.

The secret between you and me simmers away in silence and I'm prepared for the lid to blow at any minute. That's why I make sure that I text you every day. It helps keep the connection between us active even if it is from miles away. It makes me feel like I have the upper hand by keeping you sweet, but it sickens me to chat idly with you. I imagine you feel pretty pleased with yourself that you've returned home safe and sound with something you believe invaluable to use against me; leverage for a rainy day.

I haven't spent much time with the girls since we got back because I've kept them far away from the house, warning them not to show up unannounced and only meeting them for coffee or drinks in town. Often, I've lied to Jacob and told him that I was working late and just going straight to bed as soon as I got home. I can't risk any of them saying something to Jacob about what they know, and even though it wasn't their place to, I didn't trust them not to. I'm just glad things are back to normal between me and the girls. Georgia had filled them all in about our night with Jack and they all came around quickly. I knew they would anyway, because Georgia and I were fine now, and they wouldn't have seen sense in carrying on a feud without their strongest member.

I think Jacob has become a bit suspicious about why he hasn't seen any of them floating around our house – especially Georgia, which I understand because it's completely out of character for me to isolate myself from everyone. I'm the social butterfly among my friends, the host, the party planner; not the recluse I've become. Often, he would come home to find spontaneous dinner parties or last-minute Friday night drinks. For some reason, and one I'm not complaining about, he hasn't asked me for an explanation behind my peculiar shift in behaviour, and I haven't offered one.

I told him about you though – Zara of course, not the real you, obviously – and he asked the usual questions that any husband would: where did you come from and what were you like? I was more than happy to tell him to be honest because I wanted to test his knowledge of you. How much of what you had told me was the truth? Did you tell me aspects of your life that were genuine or was everything that came out your mouth just one big filthy lie?

I watched his chiselled face carefully for any flicker of desire in his eye or any hint of interest in your beauty, your personality, your demeanour, but this is where the two of you differ because his poker face is and always has been excellent. Yours on the other hand, not so much, eh, babe?

My train of thought is interrupted by my guest taking her seat at the table. It feels so good to have her here, my best friend. We've spoken over text and phone calls since we arrived home, but tonight is the first I've seen her in person. I can tell from her bright smile that she is in high spirits and she looks phenomenal. She's had her hair lightened, and her previous sun-kissed golden locks are now a strikingly sharp shade of platinum blonde. It suits her. I could never pull off such a prominent look.

There's something else different about her though, but I can't put my finger on it. The energy that surrounds her, her aura – it's vibrant and glowing. She would absolutely kill me for thinking it, but dare I say she might even have gained a few pounds. Not in a bad way though, not at all. In fact, she looks all the better for it. It's not that she was unhealthily skinny or anything, just that she is always overly careful about what calories she consumes and what the fat content of absolutely everything is. That's why I was even more surprised when she joined me in ordering both a starter and main completely overloaded in carbs. My stomach grumbled at the thought of gooey mozzarella sticks and chilli nachos covered in chunky salsa. My appetite hasn't been great since being home, but that's just down to stress, I'm sure it will pick up again soon.

I decide to stick to soft drinks seeing as I've brought the car and order a coke and she follows my lead by ordering a jug of water for the table. I can't help but laugh because Georgia never misses out on the cocktail menu no matter what time it is and especially when I have the car knowing she'll always bag a lift home. I chalk it up to nerves because as steely as Georgia Person is, she is an utter melt deep down and I guess she's feeling just as anxious as me about our first get together. She just doesn't want to rock the boat by getting wasted and spoiling our reunion.

Out of nowhere, and completely off topic, she is the first to mention you, which is a little annoying because I want to spend my time with her and just her. I don't want our nice lunch to be invaded by your nasty ass energy. I've had enough of that recently to last me a lifetime.

'So, I've been thinking about … well … you know what.'

I lean on the table with both elbows and clasp my hands at the bridge of my nose, bracing myself for what she is about to say.

'OK, shoot,' I reply.

'I think you should bring the bitch here – to London I mean, not this restaurant.'

I take a sip of my Coke, breaking eye contact between us. I know what she means, but I'm stunned at her suggestion. I don't know why she thinks that's even remotely a good idea. Bringing you closer to my husband. If anything, I want to keep you as far away from him as possible. As if she reads my mind, she answers before the question escapes my lips.

'Just think about it, Lauren. She's got something on you, and that bastard is still lying to you. It's time for you to do something about it. Something they won't forget. It's time to stop being such a pushover.'

It had never once crossed my mind to invite you here. I didn't want you anywhere near me ever again, but Georgia did have a point. I did have to do something; I just wasn't sure what. Jacob wasn't about to admit that he was still in touch with you anytime soon, that's for sure, and you were cradling delicate ammunition that could potentially destroy my marriage if manipulated in the correct way.

I take a deep breath and twirl the paper straw around my glass, rattling the ice cubes loudly.

'OK then, what do you have in mind?'

She beams at my acceptance and together we come up with the perfect plan for you, my dear friend. We spend the next few hours going over the finest of details and how to expertly get the ball rolling. My heart swelled with love for my best friend; appreciative at her newfound interest in my battle with the enemy and just how invested she was in bringing you down. She didn't once ask me if I was going to leave my husband, because she knows me well enough to know the answer to that. It reminded me just how much I would be lost without her. She was loyal, a true friend – family even – and both you and my husband could learn a thing or two from her.

CHAPTER THIRTY-TWO

T his morning when I open my eyes, I have no desire to go back to sleep. I'm eager to get the ball rolling. Jacob is lying next to me still comatose. His alarm hasn't yet sounded to wake him up for work. He looks so content, so happy, as if he doesn't have a care in the world, as if he hasn't been lying to his wife every day for God knows how long. I wonder how he does it, how he manages to look me in the eye every day and tell me that he loves me. I hope he is making the most of his slumber because this will be the last morning where he sleeps peacefully with his deceit tucked carefully away beneath the surface.

It took three failed attempts to reach you yesterday, but on the fourth you eventually answered your phone. I know you were doing this on purpose. We're always battling for that upper hand, aren't we? I do my very best to sound weak and pathetic as I explain to you that none of the girls are speaking to me because they're still so angry with me for ditching them on holiday, and that I desperately need someone to talk to. I need you to believe that 'someone' is you. I tell you everything that Georgia and I came up with; that the guilt has eaten away at every part of me and that I'm thinking of coming clean about the whole thing. I knew that you wouldn't allow that because if I did, you would no longer hold any power over me and then what would you do?

You act just as I suspected, playing the role of my new best friend, empathising with me, telling me that you wished that you could somehow be there for me. I know that you had picked up on the hint before the question was even asked, and you will probably think that this whole thing was your idea. You will believe that I've given you a fresh opportunity to worm your way into my life, but you have no idea that by asking you to visit, I'm really preparing to bring you crashing down to earth with an almighty thud.

You agree to the trip after a bit of false reluctance, but decline the offer of my spare room, which is fair enough, I didn't expect you to say yes, anyway. I mean you're stupid, but you're not that stupid. You will want a base of your own, somewhere where you can safely slide off your devilish mask and morph back into the slimy reptile that you truly are.

Although I always knew you would say yes, I was still a little surprised at just how quickly you were willing to drop everything to come down here. I don't know much about your commitments back home, but you managed to clear your schedule pretty damn quickly. That only made you look all the more desperate though, I hope you know that, and just to make sure that you couldn't back out now if you did happen to have any second thoughts, I booked and paid for your flights myself. 'A little gift,' I told you, to say thank you for being such a great friend.

Everything is now perfectly in place. You will arrive early tomorrow morning and in only a matter of days you will be sent on your merry way right back up to Scotland, defeated and devastatingly humiliated, but most importantly without my husband.

He on the other hand will spend days, weeks, possibly even months begging for my forgiveness, and I'll bathe in the chance to watch him suffer. The best part about his up-and-coming suffering is that I already know that when I'm satisfied that he has been tortured enough, I'll undoubtedly let him stay. This was never about getting rid of him; it has always been about you – only getting rid of you. I feel giddy with excitement. Georgia was right, this has to happen for everything to go back to normal. God, I'm so lucky to have her.

I gently swing my legs out of bed and pad across the hallway to the spare bedroom where I've already laid out my outfit for today. I'll wear my favourite pair of black skinny jeans with a plain white T-shirt and throw on my studded leather jacket. It's a non-complicated, no fuss look; and yet a fierce one, one I feel confident in; an armour fit and ready to tackle anything that you throw at me today.

After my shower, I tie my hair back into a sleek ponytail and push a pair of large hoops through my ears. I look tired. I am tired. I'm tired of all your shit and it shows. Usually, I would layer on that concealer till the cows came home, but not today. I may be dressed well, but I don't want to look well. I want you to really believe that I'm suffering, really believe that I'm in dire need of your help and support.

Now for that little something extra that will surely spike your interest if you notice. I pick up the unfamiliar dark purple bottle of perfume that was sitting on one of the bedside tables and spritz it over my neck and wrists. I noticed it sitting on your dresser in Tenerife one of the times I was in your room. It's funny because for the past few weeks I've been wearing your favourite perfume and Jacob has turned his nose up in disgust. Turns out, it's not to his taste, and neither are you.

I stand under the doorway of an old derelict cafe that has been closed down for several years. I stand here for a while, doing nothing but watching you. I watch as your head swivels as you turn to admire the photographs hanging on the walls. You're fiddling nervously with a gold chain that's hanging around your neck and I like that you're so nervous, because you should be. You look at your phone a handful of times, each time dropping it back down on the table in obvious frustration. I assume that you're checking the clock and wondering why I'm so late. You don't deserve my time, so if I'm giving you any of it, I'll always make you wait.

You pick up a teapot and pour yourself a cup of warm tea. I can't help but think just how rude that is of you to not wait on me. What terrible, terrible manners you have. I shouldn't be surprised though, not really, because you don't possess the qualities that resemble anything close to respect.

As you take a sip from your cup, I decide to make my move, swiftly crossing the street and pushing open the door as a gust of wind chases me inside, blowing the napkins from a handful of tables. You spot me and clamber clumsily to your feet to greet me. You hug me tightly, and I notice a distinct difference in your demeanour. It's softer, much more relaxed, like you're simply meeting an old friend, but I remain rigid under your touch. I can't help it, being so close to you is killing me. I notice that your nose twitches slightly as you pull away from me – you've recognised my new scent. I slide off my jacket and hang it over the back of my chair.

'You look amazing,' you tell me.

I shake my head, dodging your weak attempt at a compliment. We both know that my face is a portrait of stress and angst, but you just can't help herself, can you? The lies spill from your mouth so easily.

When I take my seat, you reach across the table and take my hand in yours. It feels like an electric shock, but I somehow manage to keep it together, fight the urge to pull my hand free and smack you with it. Instead, I allow you to cradle my hand in your soft palms. My saviour.

'I'm so happy you're here, Zee.' I lie.

You smile and begin to chat away, pleasantly and freely. You seem happy and genuinely pleased to be in my company. Something has significantly changed about you. I can see it in the way you look at me. There's less malice, less danger, more admiration, and more warmth. Could it be that you actually think that we are friends? Best friends even. No, surely not, even you can't be that delusional. I pop a piece of cake into my mouth to mask the laughter that has begun to escape. What a ludicrous idea; you, my best friend. That will never happen.

Our afternoon has been as good as it can be when dining with your enemy. It was difficult to enjoy the delicious treats from tea because the heavy, nauseating feeling lodged deep in the pit of my stomach wouldn't allow it. I carried on our merry little dance for as long as possible. I listened to you and joked with you and I actually surprised myself at just how good of an actress I could really be, but now I realise that we are done here, and I can't let you leave straight away. I don't want you to have any spare time on your hands to sit around your fucking cauldron, plotting and scheming of new and inventive ways to get close to my husband, so I encourage you to browse the high street with me. You agree, and I make sure that we take our time dipping in and out of as many shops as I could convince you to.

As the sun starts to fade and the wind begins to chill my face, a combination of impulse and impatience takes over. OK, let's go for this then. No time like the present.

'Why don't you come back to mine, babe? We can grab a bottle of wine on the way?'

Your eyes widen with surprise, and I could have sworn that you were just about to greedily accept my offer but instead you blindsided me, shocking me with your answer.

'Do you know what, Lauren, I'm so tired from travelling early this morning, I think I'll get an early one tonight.'

I grit my teeth and feel my fists clench by my side. I want to scream at your sheer defiance. This should have been a no brainer for you; the chance to enter my home and meet my husband. I was giving you an in, a way to finally get what you want, but you turn me down. What the hell is going on? I take a deep breath and roll my eyes, for the very first time my mask is betraying me.

'Oh, come on, babe. I won't keep you late.' I try again, but you rebuff me again.

'Fine,' I tell you sulkily. 'But tomorrow you're coming over to the salon, I'll give you a fabulous blow dry with my own fair hands.'

I force my smile to reach my eyes as I beam at you, praying that you say yes. Fortunately, you do, and I suppose you had to really because what other excuse could you have conjured up? What else would you be doing?

After we say our goodbyes, I phone Georgia immediately. This wasn't how tonight was supposed to go; you were supposed to be in our house when Jacob arrived home for a little surprise.

'Hey, George, it's me. Listen, we have a problem.'

'What's wrong, where are you both?'

'She didn't want to come back to mine, I don't know why. I didn't know what else to do, so I panicked and invited her to the salon tomorrow,' I blurt out, barely taking a breath.

'OK, that's fine. In fact, don't even worry about it. I have a better idea.'

CHAPTER THIRTY-THREE

I twist the barrel brush around Mrs Young's ash white hair as I blast the dryer. You should be here any minute now.

'Becky!' I shout across my bustling salon. 'Are there any spaces left at all today?'

'Nah, babe, totally full,' she shouts back over the noise.

Good. I knew there wasn't, but I wanted to double check. I purposely filled the diary to the max, ensuring there was no room for walk-ins or last-minute appointments, and definitely no sign of a booking for anyone named Zara.

'OK, hun. Just remember we aren't taking any strays in today, even if we get a cancellation.'

The bell jingles as the door opens and I catch your reflection in the mirror as you approach the reception desk. Your hair is scraped up into a bun and you've dressed in a playful canary yellow sundress. The dress should have been hideous, but it looks good on you because you've paired it with a black leather jacket and chunky biker boots. You've also applied a startling red lipstick, which has undoubtedly transformed the whole thing into something along the lines of a rock-chic vibe. I remember when you used to hide the way you dressed, dulled yourself down so that you appeared less of a threat, but look at you now.

I can't hear what you're saying because of the noise, but your face tells me everything I need to know; it looks mortified by whatever Becky has said to you. Becky is a terrific stylist, but her people skills are something to be worked on for sure, which is why I purposely put her on desk duty today when our usual girl phoned in sick. If there isn't an appointment for you in the diary, she won't mind telling you that you won't be seen by anyone. I wouldn't take it personally though, that's just the way she is, and she'd say the same to anyone. My lip twitches into a smile – but of course you don't know that's just how she is, and absolutely will take it personally.

I finish brushing out the tight curls on the head in front of me before applying a firm-hold hairspray, and then tap Mrs Young on the shoulder gently, letting her know that she is all done.

I swipe any stray hairs off my jeans and make my way over to the reception desk to fetch you.

'Zee!' I coo and pull you towards me, dismissing Becky and then linking arms with you before leading you over to one of the vacant basins. I pull your jacket from your shoulders and hang it on the coat stand. You do look very pretty today, and it's really not sitting well with me because I don't want you to meet him when you look so fit.

I wrap the black cape around you tightly, encouraging you to take a seat. You look a little confused, and I guess you're wondering why

I'm doing all this nonsense myself when I have plenty of people to do it for me. But what fun would that be?

I let the showerhead run for a minute to gauge the temperature, it's lukewarm, perfect for washing any normal client's hair, but you aren't any normal client, so I turn the temperature up a notch. You flinch as the burning water runs over your head and trickles down your perfectly made-up face but choose not to say anything. I scrub at your head, my nails furiously attacking your scalp. After I rinse the shampoo clear, I don't bother with much conditioner because I've spotted another opportunity to have a little fun with you. The condition of your hair up close is visibly damaged by heat and I know that it's going to be sore and tough to try to comb it through, which is why I don't give your hair a chance to soften, that would only ease the process and we wouldn't want that now, would we? I drop your head, allowing it to fall back down with a sharp thud against the white ceramic. It's a petty move and I know it is, but it feels so good.

After wrapping a towel round your head and taking you over to a chair, I begin to wonder just how far I could push you. If I don't want you to look good for my husband, then isn't it up to me to make sure that you don't?

'You know, babe, your hair could really do with a good chop to spruce it up a little, what do you think?'

'Oh, don't be daft, I appreciate the offer but honestly I'm fine thanks. I don't want to waste your time.'

OK then, not so easy. Nothing a bit of sulking won't fix though.

You hate the silence between us and eventually agree to let me take a little of the ends. Of course, my little and your little are going to be two completely different things. I smile at you brightly in the mirror as I take the first chop at your hair without even looking at your head, without drawing attention to where I'd positioned my scissors – three inches high.

This is too good, I notice your eyes begin to water, and you can't help but flinch in your chair with each snap of my scissors. I bid a joyous farewell to your lusciously long locks and silently thank you for being so eager to please me. If you had just stood your ground, insisted that you were fine as you were, maintained that you weren't bothered about a few split ends, then maybe you wouldn't have been in this predicament. It's your own fault, what's happening, really it is.

I don't however want you to think that I have in any way shape or form sabotaged your hair on purpose, so I do my best to look as focused as I can, when all the time I'm really not giving a rat's arse about how it's going to turn out. I finish off with a beautiful bouncy blow dry, which would have looked terrific on you had I not just sliced away at your length, but not now, because any girl who looks after themselves knows that curls on short hair will only make the hair appear even shorter.

'Ta-daa! All done, babe!' I squeal in pleasure.

Oh god, you look horrified by what you see in the mirror, it's bloody fantastic. I wait for you to say something, anything, but you don't – not even a simple thank you, which isn't very nice now, is it? What a rude little bitch you are.

You sulk your way over to the pink sofa at reception and I head through to the staff area to collect my things. In the safety of the back room, I slam my hands down on the table and close my eyes tightly. Being around you and acting like your friend, it just gets too much sometimes.

The destruction of your hair wasn't actually part of the master plan, that bit was all me. I just couldn't help myself though when I saw how pretty you looked, and I there was just no way I could allow you into my home like that. I can't wait to tell Georgia when I get the chance, she'll be proud of me, I know it. I use a couple of precious moments to compose myself and get my shit together before carrying on with our day.

I still have a little time to kill before taking you home with me because I don't really want you in my home any longer than absolutely necessary, so I suggest that we go for a coffee at one of the locally owned cafes down the high street. The sun is beaming from the sky, so I insist that we sit outside. You keep fidgeting with your hair, dragging your fingers through the curls, attempting to straighten them out, extending what length you've left. There's not much chit chat between us right now, but I don't try to force it because it's normal for friends to be able to sit comfortably in silence.

Two blokes walk past our table and you jerk your head towards your chest, diverting your eyes from their attention. Oh wow, you're just as bad as that song. How does it go again? You're so vain. You're so eager to be liked, so desperate for attention even from strangers, two men that you will never see again in your life and yet their opinion of you matters – it's pathetic.

'What's wrong, Zee?' I ask.

'Oh, I just, I thought I felt a drop of rain.'

I peer dramatically up at the crystal-clear sky in amusement. There is no rain, none whatsoever, but I ignore your moment of stupidity and finally ask if you fancy coming over to mine for a bit and I'm delighted that this time you agree. Everything is slowly coming together, just like we planned. There was a slight hesitation before you accepted though, that's how I know you only said yes because I told you that we'd be home alone. I must admit, I'm a little confused as to why you're so keen to avoid him. After all, isn't that really what you came here for, to be with him? Nevertheless, you can't hide the excitement that's started to spread widely across your face; anticipation blazes through your eyes in desire. That poker face again. You really need to work on that.

CHAPTER THIRTY-FOUR

When we arrive at my house, I park the car at the back door and lead you over the red cobbled path rather than present you in plain sight to my full neighbourhood because I don't want anyone asking me who my guest was. When you're gone, I want to forget about you, I don't need any reminders. I also know that by parking here, Jacob won't see my car when he arrives home as it's too far down to be seen from the front door. There's always a method in my madness.

You hesitate before entering, but now that you're inside I can see that you're transfixed on my house. You turn to close the door gently behind you and your fingers linger a little too long on the handle, which is strange. I study you as your eyes graze over all my possessions, under a jealous spell, bitterness oozing from you.

I urge you deeper into the house, through the alcove that leads us into my living room and tell you to take a seat and you pause to take your boots off, which is baffling because it's a bit too little too late to discover some manners now.

You are in a world of your own, somewhere far, far away from me; I bet you can't believe that you're really here.

'Don't be shy, sit down and make yourself comfortable.' I puff one of the cushions to entice you and then ask if you would like a glass of wine. My words startle you – you aren't interested in me right now.

'Yes please.' You accept, still not meeting my eyes, too focused on everything around you.

I head back into the kitchen and pull the bottle of rose that I bought two days ago from the fridge and take two glasses out of the cabinet. I pause before I interrupt you because your expression catches me a little off-guard. It's no longer inquisitive and childlike; it's darker, more dangerous, and I realise why by following your gaze. Our wedding photo has caught your attention. I cock my head to the side as I watch your forehead wrinkle and your jaw clench, you seem really triggered by that, as if you haven't seen it before.

I move quickly, kidnapping the opportunity for you to study it any further and pour pink liquid into your glass first, handing it to you with a wide smile. I notice that your eyes have changed colour, like a mood ring does when it senses a change in your emotions. They are a much deeper shade of blue now, almost black, and nowhere near as fragile and vulnerable as before.

You take a quick sip of your wine and put your glass down on to the coffee table with a thud before excusing yourself and asking permission to use the bathroom.

'Of course, you can, babe. Don't use the downstairs loo though, the tap ain't working. Use the main one, it's just up the stairs straight ahead. You can't miss it.'

I take a seat on my sofa, leaning back and melting into its comfort, taking a deep gulp of the floral but fruity liquid. I've left all the room doors upstairs partially open just like Georgia told me to. She said that you wouldn't be able to resist sneaking a peek inside.

I take my phone from my back pocket and click on the app that I still have downloaded from my previous plan that I imagined would be successful in catching Jacob in the act. Georgia was right about your crazy ass because as I expected, you've bypassed the bathroom and have sneaked into mine and Jacob's bedroom. I watch you so carefully, completely focused on your every move. It feels like I'm watching some weird psychological thriller on Netflix.

You run your hand over our bed and successfully identify which side is Jacob's. I knew you would, because I left his watch on the bedside table on purpose. I can't see your face now though because you've turned away from the camera, but I notice that you've lifted something into your hand. Oh surely, fucking, not! My hand slaps against my mouth as I hold back my horror, watching as you take a sip from his stale glass of water. Completely stunned, I put my glass down, jump to my feet, and begin to pace the length of the living room. You really are a whole different level of bunny boiler and it's fired something up inside me, ignited fresh fury. Stuff Georgia's plan, this is too much, I don't want you in this house any more. Time is up for you, babe. Time to face the music right here and now.

'Zee, are you OK?' I'm about four steps up the staircase when my phone rings from the kitchen. Fuck, what if it's Jacob? I quickly turn back on myself, furious that I've been interrupted.

'Lauren, you need to stop what you're doing. I need to tell you something urgently.'

Fuck's sake George this is not the time.

'George, I can't! She's upstairs right now. She's just taken a drink out of a filthy old glass of water for fuck's sake! She's crazy! I need to get her out of here!'

There is a brief pause before she replies, just as stunned as me.

'She what?' Her voice is icy and furious. 'Never mind that, call the whole thing off, I really need to see you tonight.'

The phone beeps and the line falls dead without any further conversation. What does she mean, call it off? This was her idea, to punish her.

The faintest whisper behind me catches my attention; please forgive me. It's so subtle I would have missed it if Georgia was still on the phone, but it makes the hairs on the back of my neck stand up. The front door opens and closes loudly – Jacob's home. Shit. I whip around to find you standing far too close to me and I yelp in genuine shock, dropping my phone onto the floor.

'Shit, Zee, you scared the life out of me there, babe!'

I try to laugh it off, but you don't laugh with me. You don't speak, you just stare at me, wild and panicked, a rabbit caught in the headlights.

257

'Please forgive you for what?' I ask you; a nervous smile pinned across my jaw; my whole body aware that Jacob could enter the kitchen at any minute. This isn't how it was supposed to go.

'Lauren, I'm really sorry I have to run,' you blurt out, before babbling on with an excuse about a leak or a flood and shoving your feet quickly into your boots. Why are you leaving? I thought you wanted to see Jacob; I don't understand.

'OK … but you're sweating. Are you OK?'

I step towards you attempting to grab you, to hold you firmly in position but you jolt backwards, and before I know it you've swung open the back door and fled, leaving behind the scent of our shared perfume.

Fuck, I breathe huskily. Things got a little out of control there. One minute I wanted you out of here and the next I realised that this might be my only chance to confront you. I don't know what the hell Georgia was going on about either. What could be so important right now, more important than this?

I hear Jacob exit the downstairs bathroom. Of course, there is nothing wrong with it, I just needed to give you an opportunity to venture upstairs. I rush to collect our two wine glasses, but he catches me in the act as I'm popping them in the dishwasher, so I have to admit that I've had a guest; that you've been here.

'Oh, hey, babe. You're home early,' he says. He didn't expect me to be home, that was the point, I wanted to catch him off-guard.

'Yeah, I wasn't too busy today so finished up early to spend some time with Zara.' My fingers grip the edge of the worktop. 'You just missed her actually' I spit. I don't mean to, but it's out before I could stop myself, hide the poison in my voice.

'Did I? Where did she go then?' he asks. Is he questioning me? It sounds like he is. Who the hell does he think he is?

I'm really struggling to hold it together, my anger slowly escaping my grasp. I do my best to calmly explain why you left so abruptly, but he doesn't seem to be listening to me and that only adds to my rage because he was the one who wanted to know in the first place.

I stop speaking after his reply and allow the silence to fill the gap between us that seems to be growing bigger and bigger. I busy myself by putting the bottle of wine back into the fridge, but I can feel his eyes bore a hole through the side of my skull. Eventually he walks away, rubbing his temples and sighing loudly, and I let him go. Before I would have chased after him, apologised for being so snappy, but not now.

I try to dial Georgia again, but she doesn't pick up. I try another three times, but she ignores every attempt. I don't know what the hell I'm supposed to do now; she wants me to stop, but she doesn't realise how close I came to giving up, how close I came to letting her go. I can't stop now, I need to push forward with the plan, with or without her. She won't get away again.

CHAPTER THIRTY-FIVE

In hindsight, I realise that it must have been Jacob's unexpected arrival that caused you to flee the scene. You weren't prepared to see him; you didn't have a plan of your own ready to tackle the situation. You're actually not as bold as you first appeared to be. When we first met you surprised me, the lengths you were prepared to go to were extraordinary. Even just turning up to Tenerife in the first place was a big move, and that was just the beginning – before I knew what else you were capable of.

Babe, really worried about you. Hope everything is OK? X

I press send and try my very best to wait patiently for a reply, but I just can't help myself, so I send another.

J has gone back out for the night, probs won't be home till well after we've gone to bed if you fancy a sleepover? x

Maybe I'm missing something here, because I still can't wrap my head around why you only want to come over when you know for certain that he isn't going to be there.

There's something you can't resist though, something about being in my company, in my house, and although you take your time, you eventually reply, accepting my token of kindness. The power creeps back into my possession once again. For the umpteenth time, I have the upper hand and I'm not afraid to tell a white lie or two to get it. Jacob is not going to be out tonight, he'll be at home – our home, mine and his, but it's time for our little love birds to finally meet. Well overdue, some might even say.

Around 7 p.m. I pick you up from a pub just around the corner from your hotel. I'm not late this time; I don't have time to waste any more.

Standing with my back against the driver's door, I watch as you struggle along the path towards me with your suitcase. I pop my gum exaggeratingly, almost as if it's a chore for me to even be here – I suppose in some way it is. I wonder if you notice any difference in my attitude towards you, perhaps you're wondering why I'm not falling over myself to help you like I normally would have for any friend. The difference being, you're not really my friend and right now, I really can't be bothered to pretend.

You push the release on the boot of my car and heave your oversized case onto your knee that's balancing on the edge of my car. Why do you have such a big case with you? You're only here for a couple of bloody days. It almost seems like you've brought everything but your kitchen sink with you.

'Jeez, Zee, what the hell have you got in there!' I can't help myself. 'You'd think you were here for a month.'

You smile back at me, but there's a disingenuous aura that puzzles me, I feel like I've rumbled something you didn't want me to know about.

I pop my gum some more while I think. You flinch each time, I think it's annoying you. Pop, pop, pop, some more. Ahhh, I get it now. You did have something else in mind, didn't you? Some stupid plan to ensure you could stay here for more than the intended few days. I don't know exactly what it was that you believed you had up your sleeve, but your trick isn't going to work here. You will be sent back on that plane come Thursday just like I planned, I promise you that.

On the drive back to the house, I tell myself to fill the empty space between us with nonsense. Feeding you little snippets of false information; that Jacob was acting so odd when he arrived home earlier and that we had a little falling out over it. I know exactly what to say to you; I know that you will relish the idea of us arguing, of the distance between us, a crack in our marital bliss. It's almost like I can't stop, I just talk and talk at you. I think I'm doing it so that you don't talk to me, that way I don't need to pretend that I care about anything you have to say.

'I've made the guest bedroom up for you, babe. It should be more comfortable than your hotel room.'

You and I both know that my guest bedroom was already made because you would have seen it earlier when you went snooping where you weren't supposed to be. You don't question me on it though, you know better than that.

'I'm going to totally pamper you, babe. I'll run you a nice warm bubble bath when we get back and while you're relaxing, I'll cook us something yummy for dinner.'

I don't ask what you like and what you don't like, because it really doesn't matter – I doubt anyone will be eating a meal tonight.

What a joke your excuse was for leaving earlier. As if there had been a flood in your hotel. A flood of all things. Obviously, I phoned your hotel just to double check there wasn't a faulty bathroom somewhere or a burst water pipe and the girl on the phone laughed her head off. No, there had been no flood. I feel the words bubbling in my stomach, swimming up my chest, splashing around my mouth.

'You're so lucky that none of your things were damaged, Zee.'

You nod your head in agreement, for a minute I think you know I'm on to you. I see your brain ticking over, trying to think of something else to say that will convince me that you were telling the truth, but all of a sudden you appear startled. What did I say? Did you see something alarming out of the window? I can't see a thing, the only thing that has changed in the space of a few seconds is the track on my playlist. Is it the song? Why would it be the song?

I don't want to draw your attention to anything while I try to work this out, so I mumble on about a new set of traffic lights that have been erected at the end of the street, causing far more of a build-up than there ever was before, but all the time I'm talking to you, I'm still listening. In fact, I'm listening more intently than ever before to a song that I've played time and time again while at work or at the gym or even just doing housework.

I think this song means something to you. It's a fabulous track 'Can't Let You Go', not sentimental in any way, in fact, it's about a guy cheating on his wife with – oh, I see. It does mean something after all.

I almost feel a bit sorry for you. Jacob has definitely led you up the garden path with this one, I have no doubt about it. I bet he's told you he would leave me for you if he could, that it's you he wants, that he's addicted to you. That bastard.

I keep my eyes focused on the road ahead with both hands firmly gripped to the wheel, but out of the corner of my eye I catch you swipe at your face as you brush a tear away. I sneak a quick glance in your direction, but you've turned your head away from me and are gazing out the window.

I could skip the track and spare you. All it would take is for me to press this little button beside my right hand on the wheel. I could make a joke about hating that fucking song and you would think nothing of it, but I don't. Instead, I decide to let it play, let it work its magic on you, let it awaken something deep and painful inside you. Some people might think that I'm being cruel. Some people would be right.

WE ENTER MY house through the front door this time. Jacob will be sitting in the living room and would see you straight away if I walked you through the back door. It's not time for that just yet.

I grab your hand as soon as we're in and lead you straight up to the guest bathroom where I hand you my own blush pink silk bath gown, then I pull two fluffy, fresh white towels from the cupboard that smell of crisp baby powder fabric softener and inhale their comforting scent deeply. That reminds me, I've left you a little surprise in your room. Nothing big, just a subtle clue, just for fun really. I do hope you notice it, the perfume I mean – the one you use, the one I've been wearing around Jacob for a while now and each time he turns his nose up.

I retrieve my very best and most expensive peony scented bubble bath from the cabinet and notice that the cosmetic scissors I usually keep in a glass jar on the bottom shelf are missing. That's strange, I think. I definitely haven't moved them. I make a mental note to have a little hunt for them later when I get the chance.

I leave you to your own devices now and you smile at me fondly as I close over the bathroom door, leaving you to undress in private. I'm careful not to close it completely and I stand behind it with bated breath as I watch you undress slowly, exposing a lace underwear set that I bet you bought just for him.

You unclasp your bra and step out of your underwear and begin to wander around my bathroom while the bath takes its time to fill, your dirty little fingers dipping into drawers where they don't belong.

I jump back as you turn to face the door, now realising that it hasn't been closed correctly and for a brief minute I think that you've seen me as you walk towards me, but instead you simply close the door firmly, snubbing the lock and shutting me out.

I skip downstairs, eager to get the wheels in motion for my spectacular dinner party. Jacob, as I expected, is waiting patiently in the living room for his meal. He knows we have a house guest, but he doesn't know just how special our guest of honour really is. I smile at him excitedly as I pass him by.

I told my husband to put his feet up and relax while I popped out to pick you up from your hotel. I told him that you had asked if you could maybe stay at ours for the night because of the flood, and I couldn't say no to a friend in need. I also told him that I thought it would be best to wait until dinner was ready for me to introduce you as you've had such a rough day and might be feeling a little tired and shy.

All these new lies I tell, each one of them serves a purpose and so I don't feel bad in the slightest. They are a means to an end.

I prepare dinner with the ingredients Jacob had brought home earlier, and as the herby sauce boils gently on the stove, I set the table for three. It really is a shame that this meal will go to waste because it smells delicious. I wish I'd just shoved a couple of pizzas in the oven now.

Upstairs I hear the creak of a loose floorboard as you pad around the guest room; signalling that you will be down to join us very shortly.

'Babe, come take a seat at the table, dinner's almost ready,' I tell my husband, and he obeys, like a loyal companion – except he isn't loyal, is he? This whole thing is a result of just how disloyal he is, actually.

He pulls out his chair with a scrape against the marbled floor and takes a seat, waiting patiently for me to serve him his dinner – and of course, for our guest to arrive.

Adrenaline rushes through my body, filling every vein as I lean against the worktop, glass of wine in hand, ready for my party to begin.

I hear you now, pounding down the stairs, it's happening, it's finally happening. I can't believe I've managed to pull this off, Georgia will be so proud of me.

You open the living room door and make your way towards the kitchen. Any minute now you will realise your error, any minute now you will come face to face with your worst nightmare.

You stop just as suddenly as you appear.

'How was your bath?' I ask.

You don't speak, your face has drained of colour and your eyes bulge painfully in their sockets. I take a sip of wine allowing you a moment to think of something to say, to realise that you've been caught out, to come up with an apology but you remain firm and rigid, glued to the spot.

'Please, take a seat.' I gesture towards the empty chair directly across from my husband.

You make no sudden movements, I see your eyes fleeting over the scene in front of you, trying to work out what you should do. You should have fled there and then; you should have turned on your heels and ran out the way you came, but you don't. Foolishly you take slow but sure steps towards the empty chair.

I sneak a look at Jacob as his head swivels to acknowledge your presence. He looks confused, as if he can't quite believe what he's seeing, but he doesn't however appear fearful and I'm intrigued as to why, because he really should be.

I smile and take another sip of my wine before speaking to you once again. 'Zara, are you OK?'

Jacob looks like he has just been slapped with a wet fish. He doesn't understand why I'm calling you Zara, because that's not your name, is it, Karly?

I hear my husband exhale deeply and I tilt my head in amusement. Oh my, he thinks he's still safe. He thinks I really believe you're a girl named Zara. Surely, he can't think he's going to get away with this? Surely none of you do?

I pour you a glass of wine and set it down in front of you, only now noticing that you're dressed in nothing but my silky robe. I instinctively take my stance behind Jacob, a primal move, claiming what's mine.

I clear my throat loudly. 'This is my husband, Jacob.'

I place my hand on his shoulder at the word my, just in case you needed any more reminders that he is mine – not yours. I expect you to hold your hands up now, admit defeat and apologise profusely for your deceit, but the sound of your broad Glaswegian voice causes the temperature of my blood to rocket when I realise you've no intention of apologising.

'Hi.' You smile sweetly at my husband. 'I'm sure you've heard all about me.'

CHAPTER THIRTY-SIX

I pull my hand sharply from Jacob's shoulder, like it has suddenly caught fire, and I step back into the safety of the cooking area. OK, so this is taking longer than I thought it would. None of them are fessing up or showing any hint of apology for their actions. It appears I'm dealing with two people who simply believe that I'm incredibly stupid and naïve. This has been their problem all along though, it's what's brought them here.

I pull a ladle from the utensil drawer and begin to pile dinner onto each of our plates as I consider my next move. I could continue to play along for a little while longer I suppose. I could bide my time and make them squirm as I drag out our meal, forcing them to engage in false conversation. One of them is sure to crack, there's just no way the two of them can keep this up for an entire meal.

I realise that if I want to continue down that path, I need to fill the silence in the meantime.

'Oh shoot! You must be wondering what's going on, Zee. I must have got mixed up again. I was just so sure Jacob was heading out for the night.'

I'm not thinking clearly, I scald myself as soon as the words escape my mouth. That was stupid, very stupid. All it would take is for Jacob to question me as to why I would even think that was the case, when I knew fine well, he would be here for dinner.

It's OK though, because your desperate desire to speak to my husband is what saves me.

'It's nice to finally meet you, Jacob.'

I ignore you, focusing my attention on my husband now.

'Are you all right, babe? You've gone a bit pale.'

Nothing, I get absolutely nothing back. He's not said one word since you arrived at dinner, and that's because he is a coward. He's never really had the balls to have a proper affair, I realise this now. It was all just showmanship, just something to stroke his fucking ego if nothing else. And now I'm angry again, my restraint flailing. Nah, I can't do it, I can't carry this on any longer. There's no way in hell I can sit there with the two of you making idle chitchat. My stomach wouldn't allow it. I can't watch you look at my husband with a burning arousal. I can't bear to look at his gormless face as he tries to find a way to worm his way out of the mess that he has found himself in. I can't risk this going any further than it already has. The time has come.

My hands tremble as I lift two delicate plates and turn towards my loving husband and my new friend, giggling wildly like a naughty child. The sound of my own laughter is menacing, and I almost don't recognise myself. It's a mixture of anticipation, nerves, fury, and more – so much more.

I stand at the edge of my beautiful glass table, right in the middle of the two of you, taking one final look at Jacob before peering down at the unnecessary white, creamy pasta resting on my best dinner plates that we received as a wedding present.

What a waste, I think, as I raise the plates shoulder high before launching them from my grip, sending them crashing onto the table leaving a volcanic eruption of sharp shards of broken ceramic and piping hot penne in my wake.

I gently wipe away the sauce that has landed on my T-shirt and turn to face you.

'Oh, what a shame,' I say calmly. 'Karly, would you mind helping me clear this mess up?'

Chapter Thirty-Seven

Jacob

Her eyes are wild and dark, not the luminous shade of sapphire that normally shines brightly with love and adoration.

I slowly pick a sharp piece of white ceramic out of my hand and it draws blood. It trickles down my hand and drips onto the floor, but making a mess is the least of my worries; we're already in too deep here. My stomach churns. I feel a sickness that I've never experienced before. My mind is racing frantically how the fuck has this happened? I was careful; I know I was, I never left anything behind; always deleted messages and made sure that I never stored any pictures that were sent. And yet I can't help thinking that I should have known better, should have seen the signs. She's been acting strangely for a while now, I chalked it up to hormones or a bust up with her mates but it's crystal clear to me now that she's known for a while now – but for how long? I need to fix this, do something – anything – before it escalates further.

'Babe, I can explain,' I plead as I push out of my chair and rise to my feet.

She doesn't answer me, she doesn't even shout at me, she just stares at me with so many emotions painted across her beautiful face: disgust, shame, anger.

We very rarely fight, I mean sure we bicker like any couple but nothing serious, nothing like this. She usually always has a comeback, a smart-ass remark to put me in my place, but now is different. Her silence is much worse than anything she could ever say to me, it's frightening, and I can't gauge her next move. I think she's waiting on me to do one of two things: hold my hands up and admit blame or dig myself deeper into this muddy hole.

Out of the corner of my eye I notice Karly pushing her own chair back and beginning to stand up, but I'm careful not to turn and face her. I need to stay focused on my wife's face.

'Lauren, babe, whatever you think this is – it's not,' I say gently. I need to approach this with the utmost caution. 'There's absolutely nothing going on here, you know there's not. Deep down you know that, babe. You do know that, don't you?'

My voice is soft and gentle. I need to make her believe me, make her understand that whatever is going on here is not my fault.

Finally, she speaks. 'If nothing is going on, then why is she in our house, Jacob?'

The way she says my name, it wounds me. She spat into the air, as if it were poison that she needed to cleanse herself of. I understand that she's angry, of course I do, but she's talking like I'm the one who brought her here. It wasn't me; I didn't do this. I feel my temper start to flare in the pit of my stomach.

'How would I know for fuck's sake? You were the one who invited her here!'

'No. That's where you're wrong. Sure, I mean I guess I did invite someone into our home. Her name was Zara though, never Karly.'

I can't be angry at my wife, I can't. This isn't her fault; it's Karly who's manipulated her, it's her who should be punished. It's her my anger should be directed at.

'Listen to me, babe. I understand that you thought she was your friend, really, I do. It's not your fault, and it's not mine either.'

'It wasn't your fault?' She marvels at me. 'If it wasn't your fault, then why were you still in touch with her? I saw the messages – last year. You left them on your phone. You're a fucking idiot.'

Last year? What messages is she talking about? There's been loads – too many to remember or even hazard a guess at the exact conversation. It's best not to ask any questions. I don't need to know specifics; I just need to address the root of her anger.

'It was just a few texts back-and-forth, babe, nothing more to it. Just a bit of fun. She doesn't mean anything to me.'

I step forwards, try to take her arm, but she flinches out of my reach.

'Babe, come on, you have to believe me!'

The anger I've tried so hard to suppress has started bubbling up to the surface now. She's not listening to me; I need her to just fucking listen to me for once in her life. As much as she isn't to blame here, she isn't exactly innocent in all this either I realise. A multitude of thoughts race through my mind; how devious my wife has been, how much she has hidden from me, how she orchestrated this whole dinner party from hell. No, she's far from innocent here.

LAUREN

I CAN'T LISTEN to any more of his shit, it's doing my head in. I turn my attention towards you, because you've been awfully quiet, haven't you? Standing there, clutching at my silk robe, a single streak of blood dripping down your cheek where one of the shards has grazed your pretty face – you play the victim extremely well.

'So, Karly or Zara, what should I call you then?'

You have the nerve to gawk at me as if I've asked you something difficult. You clear your throat before you speak.

'Karly. My name is Karly. Which you quite clearly know, so I don't really know why you're asking.'

Oh, would you look at that? Was that a bit of sass I detected there? I think it was. In fact, I know it was because there's no fondness in your tone any more. No, that's all gone, washed away with the rest of your lies. You never cared about me at all, not really. Sometimes I think you were confused though, perhaps thought I could become a friend, but that was never going to happen.

'Ah yes, silly me. Karly, of course it is! Well, Karly, sit back down, will you? I think we have a few things to talk about.'

'No,' you say sharply, as good as slapping me across the face.

'Sorry?' I ask. I don't think you understand what I've just said, because you aren't powerful enough to run away now.

'You heard me – I said no. You don't tell me what to do. I'd rather stand for what I'm about to say.'

I can't help but smile, for there you are – the real you. The one who left me for dust in that hotel bedroom, the one who didn't give a shit about what happened to me, the one who came to steal my husband.

'Fine, suit yourself,' I say and delicately tiptoe my way around the broken shards splayed across the floor as I fetch my glass of wine from the kitchen worktop. I swirl it around, splashing it against the glass, watching it crash like waves with the flick of my wrist. I raise it slowly to my mouth and take a large gulp, draining its entirety and sitting it down firmly before turning back to face you both.

'So, who would like to go first then?'

CHAPTER THIRTY-EIGHT

KARLY

She looks so smug, standing there with her wild eyes, looking at me like I'm the crazy one here. I won't sit back down. She doesn't get to be in control any more. She thinks she's been so smart, figuring out who I really was and putting this whole bloody thing together. I don't understand why she bothered to be honest. Surely, she should have just confronted me back in Tenerife when she first arrived. What was the point in dragging all this out when the outcome would ultimately stay the same? Anyway, I'm not sitting down to this. I won't allow her to tower over me like she has authority over this situation.

Jacob's eyes have remained glued to Lauren's face, barely even glancing in my direction, which is quite fucking annoying to be honest because I wish he would just stop pretending. There isn't a point in lying to her anymore – there's no need. It wasn't how I'd imagined us coming together, but we're here now, and so we may as well be honest about our relationship and make sure once and for all that everyone knows their place and where they stand.

I wait patiently for him to answer her; to take the lead and tell her that yes, he's sorry, but he's in love with me. There's so much he needs to tell her: it's me he wants, it always has been and always will be, and that she should leave without making a fuss, but the room stays silent.

My forehead creases in frustration. The silence is almost deafening. I don't understand his silence, I've never had him pegged as weak – but maybe I'm being unfair to him. This is a shock to him too, he's having to think on his feet here, maybe he's just a little slower than me at adjusting to surprise. I decide that I need to be strong for both of us now, guide us through this dark fog and into the light, where we can finally be happy together.

'Well, it's quite simple really, Lauren.' I sigh. 'Jacob is supposed to be with me. He wants to be with me.'

She throws her head back, laughing into the air, howling with delight, and my blood starts to boil under my skin.

'It's true. He couldn't tell you before because he didn't want to hurt you. He's putting your happiness before his own, and it isn't fair. He wasn't mean enough to upset you, so I decided it was time I did.'

I look over at him as I hold out my hand, searching his face for assurance, waiting for him to walk towards me and take my hand in his so that we can face this together – as a team. He doesn't budge, instead throws his head into his hands and starts clenching his hair tightly, rocking back-and-forth on his heels.

I feel so confused, I don't recognise this man standing in front of me. I don't understand where the confident, cock-sure man I fell in love with has disappeared to. Why am I fighting this alone? Why is he cowering behind his hands?

Never mind, I started this alone, I can finish this alone and then she can leave.

'I want you to know, I went to Tenerife with only good intentions. I swear. I didn't want to hurt you or anything, nothing crazy. I just needed you to know the truth.'

She drums her fingers on the worktop and the sound echoes throughout the room.

'But you didn't tell me who you were in Tenerife, did you, Zara? Oh no, you decided to put on a nice little show for me, didn't you?'

I bite the inside of my lip to prevent a full-blown smile breaking out across my face, and still a subtle smirk escapes me. She's right, and what a show it was, but the hypocrisy in what she is saying right now is hilarious. She must be deluded if she thinks that I'm the only one to blame here. Doesn't she recognise that she was the one who chose to play along? I never forced her to do that, I never made her pretend. If she knew who I was from the beginning, she could have prevented this herself.

I sigh dramatically. 'OK, OK, I admit there were a few white lies told – between the both of us come to think of it – but if I'm being totally honest, I started to grow fond of you. I guess you could say I thought of you as a friend or some sort, and it became harder for me to tell you the truth when we were having such a good time.'

She cocks her head and smiles, as if I'm telling a twisted joke and she's waiting for the punchline. She needs to wipe that grin off her face, she isn't whiter than white here. She has lied to me too. I could argue that hers were actually worse, more deceitful. I'm not the villain here.

LAUREN

WHAT A LOAD of bullshit. I can't quite believe what I'm hearing.

I take a quick glance in the direction of Jacob who still has his head in his hands, refusing to look at either one of us. He really is a weak and pathetic man.

'If you had grown so fond of me, Karly, you wouldn't have done what you did,' I tell you bluntly.

You look confused; a bewildered look stretching across your lightly freckled face.

'Come on!' I shriek, losing my patience now. 'You remember that fun night, don't you?'

I stride over to the chopping board that I'd left sitting on the worktop and launch it into the air, snatching the picture that I'd kept perfectly hidden. Now I'm holding it high as I walk back into the lion's den.

You didn't even realise it was gone, that I removed it from your handbag earlier on today when you were upstairs. I took your bag downstairs with me when you were bathing.

I didn't expect to find it there, I didn't know you even had it, I was simply having a little rummage and there it was.

You look shocked – hurt even – as if me going through your things without permission is the ultimate betrayal in all this.

'I know what you were going to do, Karly. I know you were going to show Jacob this picture.'

Jacob's head begins to rise, his interest has been piqued at mention of a picture. He doesn't even know half of it yet. The madness that accompanied that night, the danger you put me in.

Now you smile, but not just slightly any more. Now you aren't even trying to hide it, in fact you're laughing. Your laughter started slowly, but now it's building, ascending into a menacing cackle, and it takes every ounce of restraint that I have to resist lunging towards you and grabbing your throat. Oh god, I want to hurt you. I want to punch you, kick you, scratch you – make you bleed.

'Guess I underestimated you, Lauren.' You giggle. 'So, you knew who I was from the beginning then, eh?'

I nod as I run my tongue over the inside of my bottom teeth.

'Well, bravo for you, babe – no, really, well done.' You mock, beginning to clap your hands as you walk towards me.

My body stiffens, preparing for a sudden attack, but instead you brush past my arm with your sight firmly set on something else. I turn to see where you're going and so does Jacob. You lift your handbag from the floor and root around inside, throwing unwanted items behind you. What are you looking for? I didn't find anything else in there earlier. It's possible I could have missed something though; I stopped my search as soon as I found the picture.

I rack my brain quickly but all I can remember finding was lipstick, a pack of spearmint gum, a hair tie, and a phone charger. I'm being paranoid, there's nothing else in that you could use against me. I wouldn't have missed anything.

You stop searching, it appears you're satisfied with what you've found, what you've been looking for.

'I really hoped we could have been friends, Lauren, but I realise now that sadly we can't.'

Your back is still facing Jacob and me – still not showing us what you found in your bag. There's nothing in that bag, you're being crazy. You have nothing left, you're clutching at straws and turning a little cuckoo to be quite honest. You hoped that we could have been friends? As if. What goes on in that warped little head of yours? I think you might actually need professional help.

Jacob hasn't moved, and I'm so angry with him right now for thinking with his dick instead of his head. He could at least have chosen a girl who wasn't certifiably insane.

Why aren't you turning round to face me? I'm about to approach you, but your voice startles me.

'So, I'm not going to rush you. But I guess, you should probably pack up some things and leave us to it now eh, Lauren?'

CHAPTER THIRTY-NINE

JACOB

Slowly she starts to turn and now she's looking right at me with those big, beautiful eyes that I've only ever seen through a screen of some sorts. I know that she's waiting on me, waiting for me to back her up and defend her. She wants me to tell my wife that I don't love her, that I've never loved her – but that's not true. I love my wife; I love her more than anything. I fuck up sometimes, yeah – what bloke doesn't? But I only ever want Lauren at the end of the day. Anyone else is just a distraction, a bit of fun to pass the time when I'm bored. Nobody will ever compare to Lauren, not even Karly.

Lauren looks stunned by Karly's last words, and I don't blame her. Even I can't quite believe the missiles that are escaping her lips. Who does she think she is telling my wife to leave her own home?

I've never told her that I would leave my wife for her – not once. I've flirted around the topic. I've entertained a few 'what if' scenarios, but I've never said I would actually do it.

I know I should say something, but I just don't know what. I still can't believe this is actually happening.

Lauren begins to holler at Karly; shrieking insults by the second: calling her a bitch, trash, a home-wrecking slut, a crazy nut job. Just about everything and anything she can think of really to inflict some sort of pain, but it's not working, Karly doesn't even flinch, and that just makes her all the madder.

It's time to stop this now, I've had enough of it all. Karly needs to leave, and I need to try to pacify my wife.

'Karly, you should never have come here.'

Her smile sinks slowly, not fully understanding what I'm saying to her.

'You doing all this shit, going to extreme lengths to find my wife, lying about who you are, turning up at my house … it's crazy, it's all fucking crazy!'

Her pupils widen as she struggles to gulp down every brutally honest word. She wasn't expecting this, she genuinely thought I would choose her.

'But, Jacob, it's been ten years. It's our time now!' She screams, taking a step towards me.

I'm still aware of the strangeness that is her right hand; still hidden inside her handbag, clenched around something unknown.

I don't get a chance to respond to her, to reiterate what I've just said because Lauren beats me to it.

'No, Karly, it's not, and newsflash, it's never going to be.'

A spark of positivity ignites within me. There might just be a small possibility of rescuing my marriage after all this madness has calmed down. I recognise it in her choice of words –it's never going to be. This is a good sign, and if I have even a slither of a chance left, I need to really show Lauren that I'm on her side, that our bond is unbreakable, that nothing and nobody can come between the two of us.

'Listen to me very carefully, Karly – I don't want you. I'll never want you. I love my wife. Do you understand me?'

She doesn't answer, just stares at me in horror and so I repeat the words again; words I know will wound her deeply. 'Karly, I said I'll never want you – that I love my wife.'

Still, she doesn't answer. She lowers her head to the ground, her bare feet with red painted toes begin to fidget, shuffling from side to side, burning a hole underneath her. Slowly she raises her head back up, but her eyes are no longer on me.

Lauren is laughing at her, uncontrollably, excitedly, and I really wish she wouldn't because she's making things so much worse. She's mocking her – but boldly, and Karly's face twists horribly as the pent-up anger prepares to explode. I watch her face, the same one that I've loved to look at for so long now; that dainty nose, that crease between her eyebrows, those big beautiful blue eyes that seduce me, those luscious lips that I've dreamt of kissing, of biting. I don't see any of it any more. It's gone, all gone. All I see now is her hatred, her wickedness, her delusion – it's ugly.

In a split second, the room erupts into action as Lauren finally pops the cork on the fragile bottle that contained Karly's temper. She just couldn't help herself, she had to keep pushing her. She had to gloat at her victory, she had to dance with danger. It all happened in slow motion, at least that's what it seemed like to me. Lauren stepped in front of me, towards Karly, invading her space and spat at her five explosive words.

'He's mine, you crazy bitch.'

KARLY

STOP LAUGHING. SHE needs to stop laughing. I'm not messing around anymore. I'll do it. I swear to God, I'll fucking do it.

But she doesn't stop. She's just making things worse.

'He's mine, you crazy bitch.'

I release an almighty howl as I lunge towards her, pulling my hand from my bag and dropping it onto the floor behind me. Her stupidly smug face is all I've set in my sights, my hand wrapped firmly around the silver cosmetic scissors.

She spots them almost instantly and tries to jerk away from me, but she's too slow because now I have a fierce grip of her hair; my other hand stabbing wildly, searching for soft flesh, but she somehow manages to knock them from my grasp before they can inflict any damage and they fly out of my reach.

Now she's grabbing my hair too. She pulls at me, swiping at my face with her sharp claws, trying to kick me in the stomach with the heel of her bare foot. I roar as I try with all my might to push her away, but she hooks her arm around my neck and now we're both falling towards the floor. An almighty crack signifies the shattering of a skull as it collides with the sharp corner of the kitchen worktop. I flinch, instinctively grabbing my head and searching for signs of injury, but I'm OK.

I straddle her now as she lies flat on her back on the cold marbled floor, taking a few more furious swings at her once kind face. Punch after punch after punch, I find it hard to stop. Her face is bloody now, a real mess, far from pretty, and as my fist collides once more, I hear the crunch of her nose as it jerks and breaks.

I pause for a moment to catch my breath.

'Come on, bitch. Is that all you've got?' I shriek, but she doesn't move an inch.

Why isn't she fighting back? I need her to fight back, to show me what she's made of – but she isn't moving. Why is she just lying there like that? She's just accepting it all, every blow, every shot, making me look like the bad guy.

'Lauren, answer me,' I shout. No reply. 'Come on, Lauren. I mean it now. Fucking answer me.'

Still, she doesn't speak, she doesn't move. I unclench my fists as soon as I realise that I've done. Oh shit, oh shit, oh shit. What have I done? I didn't mean to kill her, not really. I just wanted to hurt her. Didn't I? She can't be dead; she just can't be. I can't have done this.

I cradle her head in the palm of my hand as I bend towards her face, listening intently for the sound of breath. Blood trickles through my fingers from the back of her head. I'm just about to check for a pulse when a deafening bang erupts from behind me, followed by the thud of something heavy falling onto the floor. What the fuck was that? Jacob? Where is Jacob?

I drop her head back onto the floor, but before I can successfully get to my feet – another bang. I feel something enter my body, I feel its sharp, burning heat tearing me apart. My head spins and I can't focus. I try to turn around, to see what has happened, but the pain finally envelopes me and I feel myself toppling over. The bright light of the kitchen becomes manic, the ceiling swirls like a kaleidoscope, and eventually the entire room fades to black.

CHAPTER FORTY

FOUR WEEKS LATER

Beep, beep, beep. That's all I hear these days. It's become a comfort to me; something regular, something expected, something reminding me that I'm fortunate enough to still be here. That's not an exaggeration, the doctors told me themselves that I was incredibly lucky to survive this.

The 9 mm bullet fired from a handgun ploughed into my back, narrowly missing my lungs as it ripped into my flesh. I needed urgent surgery to remove the bullet and to repair the life-threatening damage to my arteries, but my vital organs held up and here I am. I guess it's kind of cool to say I've survived a gunshot. It's definitely a conversation starter.

The same nurse who manned the ward last night is still here. She finishes at eight o'clock this morning, just one hour to go. She looks tired, but I guess you would after a twelve-hour shift.

She wraps the material around my arm, secures it tightly, and then places the little clip on my finger. The tube begins to tighten;

constricting aggressively like a python squeezing its prey. But I'm used to it by now. Nurses frequently pop along to check my observations throughout each day.

She pulls at the Velcro and releases my arm, giving me a brief but genuine smile, and then wheels the blood pressure monitor away for someone else to use.

I'm being discharged today – finally. Hannah will be collecting me from the hospital this afternoon as long as nothing changes, but I don't think it will.

It took her a couple of days to realise that something was wrong; I wasn't replying to her messages or answering her calls, but it was that fourth day of radio silence that really got her worried.

I always thought that I was good at telling a little white lie, but it turns out I never fooled Hannah. She didn't believe me one bit about this brand-new job in London and had her suspicions all along that I was up to no good with the Cruthers' family.

She obviously didn't have Lauren or Jacob's phone numbers so she couldn't phone them directly, but she realised that she did have something – the link to Lauren's Facebook account. Amongst the whirlwind of tequila and masterplans, I'd forgotten to erase my search for Lauren from Hannah's phone that night in July. That's where she went first, and what she found was far more than she bargained for.

Splattered over Lauren's Facebook was an array of messages from grieving friends and family members, all expressing how sorry they were that something like this could have happened and what a tragedy it had all been. Pictures filled her timeline of happier times, of pleasant memories, of old family photos from when she was just a little girl living life without a care in the world. Her whole life ahead of her.

There were so many messages, but not one told her the exact details of what had happened, what the tragedy was. All she knew was that it was bad, very bad.

She was never one for watching the six o'clock news, so she never heard the story break a few days earlier, but after reading all those terribly sad messages, something told her to open Google. It wasn't the messages themselves that made her panic, but the absence of her best friend accompanied by the death of Jacob's wife.

I guess I followed in the footsteps of my mum and dad because my story also ended up in the papers and on television for the world to see.

There were so many headlines: Adultery leads to young couples' tragic death – another victim in critical condition, Infidelity massacre in quiet seaside town, Family mourn dead couple as mistress arrested.

One paper shamelessly decided to print which hospital I'd been admitted to and that's how she found me; my best friend, my guardian angel, my red-headed saviour coming to my rescue. She's been the family that I so desperately needed all along, and I've been so foolish to not acknowledge just how important she really is to me. That is going to change now, of course. I'm going to be a better friend to her. If it wasn't for Hannah, I would have been left here for weeks all alone and honestly, I just don't think I would have been able to cope with everything.

She's been staying at a cheap hotel not far from the hospital for three and a half weeks now, and I plan on paying her back from my savings when I get back on my feet. It's really the very least I can do.

The first couple of weeks are a bit of a blur to me, but the nurses tell me that she's been here every single day since she travelled down here. When I finally managed to open my eyes, her beautiful porcelain face was the first thing I saw. She hasn't asked me any questions about what really happened that night, and I'm grateful for that. I don't feel ready to talk about it – not yet, anyway. Still, she's been kind enough to answer any of mine and I'm glad I heard it from her first and not some shitty tabloid reporter or even the police who frequent my ward.

It's hard to find the words to explain how I feel about Lauren's death. It was an accident. I really didn't mean to kill her – I swear I didn't. A part of me did genuinely care for her, and for what it's worth I really did enjoy certain aspects of our short but complicated friendship. I've shed many tears for Lauren when I'm left alone – but not because I feel guilty or anything. Her death was inevitable either way, fate had already decided her path. All I'm guilty of is speeding up the process. But my fate was different to hers; I was made to survive, to bounce back, and to make the most of my second chance at life. That's why I'm in the clear and why nobody suspects or blames me for anything to do with Lauren's death. There are only two people left in this entire world now that know what really happened – that Lauren was dead before shots were fired.

Obviously, I told the police that you attacked her, and that I pushed you out of the way to get to Lauren, to make sure that she was OK. I was trying to save her, protect her, but it was too late – and that's when you shot me. It's not a total lie because you did shoot me, and not just me – you shot Jacob too. I know that you were going to kill Lauren as well. Like I said, fate had already dealt her cards before I played my hand.

It doesn't matter that I didn't actually see you with my own eyes; you were caught red handed, and that's enough for me. A little fabrication won't make much difference to your life now, but I'm sure as hell not going to let mine go to shit for one stupid accident that nobody else knows about.

My feelings towards Jacob's death are a little more complicated, but not because I didn't love him, because I did. A little too much if anything. I was infatuated by him, overwhelmed by our love, completely and blissfully unaware of the harsh reality of his deceit. The most painful betrayals are served to us ice-cold by the ones we love the most. That sizzling hot intensity of unconditional love that I once felt for him has vanished, our fairy tale extinguished, and in its place lies painfully raw revulsion, bubbling uncomfortably beneath the surface.

I haven't cried for Jacob – and I won't. He ruined so many people's lives with his lies. If anyone is to truly blame for all this mess, it's him – but he's dead now, so I guess that's where you come in. Not just because you're a murderer, but because people find it difficult to stay mad at the dead. They'd rather direct their anger towards someone they can see suffer, someone who is still alive to receive appropriate punishment. What punishment is appropriate for blowing someone's brains to smithereens though? Should it be a life for a life? Should you be locked away and tortured brutally? I personally think just being locked up for two murders and an attempted murder is enough punishment for you. As I said, Jacob brought all this on himself. He deserved what you did to him. I was just collateral damage and I've accepted that. How can I not forgive you when you've granted me a lifeline?

I hope one day I'll be able to come and visit you. Maybe we could become friends, because I admire your courage. You decided on a plan and you rolled with it, no matter how crazy or dangerous it was. That's something I can get behind, after all I've done a few crazy things myself. I really do hope you're strong enough to get through this, and even though you might be a bit mad at me right now for adding another murder on to your charge, I want you to know that here is no bad blood towards you on my part for what you done. In fact, when I heard about it, I laughed. Oh god it hurt to laugh but I just couldn't help it. That bastard took ten years of my life from me, and I hated him for it. Now, thanks to you, he's gone and he can't take anything else from me, or Lauren or you – or even anyone else that I'm yet to find out about, because I suspect there'll be others lurking in the shadows too.

You're a hero in my book. Thank you, Georgia. Thank you.

CHAPTER FORTY-ONE

Georgia Pearson was arrested shortly after her wild rampage that evening. Concerned neighbours reported sounds of uncontrollable wailing emanating from the Cruthers' household and contacted the police. One gentleman felt compelled enough to pop over and check that everything was OK before the police arrived, and I just don't think he bargained for what he found.

The back door that opens into the kitchen was left wide open and inside was where he witnessed Georgia kneeling in a pool of blood cradling Jacob's limp, lifeless body. Can you imagine walking into that kitchen? Three lifeless bodies, blood spattered everywhere, an inconsolable woman refusing to let go of a dead man.

Georgia and Jacob had been having an affair for two years. Two whole years, can you believe that? Lauren's best friend and her supposedly loving husband. Now that's the ultimate betrayal. I'm just glad Lauren isn't alive now to hear about that, it's better she died not knowing.

I, however, am not that fortunate. I survived and found out more than I ever thought imaginable. It struck me like a hard iron fist to the stomach when I found out about them. I was so naively blinded by him and everything he told me, but I wasn't just angry – I was embarrassed. It had never crossed my mind that Jacob could be remotely interested in anybody else other than me. While I was busy focusing all my attention on his wife, I completely overlooked his mistress. I truly thought that I was smarter than that, and I felt foolish.

Georgia has been charged for the murders of Jacob and Lauren Cruthers, accompanied by another charge of attempted murder. She's pleaded her innocence from the beginning, refusing to confess to any of the charges while she awaits trial.

She is guilty though, no matter what she says. She might not have been the one to kill Lauren, but she quite clearly killed Jacob, and I definitely didn't shoot myself in the back. I mean, you couldn't look any guiltier than her – she was found there in such a sorry state. I don't really understand why she didn't flee as quickly as possible, why she drew so much attention to herself by crying so loudly, but I guess people react differently to shocking situations. Perhaps the reality of her actions got the better of her.

My little white lie of witnessing her attack on Lauren wasn't the only thing that incriminated her though. Lauren's phone records showed evidence of an incoming call from Georgia earlier that day. The police strongly implied that this phone call was the instigator in the madness that was to follow. It has been speculated that the conversation between the two women involved Georgia telling Lauren about the affair.

The duration of the call wasn't too long, but that in itself was enough for them to suggest that Lauren was simply unwilling to hear Georgia out, which then fuelled her into making an appearance at their house later that night.

It's quite obvious that she was mad about something; whether it was something Lauren said to her, or something Jacob had done, or perhaps it was even me she was mad at? I guess if Lauren knew exactly who I was the whole time, then she would have shared this with her best friend. Was she incensed that Jacob was playing her for a fool too? I just don't know.

To be honest, I don't know a lot about anything, not really. For some reason, I've been kept in the dark by the police and it has been Hannah who has kept me in the loop.

Despite believing it was Georgia who pulled the trigger, admittedly, some things don't really make much sense to me: I don't know why Georgia had a bloody gun with her when she came to speak to Lauren, or even where she got it from. I don't know if she actually planned on using it or if it was simply a tool to scare someone into admitting guilt. I don't know who she was intending to scare, was it me or Jacob? I don't even know what she did with the gun, because I don't think it was found anywhere in the house. Did she leave, dispose of the gun somewhere and then come back? Did she think she'd get away with it if she was the one who found the crime? I can't wrap my head around these things.

I'm going to try to let sleeping dogs lie though. It really doesn't matter what makes sense to me and what doesn't because what's done is done. As far as I'm concerned, Georgia killed Lauren and Jacob. I told the police that I saw her and I'm sticking with it. The only person who could clear her name is me, and that's something I definitely don't intend to do.

GEORGIA

'TELL US THE truth, Georgia. You will only cause yourself more stress by lying – especially in your condition, love.'

'I'm telling you the truth! I've told you the truth from the beginning!'

'You were found in a pool of Mr Cruthers' blood by the neighbour. He saw you, Georgia.'

'I didn't kill him. I could never have killed him. I loved him.'

'But you did kill Mrs Cruthers? And you did attempt to kill Miss Winters? Is that what you're saying, Georgia?'

'No. That's not what I meant. You're twisting things. Why won't you listen to me? I didn't do this.'

'OK, Georgia, OK. Say you didn't do it … then who did?'

I didn't do what they're all saying I did. Lauren is … was my best friend. I would never have hurt her, at least not physically.

When I got to their house that evening, I chapped and chapped on the front door, but nobody answered. That's why I went around the back because I knew they were home. I didn't understand why nobody was coming to let me in.

The back door was wide open, and I shouted Lauren a couple of times before I stepped over the doorway. I really wish I hadn't. I so wish I'd just turned on my heels when nobody answered the front door, climbed back in my car and went back home. But wishing I'd done things differently won't save me now.

The first thing I saw was the heap of two bodies on the floor. That little bitch was lying on top of Lauren, blood radiating outwards; both of their blood mixed together. I whispered to Lauren, but she didn't answer and so I edged closer to them, aware that something terrible had happened and that I might be in danger too by being here.

I couldn't avoid stepping in the red liquid, and at the time I didn't really think twice about doing it. I had to get close enough to Lauren to be able to check if she was breathing or not. That's when I saw the puddle that had formed around her head, her beautiful dark hair splayed around her, completely drenched.

I pressed two fingers against her neck, but there was no pulse. I put my hand over her mouth in hope that I would feel her faint breath against my palm, but there was nothing. I took hold of her hand that was lying above her head and although it was still slightly warm, I knew she was dead. My best friend was dead.

I turned away and my body catapulted forwards as I heaved over and over; my hands trembling as I pushed them into my legs to try to keep myself from toppling over.

I didn't check if Karly was breathing. I didn't even think about touching her. I couldn't see her face clearly as it was hidden by her hair; still a little wet with a towel lying limp beside her, blood greedily seeping into the cotton. I assumed she was dead too. If I'm guilty of anything, it's not making sure that she was.

I backed away from them, planning to leave the kitchen and call the police from the garden, but I was not prepared for what I saw next. A blood-curdling scream erupted from my core when I saw Jacob.

We had been seeing each other for two years and we were madly in love. We knew what we were doing was wrong, but you can't help who you fall for. I knew that the sneaking around wasn't going to be forever, Jacob assured me that it wouldn't. He was going to leave Lauren, he promised, and I believed him, but when Lauren told us about the other girl in Jacob's life I was stunned. I knew he was capable of being deceitful, but he wasn't supposed to cheat on me.

I tried my best to keep my cool in Tenerife, letting Lauren take the lead with the whole Karly situation, but it was so difficult not to come clean to her about my own affair with Jacob. If I'd told her, perhaps she wouldn't have put up such a fight with Karly in a bid to keep her husband and she might still be alive today, but I didn't. Hindsight is a beautiful thing.

Instead, I distanced myself from her and watched from afar. I know she thinks I abandoned her, but I didn't, I just couldn't trust myself to keep my mouth shut. And anyway, she really blossomed during that week. I mean, really fucking blossomed. She played the game expertly, and I admired her determination. I do think she should have done things a little differently though. She should have confronted her before that holiday came to an end, but she didn't and that was her biggest mistake. That's why when we returned home, I felt that I had no choice but to help Lauren out. I had to expose Karly – we both did.

Of course, I ended things with Jacob. I'm not the type of woman to be messed around and then beg for more. I couldn't believe he could be so fucking stupid; to betray me like that after all we were sacrificing to be together. I mean, I was really willing to burn bridges with my best friend for him. That bastard.

He didn't take my rejection well, and actually it was quite pathetic the way he grovelled. There was absolutely no chance that I would ever take him back and yet he begged and begged me to give him another chance, told me he would finally leave Lauren and also cut Karly from his life for good, but I didn't believe him.

I wasn't going to tell Lauren about our affair. I didn't see the point. She had solid evidence in Karly that Jacob was a liar and a cheat and so exposing myself didn't make any sense – but I'd no choice in the end. There was no possible way that I could hide what was about to come. He had well and truly left me in the shit, and I was not about to lose everything without taking him down with me.

I don't know what happened in that kitchen, but whatever did, it happened before I got there. I'm guilty of many things that I'm not particularly proud of, but I'm not guilty of murder.

Of course, the police found a record of my phone call to Lauren that day, I've never denied phoning her. I needed to see her as soon as I found out, I couldn't carry on with the lie any longer. I know she had all the crazy shit with Karly going on, but this was far more important.

Earlier that morning, the Midwife had confirmed that I was indeed pregnant – sixteen weeks to be exact. I'd a sneaking suspicion that something was a bit off after I'd returned from Tenerife; I'd felt like shit the whole time I was there but had chalked it up to sun stroke and yet the nausea continued when we landed back in England.

The pregnancy changed everything. I knew immediately that I wasn't going to bring this baby into this world under a blanket of lies. I had to tell Lauren everything, and that's why I called her that day, and that's why I went round that evening when she didn't have time for me on the phone. No other reason.

I did not kill anybody – but nobody believes me.

For some reason, I'm still being questioned aggressively, in spite of the fact that they've already made-up their minds about me. I've been brought to this room time and time again and sat down in front of the same two police officers.

Sometimes my lawyer is here, sometimes he isn't. I don't say anything when my lawyer isn't here because I know that they don't have a right to question me without appropriate representation present. It's a snaky move, an underhanded attempt to intimidate me into admitting guilt.

My lawyer is here today, but the tape hasn't been started yet. There seems to be something going on behind the scenes that I don't know about or they don't want me to know about. I can't put my finger on what it is, but there's just been a lot of coming and going, whispers in ears, and anxious glances between themselves.

The officers don't have the same fierceness about them today. They almost look doubtful, like they might be afraid of something ruining their case.

The door to the dark room with no windows is gently prised open and a young man with sandy blonde hair sticks his head inside.

'Excuse me, sir, we have something you might want to have a look at.'

The eldest officer, who is actually the nicer out of the two evils announces that they'll be back with me shortly and then they both promptly push back their chairs and exit the room.

'What is it? What did you find?'

'They've found something else on Mrs Cruthers' phone, sir. It looks like she had some spyware installed.'

'Spyware? What do you mean, fucking spyware? Well spit it out, what did it show then?'

'It looks like there was a hidden camera in the kitchen, sir. The recording backs up Miss Pearson's story entirely. Another woman is seen entering the property before Georgia Pearson arrived. She was captured taking fire at both Jacob Cruthers and Karly Winters.'

'Oh shit! OK, so she might not have shot the two of them, but she did attack Lauren Cruthers, didn't she? We have Miss Winters' testimony.'

'That's just it, sir. It wasn't Georgia Pearson who attacked Lauren Cruthers either.'

EPILOGUE

She wasn't supposed to survive. But as per usual, Karly Winters always comes up trumps and somehow manages to get her own way. I've always hated that about her; the way she manages to land on her feet regardless of the situation. She never understands how the underdog feels, what it's like to always live in someone else's shadow.

I've considered waiting until it was late and quiet. When all the nurses have either clocked off or are in the middle of a shift change, too preoccupied to worry about someone visiting outside designated hours. I imagine it would be quite easy to slip the pillow from underneath her head while she sleeps and push down hard on her face, smothering her to death. I chose not to though, because with her pinning everything on poor Georgia Pearson it means that I don't need to worry about a thing. She already has her mind made-up with this one, and who am I to argue with her? She's more helpful to me alive right now.

Besides, Georgia is hardly innocent in all this either, is she? A baby for god's sake. A fucking baby – his baby. The thought makes my skin crawl. Just the idea of a mini-Jacob roaming around, creating chaos, following in his father's footsteps. I don't know if it's a boy, I'm just assuming that the little bastard will be a chip off the old block – just like his dear old dad.

The thing about Jacob, well he wasn't even my type. That's what makes this whole sorry mess so bloody laughable. I only wanted him because Karly obsessed over him. She let that man consume her, overwhelm her, rule every decision she ever made. It was pathetic. And not just that, she thought that she was special. I mean, can you believe that? Special? The man couldn't bother his backside to meet up with her properly in almost ten years – how bloody special could she really be?

It started out just a bit of fun, just something for me to hold close to my chest as ammunition, a little secret trophy of my own to hold over her if necessary. My first messages to Jacob were very strategic. I pretended to be the concerned friend, someone worried for her welfare, a guardian angel who wanted to make sure that this big bad man wouldn't break her poor little heart.

He was nice as pie to begin with, but as I suspected, it didn't take long for Jacob to initiate a bit of flirting. That's the thing about Jacob Cruthers you see, he always had a way of charming the ladies and in the end, I was no exception – but I was different. You see, women fawned over him, bowed down to him, let him walk all over their weak spines. But not me. I was always in control. He was under my spell completely, wrapped tightly around my little finger, and unlike with Karly, he was always begging me to come and see him. God, I loved having that over her – almost as much as I loved saying no to him. It only made him want me more.

I did plan to eventually meet him though, more than that actually. He was the one who told me he would leave Lauren, but he had to make sure that we had somewhere to live, somewhere far from the house he currently shared with his wife, somewhere that we could start fresh with no drama. We were literally in the middle of sorting things out when Karly threw a big old spanner in the works and decided that she was going to gate-crash Lauren's girls' holiday.

I can't even explain how furious I was when she told me. She was about to ruin everything. She couldn't tell Lauren that Jacob was playing away or whatever it was they were doing together because that would give her grounds for divorce, which would then mean Jacob would have to splash out on a hefty divorce settlement. We needed that money for our own life together and Karly was about to bulldoze my dream like the wrecking ball that she is.

So of course, I followed her. She always thinks I'm the stupid one, but really, I'm far more intelligent than she cares to give me credit for. I booked a separate flight, a separate hotel, and even made some friends of my own during my little trip. There was a reason why Karly's path never crossed with Lauren's friends – I made sure we were always in a different bar or a different club. I told you, I'm smart.

There was one that one night though where I just couldn't resist. I had to meet her. I know it was dangerous, but I was standing outside having a quick fag when I spotted the two of you heading into a cocktail bar right above my head. I knew you hadn't told her yet because the two of you looked so bloody chummy. The girls were having too much fun back inside the bar to notice my absence and so I stubbed the cigarette out quickly under the ball of my foot and quickly made my way up the stairs. I made sure to avoid your eye line as I headed up to the back of the bar and stood outside the toilet. It was only a couple of minutes, but it felt like forever until she finally emerged from the cubicle. I have to say; I understood right away why you didn't feel like you could come clean to someone like her – she was a total bitch. You actually do have quite a lot in common that way.

Anyway, I didn't really have anything to worry about with you because you were too much of a coward to say anything about who you really were. By that point, though, everything had changed, and you were no longer my main concern. I still remember the sound of such fondness and adoration that Georgia had while on the phone to Jacob that night. A side of her that she very rarely let anyone see.

I'd been keeping an eye on her though, there was something off about her, I just knew it. She wasn't participating in the group's fun the way she should have been. Avoiding the sickly-sweet shots that we necked every night and purposely ordering her own drinks from the bar instead of drinking out the fishbowls that everyone had a straw in.

When she nipped outside to make a call, I decided to pay a visit to the little girl's room that was beside the door. I didn't need to go, I just wanted to hear who she was talking to. The door to the loo wasn't even a door, more like a wooden gate without a top and bottom, and so I could hear everything. Just think, if I hadn't heard that bloody phone call, none of this might have happened.

The shock of the intimate phone call was a bitter enough pill to swallow, but it was what I saw as I followed her back to the table that really turned my stomach. Some spotty teenager, who had clearly seen too much sun and too much vodka, barged into her on the way to the bar, and the way her hand instinctively clutched at her stomach in the way cautious first-time mothers do before there's even a hint of a bump to protect is what really put the nail in your coffin.

I like to think that I'm a good judge of character, but sometimes people don't take me as seriously as they should. I give myself to people wholeheartedly with no inhibitions and to my own fault; I expect the same to be reciprocated.

When I found out, I wasn't mad at you. I wasn't even sad; there were no tears shed, my eyes were bone dry. You shouldn't have treated me this way. You made a big mistake, one I privately promised you would ultimately pay for.

As the wind blows sharply across my face today and I look down at you, I'm still not mad; I'm still not sad. I'm something else, something between satisfied and amused. I know that I'm a good person. This – all of this, has no reflection on me as a person because you did this, not me.

This was all your fault.

I pull my black cap down lower, protecting my face from the icy attack. A few strands of red escape the scarf that I ever so carefully wrapped around my neck, expertly tucking in my most distinguishing feature.

Jacob Cruthers – Beloved son and brother. I bet you don't see many people smiling at a graveyard, but I can't help it. There's no holding it in after reading that gravestone. There is no mention of beloved husband – absolute zilch, and definitely nothing about a doting Daddy, and there never will be.

He never deserved love – my love in particular. He loved himself far more than anyone else could ever love him, and I don't doubt there would have been many more that would have tried.

I crouch down and take the framed picture of him in my hand, the same one I saw his mother place against the granite on the day of his funeral and brush off the droplets of rain that have landed on his face. Such a waste, all that beauty. He should have chosen me, not Lauren, not Karly and definitely not Georgia. We could have been happy.

My phone vibrates in my back pocket, but I ignore it because I know it will just be Karly. It's always Karly. There once was a time when I couldn't even get a text back and now, she won't stop messaging and calling me. She's probably just checking where I am. It's almost time for me to pick my best friend up from the hospital.

I drop the picture carelessly to the ground and drive the heel of my boot into the glass. With my free hand I reach into my black tote bag that's draped lazily over my shoulder and pull from it one singular red rose. A red rose. Not white, not black, because after all … red always was his favourite colour.

ACKNOWLEDGEMENTS

W here do I even begin when it comes to saying thank you? So many people have helped me in so many wonderfully different ways.

First of all, my thanks must go to everyone who has read this book. I thoroughly enjoyed writing this complicated tale, and a part of me isn't quite sure that I'm ready to let go of it yet. There's definitely more to come from Karly - and other unsuspecting characters.

As an indie author, it's inevitable that I'll have made a fair few mistakes – and they are all my own. Perhaps one day, I'll have a fancy editor to come to my rescue but until then, thank you for your patience.

Thank you to Emma Mitchell for taking on this debut novel for a quick polish when it needed a new lease of life.

A special thanks to my beta reader extraordinaries, Linda White and Maxine Donald for getting just as excited about this book as I was writing it.

Thanks to my early readers: Claire Docherty, Michelle Proudfoot, Kelly Hughes, Clare Dolan, Fiona Reoch, and Karen O'Reilly. I thoroughly enjoyed our little makeshift book club and hope you will join me in many more.

Thank you to Bobby Hannah for offering me invaluable insight into a male perspective. I enjoyed our regular debates over what the final title of this novel would or should be – even though I know you still aren't convinced.

Of course, I must say thank you to my wonderful family: Mum, Dad, Harry, Gran, and Grumpy Grandad, Aunt Annie, and of course, my ever so patient partner, Simon. You are without a shadow of a doubt, my biggest fans. Your unconditional faith in me when I had little in myself was truly the catalyst in me being able to follow my dream.

To my wonderful friends who have supported me all the way since the book's release. I can't count the number of times I have considered deleting the book from existence and hiding under a rock but you have held my hand the entire way and are my ultimate hype-girls: Kirsten McStay, Toni Sherriff, Ashleigh Downs, Nicole Conway and Robyn Guthrie.

Thank you to Kimberly McKenna for taking a few months out of your life to study the first draft meticulously and making edits wherever necessary before it reached the world.

Finally, a special thank you to my biggest supporters of 2020/2021 on the Instagram Book Community and my tour hosts, Love Book Tours and Insta Book Tours. You took a chance on a self-published author and her debut novel and your continued support will be cherished forever. I could go on forever about who I'd like to thank but the people who pop to mind are:

Shannon@_treatyoshelves_ Molly @mollymustreads, Robynne@robynne_reads, Sam@sambooka23, Arianne@talkingteacupsblog, Lisa@theinsomniacbookclub, Megan@lost_in_her_bookland, Kim@duckfacekim09, Danielle@asreadbydanielle, Karen@karenandherbooks, Gina@bookswithgina, Danielle@bookreviews_dw, Katie@what.katie.reads, Nicole@mrsobookstagram, Amy@amymathieson, Susan@readinginthelight and last but not least, Martin Mcneil for jumping to my rescue whenever I'm having a wobble with technicalities.

ABOUT THE AUTHOR

Paula Johnston is an indie writer in her early thirties from Scotland who managed to pen half her debut novel at her desk during lunch breaks before taking ill with a chronic illness. She continued to write from her home outside of Glasgow, and the rest is history.

Not only did Paula write the book, she also designed the front cover which has received great praise from both authors and readers.

Having always worked around people, Paula Johnston has a fierce and keen ability to not only read those standing before her but cut to the core of their true intentions. Believing in creating characters with raw flaws, her fascination with the human psyche crosses over into her debut novel, *The Lies She Told*, and has proven to be the start of something big for Paula, as she finds herself climbing up the Amazon Top 100 list without a large publishing house behind her. Since publication, Paula's book has found its way into local libraries, Waterstones and was signed by American media company, Tantor, to create an audio version.

Paula intends to write and publish more psychological fiction titles and perhaps move across to a different genre when the time feels right.

Until then, readers wait patiently for more from Paula after a fantastic write-up in *The Herald Newspaper* and *The Daily Record.*

Stay in touch:

#Theliesshetold

Twitter – Facebook – Instagram

paulajohnstonauthor

Printed in Great Britain
by Amazon

76258005R00183